REMO KEPT HIS MOUTH SHUT AND HIS HEAD ABOVE WATER.

He turned back and forth between the rapidly receding vessels and the shark that was approaching from the north. Another moment, and the gliding dorsal fin was passing in between the swimmer and his fleeing enemies. Until it stopped.

No, it didn't stop exactly. He had heard that sharks were always moving, even when they slept; but it was definitely turning—toward Remo. He was bound to lose the pirates now, but his more immediate concern involved the shark, now rapidly approaching him.

Remo willed himself to relax, preparing for mortal combat with an enemy approximately twice his size, uneasy in the knowledge that his adversary had not lived this long or grown so large by losing any fights.

Created by Murphy & Sapir

THE Destroyer™

TROUBLED WATERS

A GOLD EAGLE BOOK FROM

WORLDWIDE®

TORONTO • NEW YORK • LONDON
AMSTERDAM • PARIS • SYDNEY • HAMBURG
STOCKHOLM • ATHENS • TOKYO • MILAN
MADRID • WARSAW • BUDAPEST • AUCKLAND

First edition October 2003

ISBN 0-373-63248-7

TROUBLED WATERS

And for the Glorious House of Sinanju
sinanjucentral@hotmail.com

1

The woman was lost but tried to deny it, as if by withholding the information from herself she could somehow magically discover an exit from her private hell on Earth. She was a city girl and proud of it, dependent on street signs and landmarks to negotiate her way through daily life. The jungle that surrounded her seemed vast and alien.

She made a conscious effort to control the fear that stalked her like a silent predator. Panic would finish her, destroy whatever tiny, fragile hope she had of breaking free, saving herself. They might be after her by now, and if she didn't keep her wits about her, she was dead—or something infinitely worse.

Her body ached from the abuse she had endured since being taken prisoner. Was it three days? A week? A lifetime? She had no idea what day it was, but dawn was approaching to mark another morning of captivity, another day and night of torment.

Only this time, when her jailers came for her, they would be in for a surprise. She knew that her impression of the jungle's vastness was illusory. Her prison was an island—that much she was certain of—and not a huge one, from the way her captors spoke of it. An island meant the jungle was bounded by the sea on every side, and all she had to do was strike a course, stick to it, keep herself from wandering in circles to escape the brooding darkness of the trees.

And then what?

She had never been an athlete, even though she kept herself in decent shape, a trim size six, with just a bit more in the bust than most women her size. But on the best day that she ever had, it would have been impossible for her to swim an ocean. Going where? From where?

She didn't have a compass and couldn't have read it accurately if she had. Besides, direction was a useless concept when your world was ringed with fathomless green water, the depths teeming with predatory life.

Swimming was suicide, but she would risk it anyway before she let herself be dragged back to her cage and what was waiting for her.

A root or vine reached out to trip her, and she went down on all fours, unable to suppress a muffled yelp of pain. Her bruised, aching body protested the jolt, and now her palms were skinned, her knees raw, a small but nagging pain radiating from her ankle, where a splinter or a thorn had pierced her flesh.

It wasn't the first time she had fallen since she fled

her captors, and she had a feeling that it wouldn't be the last. Each time she fell, she hesitated, braced on hands and knees or sprawled on the forest floor, listening for sounds of pursuit, anything that would tell her the men were behind her, drawing closer, perhaps homing in on the sound of her fall.

Perhaps there was a way that she could make them kill her, if they cornered her and she resisted to the point that taking her alive was too much effort. That was a hope she could cling to, as a last resort, but she preferred to think of the slim chance of escape that remained.

At the moment she was taken, she had logically assumed that ransom was the goal of her abductors. Why they had not spared her husband was a mystery that haunted her, the image of his violent ending branded on her soul, but she supposed men were more difficult to manage. And they offered less amusement to their captors while they waited for the final payoff.

Scrambling to her feet, the woman started moving once again, following what seemed to be the ghost of an old game trail, barely visible now, overgrown completely in spots.

IT WAS IMPOSSIBLE TO SAY when she first smelled the ocean. When she stopped, she could hear the first faint sound of breakers crashing onto sand.

Armed with a new, improved sense of direction,

the woman veered left, leaving the vestigial trail as it wound away through the trees—curving, she now saw, away from the sound of the ocean. If she had not paused then and there, at that precise moment, she might well have missed her goal entirely and continued on through the jungle until she was cornered or simply collapsed from exhaustion.

She emerged from the jungle and turned right, then began to move along the beach as quickly as her legs would carry her. She stayed close to the tree line, walking on sand to give her lacerated feet a rest, still close enough to cover that she could vanish in a heartbeat if she saw trackers in front of her or heard them behind her.

In the sunlight, growing brighter by the moment, she possessed a stronger, clearer sense of time. Her watch was long gone, with the other jewelry and cash aboard their yacht, and while she had no fixed idea of what time she had fled the camp, she knew it had to be coming up on 6:00 a.m. by now. Each moment with the sun above her multiplied her odds of being spotted, run to ground, but it was still her only chance, as slim as it might be.

The woman guessed she had been following the island's coastline for an hour and a half, at least, before she struck the river. It was small, as rivers go—more of a creek, in fact—but it supplied fresh water, and she fell to hands and knees once more, burying her face in the sweet, cool current, splashing water over her hair and the back of her head with cut and bleeding hands. She drank deeply, unmindful of old movies she had seen, in which parched travelers were warned to sip a little at a time to ward off some calamity never specified. She filled her belly with the sweet, fresh water, taking it in place of food, to stop the growling in her stomach, feeling it revive her like a draft from the mythical Fountain of Youth.

And when she raised her dripping head, to shake it like a dog's, she spotted the canoe.

It wasn't native craftsmanship. If anything, in fact, it looked like something from an old Sears catalog that had been roughly used for years, perhaps for decades, and abandoned on the rough bank of this island creek. A paddle was lying in the old canoe, with scars around the blade, its handle satin smooth.

Stepping into the middle of the creek, surprised at the sudden chill of its water on her bare feet and legs, the woman dragged her only means of transportation into the gentle current. The creek was shallow, and she had to stoop painfully, pulling the old canoe along, but it was infinitely better than trying to carry the boat fifty yards to the sea.

Gentle breakers curled in toward the shore at the point where creek spilled into ocean, fresh and salt water mingling briefly before the former was lost. Without another backward glance to check for spotters, she plunged into the surf, dragging the canoe behind her until it was suddenly buoyant. The old canoe was thirty yards from shore when the woman finally succeeded in crawling over the gunwale and dropping inside, almost tipping the boat in the process. She shifted to prevent the paddle gouging her back, then reluctantly sat up and stared back at the island.

There was no one on the beach, no sign of movement in the shadows of the tree line. Could it be that she had managed to outwit her captors after all? It seemed impossible, but the woman was wasting no more precious time. Facing the sea, she lifted the paddle and began to dig in, remembering to shift her strokes from port to starboard to prevent the canoe from circling back toward the island.

Muscle cramps set in eventually, and she was forced to stop paddling, almost collapsing where she sat, pain-racked and sobbing. Even then, the ocean carried her beyond sight of the island, and no ships came after her to drag her back or sink her, let her drown.

By slow degrees her strength returned, and the agonizing cramps began to fade. Now thirst and hunger took their turn, but there was nothing she could do except force her mind to concentrate on escape, find a new rhythm with the paddle, hold exhaustion at bay by the sheer force of her will.

At some point in the endless afternoon, she slumped against the gunwale, briefly losing consciousness, revived when water slapped her in the face. She roused herself, tongue thick enough to nearly fill the dry cave of her mouth, and reaching for the paddle, found that it was gone. She had to have dropped it overboard when she passed out. With no means of propelling the canoe, she was completely at the ocean's mercy, as she had been in the hands of her abductors.

No, that wasn't right. The sea would kill her, certainly, and it would not be gentle in the process, but at least it wouldn't rape her, make her a slave to filthy strangers who could use her at their will because they had the knives, the guns, the power.

As SHE DRIFTED ON THE ocean, the woman drifted in and out of consciousness, with frequent detours into stark delirium. The sun went down, replaced by an impressive moon, and she was still alive somehow, although not certain she was sane.

In time, the sun came up and started baking her again, leaching the final, precious moisture from her body, leaving her a blistered shell.

The sharks turned up that afternoon, following the canoe for miles, rubbing their flat snouts and rough hides against the drab metal hull, rocking the woman in her cradle, barely conscious of the changing rhythm. One great fish turned on its side and raked the canoe's flank with its teeth before giving up, deciding there was no food there. Reluctantly, the killers turned away and left her, moving on to more productive hunting grounds.

Too late, the woman rose from her delirium and found the sea around her flat, apparently devoid of life. She would have welcomed dorsal fins at that point, any promise of relief, but as it was, the sea would have to do.

She dragged herself across the gunwale, somehow managed to avoid capsizing the canoe. The water swallowed her, then spit her out again, the buoyancy of her slim body dragging her back to the surface. She was floating on her back, the sun bright in her eyes, and tried rolling over, the better to drown, but the sea had a mind of its own, rejecting her sacrifice, tossing her onto her back and forcing her to breathe again.

She started weeping, tearless, since her body had no moisture left to spare. She didn't see the cabin cruiser coming, barely registered the throbbing of its engine, the churning of its screws in the water. A part of her mind acknowledged the shadow that fell across her face, but she had found the secret weakness of her adversary now, and she was sinking, expelling the breath from her lungs to prevent herself from floating, ready to suck in the water she needed to carry her down.

A sudden pain almost revived her, lancing into the flesh and muscle of her armpit, and she struggled as some unknown force again brought her back to the surface. Her flailing arm met something like a strand of a spiderweb, the contact sending a fresh jolt of pain through her flesh.

Above her, miles away it seemed, she heard a gruff voice whooping. They had found her after all, but she took refuge in the thought that she would surely die before they had a chance to take her back, make her their slave again.

"Hot damn!" the voice above her crowed. "Come look at this, Joe Bob! I done caught me a mermaid!"

2

His name was Remo, and he didn't play well with others. He especially didn't like mixing with amateurs—and to him, *everybody* was an amateur, except for this one old grumpy guy he knew.

That wasn't strictly fair, of course. The U.S. Navy SEALs were specialists, presumably the world's best at the job they had been trained to do. But they were a long way from the ocean, several hundred miles in fact. The New Mexico desert seemed a world away from the SEALs' normal operating environment.

The decrepit ghost town—once a thriving population center in the days when silver virtually streamed out of the nearby Sacramento Mountains into greedy, waiting hands—had been refurbished somewhat for its modern role, but no one would mistake it for a seaport. Situated in the northeast corner of the Fort Bliss Military Reservation, it was used for special training exercises when a desert setting was required. Away to the northwest, some eighty miles, stood Roswell, Mecca to the tired old UFO believers who were still convinced the truth was out there, hidden by a shifting veil of desert sand and the fluid denials of the Federal Department of Obfuscation.

The SEALs were not, in fact, restricted to naval operations, even though their roots lay in the old UDTs—underwater demolition teams—that had cleared invasion beaches for the Army and Marines in World War II. Today the Navy SEALs were scuba divers, paratroopers, all-around commandos who derived their name from their sea-air-land proficiency in combat.

Hence the desert, which had been selected as a likeness of the Middle East, North Africa—wherever Allah's warriors waged jihad against the West, assassinating diplomats and tourists, snatching hostages. The call could come at any time, and they had to be prepared for anything.

Which still didn't explain how Remo happened to be standing in the dusty foyer of the ghost town's three-story hotel.

Remo blamed it on Dr. Harold W. Smith, director of CURE, the supersecret government intelligence agency. Or maybe the fault actually lay with Mark Howard, CURE's assistant director. One of them had dropped a great big ball, and dropped it right on Remo's head.

While the SEALs were practicing war, Remo Williams, Reigning Master of the world's original martial art, Sinanju, and the greatest assassin currently living on the planet, was doing dog-catcher duty.

The SEALs didn't know that. They thought he was an observer and behind his back had labeled him a spook. They didn't care as long as he didn't screw up their playtime.

The game was rigged, of course. Both prey and hunters were restricted to a given area, with no real practice in the art of tracking over open ground. The ghost town, for its part, bore no resemblance to a Middle Eastern village, other than the fact that both included man-made structures baked by desert sun and cloaked in gritty dust. It would have been more helpful if the Navy SEALs were training for a trip backward in time—perhaps to face the Clayton gang at the O.K. Corral.

The sun was setting, casting purple shadows in the dusty street, bringing premature twilight to the hotel lobby where Remo stood, waiting and watching. It would take some time for the 115-degree temperature to drop out there, and even in the ancient, shady building it was hot. But at least it was a dry heat. Remo didn't sweat. Partly because he wasn't weighed down by the equipment load the poor SEALs were waddling around with. He was in khaki Chinos and a white T-shirt. His shoes were hand-stitched leather—he didn't give two hoots about fashion or style, but he did like his shoes to last through the weekend. Remo had proved the quality of the Italians' workmanship by putting their products through field-testing beyond the shoemakers' wildest imaginings.

Remo was bored. He'd already scoured the ghost town and had found what he was looking for. Dog poop. Well, actually, wolf poop. Specifically, poop from a genetically mutated *Canis lupus baileyi*, or Mexican Gray Wolf.

The wolves themselves were nowhere to be found, and by all reports this pack was nocturnal. So he had to wait for darkness, when the pack might—just might—come sniffing around. Remo wanted to be there if it did.

He had a thing or two to discuss with this particular pack of mutant, nocturnal, man-eating canines.

The war games couldn't have come at a more inconvenient time. Remo had asked Upstairs to cancel the games so that he could find his wolves, but Upstairs—which had the capability to wield such far-reaching powers in the military—said no.

Upstairs consisted of Dr. Smith the Really Old and Mark Howard the Young and Dopey. That was all there was to the CURE intelligence-gathering apparatus and bureaucracy. The mountains those two could move with a few keystrokes was impressive, but this time they weren't giving in.

"It would be most difficult to come up with a rationale for canceling routine war games," Dr.

Smith had said. He had the sour voice of a man who had just chomped down on a lemon wedge.

"The pack's gonna stay out if there's a bunch of paramilitaries romping around," Remo argued.

"So wait until the games are over," Smith countered.

"No," Remo said. "First of all, the wolves may still be migrating for all we know. We know where they are right now and I'm gonna grab them right now, before they move on. Second, if the wolves do show themselves, the SEALs are gonna go get their real guns and start shooting. Third, I don't wanna."

"You have no choice, really," Smith said.

"Yeah. Put me inside."

"What?"

"You know. An observer or something."

"That's not plausible," Smith replied curtly.

Remo sighed. He was at a phone booth at a convenience store in some small town in Arizona, already on his way to New Mexico. "Better to go in with an implausible cover than with no cover at all," he stated flatly.

"Remo—"

"Because—listen very closely to this, Smitty—I am going in, one way or another."

Smith relented, but by the time Remo called him back a hundred miles later, he had thrown a wrench into the works.

"I anticipated all manner of red flags showing up

when the order was issued,'' Smith said. ''I could not hope to quell them all without giving you better cover.''

''Yeah. So what's my cover?''

''Department of Homeland Security Special Forces Special Scenario Evaluation Specialist,'' Smith said.

''Uh-huh.''

''Your role is to offer Special Forces experience with out-of-the-ordinary field events and capabilities,'' Smith explained.

''You want me to try to trip up the SEALs while they're wargaming one another?''

''I want you to engage the SEALs. You'll be one of the teams.''

''You're right. One guy taking on a freakin' army will be much more low-profile than if I was going in as an observer,'' Remo said.

''Specialists of this type exist, Remo, and they're being used in just this way to prepare our military for field scenarios they might not expect. Just don't let them see you do anything too, er, unusual.''

''Whatever,'' Remo said. Of all the cockamamy situations he had found himself in courtesy of Harold W. Smith, this one ranked way up near the top.

So here he was, trying to hunt wolves while taking on the Navy SEALs. Single-handedly.

Those SEALs had better not distract him from the wolf hunt.

The SEALs were late. They had been air-dropped north of town, a HALO jump from a Lockheed C-130 Hercules. They came loaded for bear—or, in this case, for Remo—packing the usual assortment of firearms, knives, garrotes, explosives, night surveillance gear, whatever. It was certain that each member of the team would have a watch and compass of his own, and since there were no other "enemies" participating in the exercise who could have slowed them, Remo was forced to think of reasons for their tardiness.

One possibility a casual observer might have raised was that the SEAL commandos were not late at all. They could have closed the gap between their LZ and the ghost town right on schedule, infiltrated silently, and were stalking Remo through the dusty shells of buildings even now. But a Master of Sinanju was difficult to sneak up on. He'd hear them coming. If they muffled their footsteps, he'd hear their breathing. If they held their breath all the way into town, he'd hear their heartbeats—two or three buildings away.

Unless they had crashed or gotten lost, both highly unlikely, Remo assumed the SEAL team was trying to outfox him with an indirect approach, perhaps circling wide, north of town, to approach from the west or east.

Oh, well, here they came now. It wasn't the noise

of their approach that alerted him; he could smell them.

You load some poor sap down with enough hardware to have his own gun show and put him out in the hundred-degree-plus heat, and he's gonna sweat a little. And that's the kind of smell that carried for miles, notably when the hunter came in with the wind at his back.

The approaching perspirer made his way into town. Remo listened to the thumps of his boots as he took cover in the building at the west end of town. Remo had already been there and had swiped at the floorboards with his short but surgically sharp fingernails. They scored the wood in a thin, invisible line.

The SEALs, who had conducted exercises in this ghost town before, would have no reason to doubt that the floors at Sundberg's Mercantile weren't sound. However…

Remo heard the minute creak of the floorboards as the SEAL took a careless step. Then there was a crash—loud enough for everybody to hear—and while no startled cries or curses accompanied the noise, Remo was satisfied that he had bagged an "enemy." The Navy SEALs were too well trained to cry out in a combat situation if they suffered injury, but it was also possible that the commando, who had plunged twelve feet into the basement of the mercantile, was now unconscious from the fall. In either case, he would be in for more surprises if and when he tried the ancient wooden stairs.

One down.

Squads varied in their sizes, depending on the branch of service and the mission, but he had been told that he was up against a dozen Navy SEALs. Their guns were loaded with paint rounds, the seriousness of a "wound" determined by location of the splash, with any hit between the neck and groin considered a "kill." Before the game had started, Dr. Smith had cautioned Remo to remember that it was a game.

Remo didn't even really care about the game. He'd like to herd every last one of the SEALs into some dusty basement for the duration so he could concentrate on his real purpose here—find those wolves.

Remo left the old hotel through a side door, emerging in an alley where the pent-up heat of the afternoon still simmered wickedly. Long strides brought him to the main street—the ghost town's only street, in fact—and he stood waiting in the shadows, watching for his adversaries. He could hear them scampering around town like a bunch of parade marchers.

A man-sized shadow dodged between two buildings on the far side of the street, immediately followed by a second, then a third. It made sense that the team would be divided, sweeping both sides of the street and working house to house until they found their prey.

Or he found them.

Another group was coming in behind him, to his left, advancing from the west. Remo fell back to meet them, barely conscious of the dusty, almost stifling air in the narrow alleyway.

Using a hole in the wall as a stair, Remo ascended to the hotel roof quickly. The hotel was just one story. Remo felt the sagging roof with his feet and decided it was sound enough to support his weight, despite enduring the years of sun and wind and insects that had been working on all the town's predominantly wooden buildings. At the southwest corner of the roof he knelt and glanced below.

Three men in desert camouflage, with dusty faces, were advancing toward him, proceeding in spurts of motion followed by statuesque stillness, ready for incoming fire each time they changed position. Apparently, they thought the "specialist" they were hunting would be armed as they were, but in fact his hands were empty as he casually watched them making progress on the ground. They didn't pause to enter any of the buildings that they passed, and Remo wondered what their plan was. Were they moving toward a rendezvous with other SEALs, somewhere behind him? Three on one side of the street and two on the other left five guns unaccounted for, but he would deal with those in front of him before he went in search of others.

REMO WAITED UNTIL THEY were just below him, then stepped off into space. The drop was not a long one, no more than eleven feet, and he landed directly in their path.

"Evening, boys."

Just in front of him, the middle of the three SEALs gaped at him, but recovered from his surprise to swing his stubby CAR-15 toward Remo's chest. A burst of paint at point-blank range, and it was over, but he never even got the weapon aimed. Remo's hand flicked out and tapped him in the center of his forehead, just above the space between his eyes. It could have been a killing strike, but Remo imparted only force enough to slam the SEAL against the dusty clapboard wall, out cold before he slumped into a seated posture in the dirt.

His companions were reacting to the unexpected threat. On Remo's left, an automatic carbine was leveled at his abdomen. Remo waited until the finger was pulling the trigger, then deflected it with his left hand wrapped around the barrel, tugging even as he changed the gun's target. Half a dozen rounds spit from the muzzle, spattering the SEAL on Remo's right with yellow paint.

That should have been enough to take him out of play, according to the rules, but Remo wasn't taking any chances. Even as the paint rounds were still bursting on his adversary's camou shirt, he threw an open hand that struck behind the young commando's ear and took him down.

The last man standing fired another burst, apparently in hopes that barrel heat would break the stranger's grip, but Remo twisted and turned the rifle in his "enemy's" hands, put the man's finger on the trigger and helped him pull. The SEAL gave himself four paintball rounds in the belly. Remo pinched the very surprised looking commando behind the neck.

"Sweet dreams," he said as he lowered the unconscious man to the hot ground.

And that left eight.

Remo made his way to Sundberg's Mercantile and went in through the back. He found that his sabotaged wooden floor had collapsed under not one but two SEALs. A third was standing on the edge of the rough pit as Remo entered, lowering a rope to those below.

"Come on," the commando said, keeping his voice down. "Snap it up, you guys!"

Remo drifted up behind him, reaching for the CAR-15 slung across the young man's shoulder as he planted a foot on his backside and shoved. The SEAL plunged headfirst into Remo's trap, an old root cellar with the stairs long since collapsed, and landed with a squawk ten feet below.

Three faces craned to greet him as he stepped up

to the edge. Before they could react and bring him under fire, he raised the captured CAR-15 and hosed them with a stream of paint rounds, watching them recoil as they were spattered with bright baby-blue.

"You're dead," he told them, dropped the CAR-15 into the hole and turned away. "Stay put."

Six down, and that should leave him squared off with a pair of three-man teams. The CAR-15s were fitted with suppressors, part of any well-equipped commando's ensemble, and he had no reason to believe that the six remaining SEALs had picked up on the gunfire. They would still be searching for him, both teams more than likely on the north side of the street, and Remo needed to cross in the open.

Remo left the mercantile establishment, stepped through the front door with its squeaky hinges as if he were going for a quiet evening's stroll. No movement greeted him from windows on the north side of the street, but he couldn't rule out the possibility that one or more of his opponents had already spotted him.

He crossed the main street in a sprint that was so smooth and fast it would have looked unreal, had anyone seen it, and he barely left a dust trail in his wake. He drew no fire and reached the rotting wooden sidewalk on the north side of the street, ducking into the recessed doorway of what had once been a barbershop. Gilt lettering had long since faded from the windows, leaving ghostly outlines in its place, and the interior, as far as he could see, had been stripped bare, abandoned to rodents and insects.

Remo listened, ears pricked, at the sounds of approaching SEALs on the wooden sidewalk. No matter how carefully you walked, you couldn't be too quiet walking on a wooden sidewalk.

The SEAL appeared in Remo's doorway, glancing into darkness, seemingly alert. But when the darkness seized him, dragged him off the sidewalk and enfolded him, the soldier gave a yelp of complete surprise. He lashed out with the buttstock of his rifle but only succeeded in handing his weapon to the enemy, who plastered him collar to crotch with paint balls.

"Oh, man, you're *really* dead," Remo said, then tapped him in the head, sending him into unconsciousness in the doorway.

A couple more had been tagging along with the commando and they started rushing to the barbershop, boots clomping on the wooden sidewalk. Remo left the snoozing SEAL where he had fallen, slipping into the darkened barbershop and leaving the door ajar behind him as a lure. Bait for the trap.

One of the SEALs checked out his fallen buddy, while the other kept them covered, edging toward the open doorway to the shop. "In here," he whispered, and the words reached Remo's ears as if the young man had been shouting down the silent street.

"Jeff—"

"Is he breathing?"

"Yeah."

"So, leave him," said the point man. "He's all right, and we've got work to do."

It was a textbook entry, one SEAL close behind the other, breaking left and right, their weapons sweeping, covering the room. They didn't fire—wouldn't, without a target, or at least a noise to help them focus—but they were prepared for anything.

Except what happened next.

Remo had climbed the warped and weathered clapboard wall to cling there like a giant spider, perched above the doorway. He was thus above the two SEALs and behind them as they entered, swooping down to join them.

Both young men heard Remo land behind them, knew the sound meant trouble even as they turned to face their "enemy," but they never even saw Remo's face. Their heads suddenly collided into each other as if they'd become magnetized, and they slumped to the ground. Remo extracted paint rounds from their weapons and shattered them on the floor, then quickly painted on blue clown faces.

He went to find the last three SEALs, conscious of the deepening of the night. He wanted the fun and games to be over. He had canines to converse with.

He found the trio of remaining SEALs in what used to be the mining town's saloon. No fancy pleasure palace this. Even before the furniture was stripped away and time began to gnaw around the building's edges, it had been a spartan place. He pictured sawdust on the floor to soak up booze and blood from gun and knife fights over cards or cut-rate women.

One of the SEALs was on his way upstairs to check the rooms where two-bit whores had once serviced their clients in something less than total privacy. The other two were waiting for him below, near what had been the bar until some human scavengers had stripped most of the paneling and left it skeletal. Both eyed the shadows warily and held their weapons ready, anxious for a chance to fire.

Remo circled the old saloon, finding a drain pipe fastened to the wall, descending from the roof's rain gutter, and he scrambled nimbly up it to the second floor. He chose a window with the glass long-ago broken out and made his entrance.

The small room smelled of dust, rat droppings and age. The age aside, Remo guessed that it had smelled little different in the old days, when its clientele consisted of unwashed miners and the occasional trail hand. Waiting in the darkness now, errant moonbeams lighting the way, he listened to his adversary on the landing outside, making his way toward the room's open door.

When the tall, young SEAL edged through the doorway, Remo snatched the automatic carbine from his grasp with ease, surprise doing half of the work.

His free hand flicked toward the SEAL's temple, barely light enough to register as a caress, but it was still enough to do the job, the young man going slack in Remo's arms.

Then Remo shot him with his own weapon. One dot for each eye, one for the nose and a few more for the mouth, and Remo had created a big sloppy paint-ball smiley face on the SEAL's chest.

The last two SEALs still waited below. Remo went down to join them.

He went down fast. So fast they could barely see the bounding black form that was suddenly in their midst. Before the last two SEALs knew what was happening, he was between them, striking left and right with his pinching fingers and putting them to sleep.

He couldn't leave them undead, so he shot them, too.

Now he had the place to himself and everything was quiet. It would stay that way until the exercise ended—when one of the teams called into the commander or 6:00 a.m., whichever came first.

Remo decided the saloon was his best lookout. He went back upstairs and climbed to the roof, finding it gave him the best view of the desolate reservation terrain in all directions.

He sat cross-legged, under the clear sky with more stars than he could count. But he didn't see the stars;

he had other things to look at. The horizon. The land. And everything that prowled it.

"Come along, little doggies," he said to the night.

THE NIGHT WAS COOL BY comparison to the day. The stillness was almost like a presence in the night desert. Sound carried far. Remo heard far. But he didn't hear the sounds he wanted to hear.

There was a small crash at about midnight from Sundberg's Mercantile. Remo had left the SEALs in the cellar conscious because they were trapped. Trying to get out was against the rules. "If those kids make one more noise, I'll go over and put 'em to sleep," he muttered to himself. But the SEALs in the cellar were silent after that.

At 2:15 a.m., by the clock in the sky, Remo heard a sound that stirred his blood. It was far off and coming closer. Four paws moving on the desert soil. Canine. And then there was another. And another. It was a pack.

But what he heard warned him to be disappointed. The paws sounded too light.

The pack appeared, and it was easy to make out the tail held low to the ground, not quite between the legs, and the small build.

Coyotes.

Six of them were approaching warily, sniffing everywhere, their bodies stiff with their awareness of danger. They marked their territory at every bush and rock, and gradually they relaxed and began yipping to one another. Remo cursed silently.

He knew exactly what he was seeing.

The coyote family had recently been frightened off this patch of territory by the arrival of the Mexican Grays. They were cautiously returning, sniffing out the terrain—and deciding that the interlopers had moved on.

The coyotes were telling Remo that his wolves were gone.

He felt angry. But mostly he felt defeated. He had picked up the trail of the wolf pack twice in the past three months as they made their bold, bloody migration across Texas and New Mexico. But these weren't ordinary wolves. They were intelligent. They were cunning. They knew they would be tracked. Time and again they had foiled the trail, mostly by stowing away on vehicles at gas stations and rest stops.

It looked like Remo would be going after them again. On foot, if necessary. The people who ran this summer camp might have a problem with that, but he'd let Smitty pave the way.

But now it was time to end the little game. He powered up a walkie-talkie appropriated from the SEALs and phoned their CO.

"All finished. Come and get 'em."

The coyotes fled when the sound of whining aircraft interrupted the night's natural noises. The officer in charge was red-faced, glaring hard at Remo as he walked through swirling dust, ducking below the helicopter's swirling rotor blades.

"Where are they, dammit?" he demanded.

"Here ya go," said Remo. He had gathered the unconscious SEALs and sat them in a long row on the wooden sidewalk. Each had a hand on his neighbor's right shoulder, just to make them look less menacing. "Here come the others."

Two SEALs, paint splashed, had extricated themselves from Remo's pitfall in the old mercantile store with the ladder he tore off the side of a building and lowered to them. Their third companion was being dragged between them.

"Jesus Christ, I wouldn't have believed it," the commander muttered.

"Wonders never cease," said Remo.

"Bullshit!" the older man snarled. "These children will be going back to school."

"They're not all that bad, really," Remo said.

"Not that bad? How do you explain this mess?" he demanded.

"Oh, well, it's because I'm so damn good, ya see."

"You're not *that* good!"

"Am too!"

"By the way," the officer informed him, glaring balefully at him, "you've got a message waiting for you back at my HQ. Eyes-only, urgent. Better check it out.''

"Aw, crap." Remo sighed. "I'll need the chopper, I guess."

"No sweat." There was a softening, however marginal, about the Navy officer's attitude. "I've got a full night's work ahead of me right here, just cleaning up your mess."

Remo strolled toward the chopper and called from just below the whirling rotor blades and flicked the object in his hand with one finger. It rocketed at the Navy officer.

"Hey!" Remo shouted.

The officer practically bounced off the ground and spun in place, almost losing his balance and desperately trying to crane his head to see what had just happened to his rear quarters. He discovered the seat of his trousers was wet with fresh blue paint.

The officer shot Remo a look that was disbelief and fury. He didn't know what to do first: ball him out or demand to know how he'd fired a paint ball without actually having a gun.

"Am too!" Remo shouted over the rotor noise.

3

The red-eye into White Plains managed to arrive six minutes earlier than its absurdly precise ETA of 6:13 a.m. The plane was nearly empty, leaving Remo thankful for small favors, even though a fat man in a rumpled polyester suit had snorted, wheezed and rumbled in his sleep throughout the flight, directly opposite the seat in coach that Remo occupied.

A rental car was waiting for him at the airport, subcompact, no doubt the cheapest one available. Economy was critical to Dr. Harold Smith and CURE, the supersecret crime-fighting agency that Remo served, although its budget was so well disguised that only Dr. Smith himself had any real idea of the resources at his fingertips.

Remo had an odd relationship with money by the standards of most people, in that he didn't care about it. He had a lot of it, certainly. Being Reigning Master of Sinanju made him, technically, the custodian of Sinanju's wealth. He had no idea how vast his resources actually were. Chiun, Reigning Master

Emeritus, smacked his hand if he tried to get anywhere near the money.

To Remo, you bought things with various plastic
cards that were issued to him by CURE. The cards
had lots of names on them. Most of them had the
first name Remo, and they never ever had the last
name Williams.

He didn't mind flying coach most of the time. He
would have upgraded himself if he wanted to and
nobody, but nobody, would have stopped him. He
didn't mind driving an inexpensive set of wheels if
it got him where he needed to go. But when he saw
the three-year-old Beetle with a partially detached
fender he went back to the Rent Cars Cheap! desk
and said no thanks. "Got something a little bigger?"

The pretty young Rent Cars Cheap! clerk looked
doubtful.

"Newer?" Remo asked.

The clerk looked sad.

"Do you have a car without metal parts hanging
down far enough to drag on the pavement?"

The clerk looked despondent.

Remo moved on to the next car-rental booth in the
airport concourse and asked for something nice.

"Yes, sir!" said the middle-aged man in a but-
toned double-breasted jacket and neat tie, with gold
tie clip. He looked more like a bank president than
a car-rental clerk. "What are you looking for?
Sporty? Luxury? An SUV?"

"Sporty?" Remo asked. "Define sporty."

The bank-president-type got a gleam in his eye. "Define sporty? I'll define sporty. V-12 engine, 6-speed stick, 580 horsepower and a top speed of 205 miles per hour."

Remo looked at the clerk, then took a step back and looked at the sign on the desk. The name of the car-rental agency didn't have the word "budget" or "cheap," and there wasn't an "econo-something" to be found. The name was something like Alucci— Fine Motorcars for the Discriminating Driver."

"You Al?"

"Pardon me, sir?"

"I guess that sounds kind of sporty, if it's red," Remo said.

"It's bright red," Al said. "Cherry strawberry bloodred. It is—" he inhaled before he spoke the words "—a Lamborghini Murciélago."

"Smitty'll have steam coming out of his ears," Remo said.

"Pardon me, sir?"

"Nothing. I'll take it if you don't ask me to pronounce it," Remo said.

Al couldn't have been happier. "An excellent choice, Mr....?"

Remo glanced surreptitiously at the credit card as he slid it over. "Quartermaster. Remo Quartermaster."

"I just need to check and be sure your card will take the security deposit."

"Okay."

"The deposit required is—"

"Whatever."

Al was visibly surprised and greatly pleased when the card was authorized.

"Sign here, please," he said, slipping over the company's standard contract. "And here. And here, here and here."

Al noticed that the man slapped his hand over the rental fee and the security amount before signing the document. Al couldn't care less. He had his credit-card approval.

BEFORE HE GOT INSIDE the sleek, stubby, scarlet Lamborghini Murciélago, Remo walked around it. He couldn't help but notice that none of its fenders was dragging on the pavement.

He pulled out onto the road, and the Lamborghini did something unusual when he hit the gas. It didn't go faster; it sort of *burst* ahead. He wondered if there was an exhaust pipe with flames shooting out like on the Batmobile.

It had been a while since he had driven anything like this, and he found himself liking it. The speedometer needle nudged up to the hundred-miles-per-hour mark and still had lots of little numbers to the right of it. Remo wondered if he could make the little needle move all the way over to the right-hand side of the speed indicator. He maneuvered around the traffic on the highway as if it were standing still. When he got ahead of the traffic, he really let the car show itself off.

A state trooper was impressed by his efforts and tried to catch up. Remo left the guy behind and exited quick when the trooper was out of sight, then took side streets for a while. The rest of the drive was on smaller roads where he never had the chance to get the car over 120.

A CASUAL OBSERVER WOULD have guessed—and rightly so—that Folcroft Sanitarium was a retreat for the elite who needed someplace to dry out, unwind or simply get their act together in an age when wealth and social standing were no guarantee against the standard nervous breakdown. It was also home to many patients with more serious psychological or psychophysical problems.

Dr. Harold Smith had earned his reputation as an extremely efficient administrator, but none of the Folcroft clientele—not even the most savvy, well connected of them—would have guessed his secret.

Smith was the director of CURE, probably the most secret intelligence agency in the world. The President of the United States knew about CURE. Dr. Smith and his assistant, a young ex-CIA analyst named Mark Howard, knew of it, of course. And then there was Remo—and Chiun.

And that was all. Even the former presidents who had overseen CURE activities no longer knew that they had done so, their memories purged of the information.

The problem was this: CURE was fundamentally illegal. The methods it employed were almost always in violation of the United States Constitution—the very document that CURE was intended to protect.

The gates at Folcroft Sanitarium were open, and Remo parked out front in the visitors' lot, then jogged around to the side entrance he typically used to avoid attention.

A CIA PSYCHOLOGIST HAD once stated, officially and on the record, that Dr. Smith had "no imagination whatsoever." That was not strictly true, of course, but he was perhaps the most bland, gray individual one was likely to meet, ever. He was gazing at his blank glass desktop when Remo walked in. Mark Howard, his assistant, was in one of the chairs in front of the desk.

"Hey, Smitty. Hey, Junior."

Howard gave Remo a meaningful look and said nothing. Smitty seemed not to notice Remo's arrival, staring dumbly at his desktop like one of the patients in Folcroft's Veggie Ward.

"Fine, thanks," Remo said. "Spent some time

with the kids and the biological dad, you know. Had a few laughs out on the big res. Got some sun. Got some SEALs in New Mexico. Didn't get any wolves, though.''

Mark Howard glared.

''Thanks, I'd love to sit down,'' Remo said as he sat. After a moment he nodded at Smith and said in a stage whisper to Mark Howard, ''Better run for a drool bucket, Junior.''

Howard responded by lifting up several sheets of Folcroft Sanitarium paperwork to reveal a printout of a Visa bill. It was dated that day. The charge amount had a bunch of numbers, a comma, and a bunch more numbers. Remo saw the words ''Alucci—Fine Motorcars for the Discriminating Driver.''

''What do you know about the Devil's Triangle?'' Smith asked abruptly, looking up from his desktop.

''Some porn movie?'' Remo asked.

''As in Bermuda Triangle,'' Howard clarified.

''Oh,'' Remo said. ''I know it was a popular unexplained mystery in the sixties and seventies, but I thought the gullible masses were off that kick.''

''I will assume you know the basic legend,'' Dr. Smith went on. ''Ships and planes that disappear without a trace, or sometimes turn up drifting without passengers or crew. Speculation has fingered every conceivable explanation from flying saucers to magnetic vortices and time warps.''

Remo snapped his fingers. ''There was an old TV

movie with MacMurray called *Devil's Triangle*. Pee-yew.''

"Of course, official explanations have been more mundane," Smith continued. "The Caribbean—indeed, the whole Atlantic—can have sudden storms. Some pilots and sailors are clearly less than competent. Without beacons or other homing equipment, there's no reason to assume that searchers would locate wreckage or survivors in time to effect a recovery."

"Makes sense," said Remo.

"More recently," Dr. Smith continued, as if on cue, "the Coast Guard, DEA and CIA have suggested another cause for some of the regional disappearances, at least where surface ships are concerned. Piracy."

"Piracy?"

"Indeed."

"Yo-ho-ho and a bottle of rum?"

"Nothing so quaint, I'm afraid. It's believed that certain well-organized rings may be involved in the theft of private pleasure craft and murder of their crews, with an eye toward resale of the vessels or conversion into smugglers."

"That should be right up the Coast Guard's alley," Remo said. "Glad we got the whole jurisdictional thing figured out. Can I go home now?"

"In theory, yes, the Coast Guard and DEA would handle this." Smith said. "Unfortunately, for all their discussions of the problem, none of the agencies involved have managed to prove their case. To date, they have no pirates, no hard evidence of their existence. That is, until last week.''

Remo was pretty sure he wasn't going to get to go home.

''Are you familiar with Senator Chester Armitage?'' Smith asked.

''Is he the guy who said he wished Strom Thurman had won his presidential bid in the 1940s and resegregated the U.S., then tried to claim he wasn't a racist?''

''That was another senator. Armitage is vice-chairman of the Senate Appropriations Committee, heavily involved with half a dozen other major Senate groups. As if that weren't enough, he's an intimate friend of the sitting President, dating from their college days. Altogether, a man of great influence.'' As Dr. Smith spoke those final words, the corners of his mouth turned downward in a clear expression of distaste.

''So what? I hear the President dated a lot of people in his college days.''

''Two weeks ago, Senator Armitage lost his son and daughter-in-law in the Devil's Triangle,'' Smith said morosely. ''That is, both were presumed lost until Saturday, when Kelly Bauer Armitage was pulled from the water west of Fort-de-France by a pair of sport fishermen from South Carolina. She was half-dead from exposure, nearly drowned and she had suffered…um…extensive physical abuse. It's no immense surprise to learn that she was—and remains—nearly incoherent.''

"Nearly?" Remo prodded, sensing that he was about to hear the crux of Dr. Smith's unusual problem.

"She was able to report her husband's death—a homicide—and to describe her own abduction by… well, that is…by a group of pirates.''

"Hijackers, you mean," said Remo.

"Not exactly," Dr. Smith replied. "From her description, sketchy and disjointed as it was, it would appear that her assailants were, in fact, for all intents and purposes identical to pirates of the seventeenth or eighteenth century.''

"Identical?"

"I'm filling in some gaps, of course, but from the woman's somewhat fanciful description of their primitive lifestyle—boats and weapons aside, I believe we may safely assume—they appear to emulate the tactics of such men as Blackbeard and Captain Kidd.''

"So we *are* talking yo-ho-ho and a bottle of rum,'' Remo said. "So what's CURE got to do with it? Why can't the FBI and Coast Guard handle this?''

"Normally, I would assume they would," Dr. Smith allowed. "They've tried and gotten nowhere. They have no leads, Remo. The woman can't provide them with directions or locations, names or any meaningful descriptions—anything at all, in other words. She doesn't know or can't remember where her husband's yacht was captured by the men who killed him and abducted her. There's a suggestion that a newly added member of the crew was possibly involved, but the only name she can offer is Enrique. After the murder and abduction, of course, she has no clue where she was taken or exactly how long she was held or by whom. In short, she's virtually useless."

"So the Feds are giving up," Remo said.

"But not the senator," Mark Howard chimed in.

Remo could guess the rest: an urgent phone call to his college chum on Pennsylvania Avenue, demanding justice. If he played the angles properly, there was a decent chance the senator could parley private tragedy into a winning hook for his next election campaign, combining the tried-and-true sympathy vote for a grieving father with support for a tough, no-nonsense law-and-order candidate. A diehard cynic might suggest that a dead or missing son was a reasonable down payment on six more years in Washington, sitting at the right hand of power.

Or maybe not.

The man could just be grieving, like any other outraged father, pulling any strings within his reach to gain justice, revenge, satisfaction—call it what you like. Who would deny him that, except for certain bleeding hearts who still regarded vicious criminals as the moral superiors of their victims?

Still. "Smitty," Remo said testily, "don't tell me we're doing a freaking favor for somebody."

The expression of distaste was back on Dr. Smith's face, as if a reek of flatulence had crept into his office. "We're not in the business of doing favors," he said tartly. "That's not what CURE is for."

"Oh, sure, I know that. And you know that. But every good old boy who gets into the White House has a hard time figuring out this is the one and only thing in their lives that can't be treated as a political tool."

Smith looked sharply at Remo. "We're not being used as a political tool, but you've raised a good point."

"Huh?"

"I was called by the President and he suggested CURE look into this," Smith said.

"So it *is* a favor," Remo said.

"Once we started looking into it, we began seeing the possible true extent of the damage being done in the Caribbean to U.S. interests," Mark Howard explained. "Since we don't know who or what is behind this, we can only make assumptions about their implication in various losses throughout the region going back over the past few years. But the scale is staggering."

"That qualifies it as a threat to U.S. security?" Remo probed. "Convenient justification."

"We don't *do* justification, Remo," Smith retorted seriously.

"Sure. I believe you."

"We're going to have to make sure the President believes that, too," Smith said to Howard. "But that doesn't mean we're not going to check into it."

"Check into what?" Remo said. "I mean, if you're expecting me to search the whole Caribbean, it just might take a while."

"Richard Armitage and his wife departed from Miami aboard their private yacht, *Solon II,* on the morning of March seventeenth. They stopped at Nassau and at Caicos on their way to the Dominican Republic, where they apparently hired an extra crewman, an elusive figure named Enrique, at Puerta Plata, on the twentieth. We've no idea why he was needed, how they met him—anything at all, in fact. You may be able to learn more from the woman herself."

"Say again?"

"You have a scheduled interview this afternoon," said Dr. Smith.

"You told me she was incoherent," Remo said.

"It's relative. You may get lucky," Smith replied. "I'm hoping that you can draw her out in ways the authorities could not."

"Uh-huh." Remo was clearly skeptical. "You

said they found her west of Fort-de-France. No sign of the yacht or her husband?''

"None so far," Dr. Smith replied. "Of course, if the DEA and Coast Guard suppositions are correct, the *Solon II* will have a new paint job by now, perhaps new ID numbers. Nothing that an expert couldn't spot, but ample change to get it through a cursory inspection. With any luck, it could make two or three smuggling runs into the Keys before it has to be replaced."

Remo didn't have to ask about Richard Armitage. The Caribbean was wide and deep enough to hide countless bodies, its shark and barracuda hungry enough to make short work of human remains. Pirate victims in the old days had traditionally gone over the side. It would be simple for a modern-day practitioner to emulate their lethal methods.

"Who was Richard Armitage," Remo asked, "besides an influential politician's son?"

"CEO of a smallish but expanding software company in his own right, Harvard educated, with a trust fund and family stock portfolio to see him over the rough spots."

"It's a tough life," Remo said.

"From all appearances, his life is over," Dr. Smith replied.

"Well," said Remo, "what kind of an investigation did you have in mind? Am I supposed to drift around the islands until Long John Silver tries to take me off, or what?''

''Essentially,'' said Dr. Smith, ''you'll be provided with a boat, of course, and cash enough to make your cover stick.''

''Which is?''

''You'll be executive material, well-bred and groomed. I hope that won't be too much of a stretch.''

''I'll try to manage,'' Remo said. ''There must be more to it than looking rich, though, or the Coast Guard would be losing half the tourists in the islands.''

''You'll attempt to duplicate the Armitage itinerary, inasmuch as possible from information we possess. Leave from Miami, make the stops at Nassau and Caicos. See about hiring a crewman or two at Puerta Plata, if the opportunity presents itself.''

''Not too obvious,'' said Remo.

''Let's assume our targets may be something less than brilliant,'' Dr. Smith replied. ''If nothing else, it may be safe to say they stick with a technique that works.''

''Except the woman got away,'' said Remo.

''Yes, which brings me to your next stop.'' Dr. Smith paused for a moment, his blunt fingertips shuffling invisible papers around the vacant, polished desktop before he spoke again. ''They've got her in a private room at Walter Reed.''

"Not here?" The surprise in Remo's tone was strictly shammed.

"Unfortunately, no," said Dr. Smith. "It would have made things more convenient, I admit."

"The senator's a Navy man?"

"The next best thing. Remember that appropriations seat."

"I see."

"If you leave now, you should have ample time to catch your flight from White Plains to Bethesda."

"Marvelous."

"I trust you'll show the proper respect at Bethesda," Dr. Smith cautioned, the expression on his lemon face revealing very little trust, in fact.

"I always try to show respect for innocent victims," Remo replied. "On the other hand, if we're discussing those who abuse them for profit, financial or otherwise, well, I'd say all bets were off."

Dr. Smith seemed to take his meaning at once. He said, "Perhaps you should give Senator Armitage the benefit of the doubt."

"I already have," Remo said as he rose from his chair. Mark Howard handed him an itinerary with his flight number, which Remo wadded into his pocket.

"Please hurry," Smith said to Remo. "Miss that flight and you just might miss your opportunity to visit with the patient today."

Remo grinned at Mark Howard, who gave him a dark scowl. "I'll hurry like a bunny."

4

Best known as a bedroom community of the nation's capital, Bethesda, Maryland—or, more properly, its Woodmont suburb—is also home to the sprawling U.S. Naval Medical Center and its equally vast alter ego, the National Institutes of Health, situated on the west side of the Rockville Pike. Between them, the two research-and-treatment facilities cover an area of several square miles, teeming with doctors, nurses, technicians, orderlies and patients.

Teeming with security, as well, from what Remo could see as he made his approach in a year-old rented Nissan. It was a nice enough car, but it was no Lamborghini Murciélago. But Remo had barely dropped off the keys and fled the car-rental desk before the small army of state troopers, traffic cops from various jurisdictions and airport security descended on the place.

"Hey you!"

"Freeze!"

"Stop right there!"

They came from all directions. They had him

trapped. This guy had been witnessed flagrantly committing more traffic violations in the past forty-five minutes than most of the law-enforcement personnel on the scene could recall seeing on the worst day of their lives.

And he was going to pay. He was surrounded. There was no escape.

And yet, he *had* escaped. The army of badges converged on the desk and the startled car rental clerk, and found the perpetrator had vanished.

An all-points bulletin had instantly gone out up and down the East Coast for a traffic criminal whose name, according to his car rental documents, was Remo Quartermaster.

The airport search came up empty.

Arriving at the other end, Remo had decided a Nissan would be just fine and less trouble. It didn't even occur to him that the per-day rental was just a fraction of the bill for the LamboGenie Whateverit-was.

The young SPs on duty at the front gate were also the type to notice a car like that. One of them examined his driver's license.

"Remo Rubble?" The guard looked at Remo as if he knew the name was a lie, just by his appearance. But he checked Remo off a list of names he carried on a shiny metal clipboard, then provided Remo with a photocopied map of the facility and traced his line of travel with a yellow highlighter pen.

The installation was laid out with the military's usual concern for detail, meaning that each intersection featured signs, and most of them directed visitors to destinations labeled with a bizarre alphabet soup of Navy acronyms. Remo imagined a group of officers penned up in a basement somewhere, being paid by the hour to concoct labels like MACVSOG and COMSINTEC. He finally decided to ignore the signs and concentrate on counting intersections, following the yellow-pen road on his map.

Somehow, he reached the hospital facility he sought. Another SP, this one young and female, waited for him in the lobby with another clipboard.

"Boy, I really feel expected," he told her as she officiously checked him off her list.

"It's our job to welcome visitors," she retorted with perfect seriousness.

"Hey, I never said welcome."

The blond SP directed Remo to a bank of elevators on the far side of the crowded lobby and instructed him to choose the seventh floor.

The Reigning Master of Sinanju and the world's most accomplished assassin did as he was told. On seven, Remo found the nurses' station located conveniently near the elevators. His clearance to visit was confirmed for the third time in fifteen minutes, another SP peering over the head nurse's shoulder as she checked her own clipboard, and a skinhead power lifter disguised as an orderly escorted Remo to a beige door labeled 725. The metal slot designed to hold a name tag was conspicuously empty.

"Take it easy, 'kay?" the skinhead cautioned him. "She's been through hell."

"Sure," Remo said.

The private room contained a single bed, hospital style, with shiny rails on either side and enough peripheral attachments that it resembled the captain's chair aboard some movie space-fighter ship. A television mounted near the ceiling, in the northwest corner of the room, displayed a frantic game show with the sound turned off. The idiots on the show were bitterly banishing one of their teammates. Once upon a time, Remo recalled, game shows had been full of happier idiots who jumped up and down with hysterical joy when they correctly guessed the suggested retail price on a five-pound canister of Folgers coffee. The world, he thought, was a meaner place without Bob Barker's conspicuous presence on the boob tube.

The woman in the bed could have used some ecstatic idiocy. She could have used any sort of a pick-me-up.

He guessed that Kelly Bauer Armitage had once been beautiful, and might well be again someday. At present, though, she could have been a refugee from Iraq, the sole survivor of a tragic airline crash, perhaps a poster girl for AIDS. Her sunken cheeks revealed a model's bone structure, but she was thin and blistered from exposure to relentless tropic sunshine.

Long blond hair that had to have drawn admiring stares in better days now spread across her pillow like drab seaweed clinging to the body of a woman who has drowned. Her body, underneath the sheet, would doubtless be alluring, if and when she got herself in shape again, but at the moment she looked wasted, drained of all vitality.

"Ms. Armitage?"

Although he tried to keep his voice down, Remo thought it came out sounding harsh, unnaturally loud inside the nearly silent room. Despite his own perception, though, the woman in the bed didn't appear to notice him or recognize her spoken name. Her green eyes—once vibrant, he imagined, but sadly faded now—were fixed on a point to the right of the silent television, seeing God knew what on the pink pastel wall.

Remo moved closer to the bed, not rushing it, making sure that he was well within the woman's range of peripheral vision. The last damn thing she needed was a strange man popping up from nowhere, at her bedside, peering down at her as if she were some kind of specimen prepared for mounting.

"Kelly?"

Jumping to the point of first-name intimacy was a risk, he knew, but it appeared to break the ice. The woman turned her head to face him, frowning slightly, but at least she didn't flinch or scream. In fact, her eyes appeared to focus clearly for the first time since Remo had entered the room.

"I've told you everything I can remember," she declared.

There seemed to be no point in telling her that they had never met. As an alternative, he said, "I hoped that if we went through it again, just one more time, you might remember something else."

"Is that the way it works?" she asked. Her voice was small and faraway.

"Sometimes," said Remo.

"Oh." She thought about it for a moment, vision fading in and out of focus on his face, before she said, "All right. Where should I start?"

"At the beginning," Remo told her, "if you wouldn't mind."

"Okay."

She hesitated, whether marshaling her thoughts or simply losing track of them, he couldn't tell. At least a minute passed before she spoke again, but when she did, her voice was firm and clear.

"We started from Miami on a Friday," she began, and Remo wondered what the problem was, how anyone could call her incoherent. "First vacation in a year. My Richard works so hard. Not anymore, of course. He's resting now."

Tears shimmered in her eyes, prepared to spill across her blistered cheeks.

"You stopped in Nassau and at Caicos," he reminded her.

"I'm getting there," she said. "Who's telling this?"

"I'm sorry." Remo was encouraged by the flash of anger, the display of spirit.

"So, we stopped in Nassau, and at Caicos. Richard likes to gamble. He knows how to play. He's lucky. Used to be."

The first tear left a shining path across her face. If Kelly noticed it, she gave no sign. Her eyes were focused somewhere in the distance now, beyond the pale acoustic ceiling tiles.

"We had a great time, really. Nassau…Caicos… Richard needed to relax. All by ourselves…"

"You went to Puerta Plata," Remo said.

The woman grimaced, flicking her eyes toward Remo with a reproachful glare, as if the very name left a foul taste in her mouth, but she didn't reproach him verbally.

"We went to Puerta Plata," she agreed.

"And met Enrique."

"Filthy bastard!" Kelly startled Remo with her sudden vehemence. "He was a part of it, you know. Oh, yes. I didn't trust him from the first, but Richard told me everything would be all right. It wasn't, was it?"

"No," Remo agreed, "it wasn't. How'd you meet him?"

"Richard?"

"Enrique."

"Bastard!" This time, Remo wasn't sure if Kelly was addressing him directly, or referring to the missing crewman. "Richard found him. Tried to warn him, really. Didn't like the way he looked at me. He always smirked, the little shit! We never should have hired him."

"Where did you go from Puerta Plata?" Remo asked.

"East," she replied, "and south. Down through the passage."

That would be Mong Passage, Remo thought, the stretch of water separating Puerto Rico from the eastern coast of the Dominican Republic. He had learned that much from checking out a map in the in-flight magazine while airborne between White Plains and Bethesda.

"After that?" he prodded as gently as possible.

"It was supposed to be a real vacation," Kelly Bauer Armitage replied, slipping gears. "No plans, no reservations. Living on the water. It was just supposed to be the two of us, but Richard took him on, in case we hit bad weather. There was nothing in the forecast, but he worries. Used to."

Both of Kelly's sunburned cheeks were wet with tears now, but her voice was steady. One hand had

worked its way out from under the crisp sheet that
covered her, fingers curling around the side rail of
her bed and tightening until the knuckles blanched.
Remo noted that her nails were bitten or broken off
down to the quick. Long scratches on the back of her
hand had scabbed over, already healing, while the
skin between her fingers was chapped from exposure
to sun and salt water.

Remo took a gamble, asking, "Where did the attack take place?"

"I don't know, dammit!" Fury and frustration
mingled in her voice. "A day beyond the passage,
was it? Maybe two. What day is this?"

He had to think about it for a moment. "Wednesday," Remo told her.

"Wednesday. No, that isn't right. It wasn't
Wednesday. You're mistaken."

"When the men came—"

"Men? You call them men? Those filthy animals?
You still have no idea." Her eyes were wild now;
she was trembling on the edge of panic. "They killed
Richard, did you know that? And they…they…"

Her tears were flowing freely now, her shoulders
jerking as she wept. Remo moved quickly, touching
her gently on the neck before she could notice what
he was doing. The woman relaxed into the bed like
a deflating hot-air balloon. The hysteria drained out
of her, but the horror still lived in her eyes.

"You said they dressed like pirates," Remo reminded her.

"They *were* pirates," she said, her voice like someone whose mind was far away now. "You didn't see them. You don't know."

"I'm trying to find out," he said.

"The island where they live...it's like another world. Like nothing from this century. No lights except for fire at night. No roads. Those bastards... what they did...you couldn't know."

"And no one mentioned a location, anything like map coordinates?"

"No, no, no, I told you no."

Remo felt grim. He couldn't help her. She was traumatized in some permanent, or at least semipermanent way. Maybe with time she would heal that part of her mind that had been locked up, but he couldn't do it for her.

All she had to tell him now was one word. "No, no, no, no," she said, her head shaking somberly back and forth. "No, no, no, no..."

Remo touched her neck again and gave her the gift of unconsciousness.

The shouting had attracted attention. The orderly was almost to the door of number 725 when Remo exited the private room. "What's going on in there?" he growled.

"She fell asleep," said Remo. "I suppose it was a waste of time."

The hulk glanced inside Kelly's room and gave Remo a glare. "I could have told you that."

"Next time I'll ask," Remo said as he strolled to the elevator, feeling a pair of eyes on his back. They weren't the eyes of the orderly. They belonged to a slim, attractive redhead he had noticed standing at the nurses' station, a prim frown on her face. He wasn't surprised when he heard her fall into step behind him and increase her pace when he hit the elevator call button. A moment later, when the door hissed open and he stepped in she was right beside him, stepping back against the other wall as he chose the button labeled L for lobby.

"Who the hell are you?" she challenged as the doors closed.

"Who's asking?"

"I'm Stacy Armitage. You were with my brother's wife, and I heard her crying, then it goes dead quiet and you make a beeline for the exit. Now, I want to know exactly who you are and what the hell is going on, or you can bet your ass you won't be getting past hospital security."

"I'm Remo, and I've been assigned to look into your brother's case."

"Remo? What kind of name is Remo?" Stacy Armitage demanded.

"Mine," he told her.

"Remo what?" the angry redhead challenged.

He thought about that for a moment. Who was he today? Oh, yeah. "Rubble."

"Remo Rubble of which agency?"

"CIS," he told her, picking the letters out of thin air.

"I never heard of it."

"That's good. You weren't supposed to."

"Cut the crap, okay? We've had the FBI in here, the Coast Guard, DEA, you name it. What are you supposed to have that they all lack?"

"A winning personality," he said.

"I must have missed it," Stacy said, sneering.

"You caught me on my coffee break."

They reached the ground floor and the elevator door slid open. Remo started for the exit, leaving Stacy Armitage behind, but she caught up to him at once, heels clicking on the shiny marble floor.

"You don't get off that easy, pal," she said.

"Oh, really? Maybe you should try a citizen's arrest," he said. "It's worth a shot, you want to make a total ass out of yourself."

"I don't like strangers badgering my sister!"

"Sister-in-law," he corrected.

Stacy grabbed his arm, and Remo let himself be turned to face her. "Listen, damn you! We were friends before she ever met my brother. Christ, I introduced them! Now, the cops and Feds are acting like there's nothing they can do about my brother's murder or the things those bastards did to Kelly, but

I don't believe it. It's not good enough, you hear me? Someone has to pay!''

He stared into her blue eyes for a moment, seeing love and hate mixed up there. He didn't take the animosity personally. She just needed somebody to vent on. "Okay," he said, "let's take a walk."

Outside, she kept pace easily with long, athletic legs. In other circumstances, Remo might have complimented Stacy Armitage on her appearance, but today, it would have felt like hitting on a widow at her husband's funeral.

"We're walking," she said at last. "Now what?"

"I want you to relax and trust me when I say that someone's working on the case. We haven't broken it, but I don't give up until I get results. You have my word."

"Your word? Trust you? For all I know, you could be someone from the tabloids. They've been sniffing after Kelly since those fishermen—"

"I'm not a newsman," Remo said.

"So, you're some kind of cloak-and-dagger character, is that the deal?"

"No cloak, no dagger," Remo told her. "But I get—"

"Results, I know. You said that. But these bastards aren't American. Suppose you find them in some pissant country where we don't have extradition treaties?"

"I'll come up with something," Remo said.

She stared at Remo for a moment, then she said, "I'll help you."

"Not a chance."

"Why not?"

"Because you're a civilian. Does that ring a bell?"

"My brother's dead! My best friend kidnapped, raped and God knows what else! So far, no one from the mighty FBI or any other federal agency has got a freaking clue about who did it, and you're telling me you don't need help?"

"Help, I can use," said Remo. "But an angry relative with no authority or diplomatic standing who starts raising hell with foreigners on their own soil doesn't qualify as help. You'd be a problem, and I've got enough of those already."

"And how do you propose to stop me, Mr. Remo Rubble?"

"Well, for openers, I think I'd call your father on the Hill and tell him that you're interfering with official business, jeopardizing any chance we have of tracking down the men who killed your brother. I don't think he'd take that very well, do you?"

Stacy went pale, and then her cheeks flushed brilliant crimson, anger leaping from a simmer to an instant, rolling boil. "You wouldn't dare!"

"There was a pay phone in the hospital lobby," Remo said. "I'll have it done in the next three minutes."

The angry color faded back a shade or two, her

shoulders slumped, and for the second time in twenty minutes Remo found himself about to watch a woman cry.

"I have to do something," she said between clenched teeth. "I can't take any more of this infernal waiting, sitting on my hands while someone else goes out and sniffs around, then comes back saying that he can't do anything."

"You haven't heard me say that," Remo told her.

"Not yet."

"And you won't, I promise you," he said, all the while wondering why he was being sympathetic instead of trying to shake the woman loose. "I'm on this job until it's done. I can't think of a single reason why you should trust me, after what you've been through, but you can."

"I don't want them in jail, you understand? I want them dead."

His shrug was casual, but at that moment Stacy Armitage caught a glint of something in the face of the man who called himself Remo Rubble. It was the slightest muscular change along the corners of his mouth, like the start of an ironic smile that never came into being. She noticed his eyes then.

She had heard men described as having cruel eyes and harsh eyes, and that was always considered romantic. Rugged. The eyes of the man who called himself Remo were at once sardonic, and maybe a little friendly, and very, very dead.

Stacy Armitage was afraid for a fraction of a second when she knew that her remark had hit home with this man. She had said she wanted the perpetrators dead. This man had committed himself, before he even knew her, to accomplishing just that deed. This man was a killer. And if he was on the case, if he was working for the U.S. government, that meant he was a hired assassin.

Stacy Armitage was pretty sure that was against the rules. But at that moment she couldn't have been more pleased.

The man with the ridiculously false name of Remo asked, "Can I drop you somewhere?"

"No," she said. "I'm going back inside to spend time with Kelly."

"She's asleep."

"Maybe I'll wait," said Stacy Armitage, and Remo knew she was not referring to her visit at the hospital.

"That would be best," he agreed.

"But only for a little while."

"Let's hope," he said, "that's all it takes."

He left her standing on the sidewalk, and was pleased to find that his boring little Nissan rental car had attracted no hordes of angry civilian or military law-enforcement personnel. The shiny red Italian sports car he had rented in New York, he decided, was a lot like the handmade Italian shoes he wore—

they were good for about a day's use before you got rid of them.

When he glanced in the Nissan's rearview mirror, Stacy Armitage had disappeared inside the hospital once more. Grimly he hoped that she was a problem solved.

All he needed was an emotionally involved relative-slash-friend mucking things up while he went hunting pirates.

5

"You wanna check the damn chart again?"

"I checked the damn chart a dozen times already," Jon Fitzgivens answered. "It doesn't tell me anything. You want to check the damn compass?"

"Smart-ass."

Tommy Gilpin wasn't absolutely frantic yet, but Fitzgivens could tell that he was getting there. Beneath the deep suntan his cheeks were flushed an angry pink, verging on salmon, and he gripped the *Salomé*'s wheel with one big hand—the same one that had served him so well hurling footballs downfield for the Princeton Tigers before he had moved on to Harvard Law School. He had a kind of "sue the bastards" look about him now, but even after three years of the paper chase, he couldn't think of anyone to blame for getting lost at sea through his own negligence. Not yet, at least.

"Still lost there, Tom-Tom?" Barry Ward was annoyingly cheerful as he emerged from the *Salomé*'s companionway, leading to the staterooms below-decks. The reason for good humor was close behind him, still adjusting her bikini top and patting at her cheeks to help disguise the flush of sex. As if they all wouldn't know she and Ward had just been doing the nasty belowdecks—if for no other reason than she never wore her bikini top except for an hour or so after getting laid.

"Looking good, Meg," Jon Fitzgivens told her with a rakish smile.

"We are not lost," Tommy said, glaring out to sea as if he were expecting helpful signposts to appear above the waves. "I know exactly where we are."

"Then share, by all means." Barry was goading him and enjoying the game, but took the precaution of remaining outside their self-appointed captain's reach.

"We're west of Saint Lucia, roughly southbound."

"Roughly?" Barry said. "Is that one of those nautical terms they taught you at yachting school, little buddy?"

"Listen, Bare, old chum, if you think you can handle this, by all means, step right up. I'm sure we'd all enjoy the show."

"I wouldn't dream of it, Tom-Tom," said Barry. "Not when we've all come to trust your navigating skills so much."

"Leave him alone for Christ's sake, Bare." Felicia Docherty was glaring back at Barry from her place on the forward deck, where her long brown body lay almost fully exposed to the Caribbean sun, her small bikini top untied, the thong between her buttocks looking more like a sensuous bookmark than swimwear.

Barry was considering a comeback when his own squeeze, Megan Richards, caught him with a graceful elbow to the ribs and shook her head in warning. Barry grinned at her and shrugged, leaned in to kiss her lightly on the lips, apparently deciding that he could afford to let it go—at least until they sighted land again. If Tommy lost his head and pitched somebody overboard out here, God knew how many miles from anywhere, there could be hell to pay before the others tossed down a life preserver. And how would they explain a missing person to their parents, much less to the staid authorities in West Palm Beach?

It should be easy, Jon considered, though he kept the observation to himself. If they were really west of Saint Lucia, all they had to do was turn the *Salomé* due east, or thereabouts, and hold a steady course until they struck landfall. Even if Tommy's calculations fell short of precision—which was more or less a given, when you thought about it—they could still raise someone on the radio.

But the radio wasn't working too often. They'd get it going for a while, then nothing. That was a minor inconvenience, Fitzgivens thought, compared to the navigation computer, which was totally fried. It had started acting up their first day out of port, but Tommy wasn't having any of that crap about returning to the source for a replacement, wasting time on the vacation all of them had planned and waited for throughout a grim semester in the halls of academia. No way. So what if it was telling them they were in the Arctic Circle? Tommy could navigate them the old-fashioned way. Or so he'd claimed.

Christ, Fitzgivens thought, he didn't even have his mobile phone. He had accidentally on purpose left it behind. He didn't need his damn mother checking up on him every damn night. But it had a GPS in it and at least he would have known where they were.

So they were lost at sea, and everybody knew it, although Tommy Gilpin had yet to admit that anything was wrong. He seemed to think determination was enough to see them through, and Jon Fitzgivens prayed to nameless gods that he was right. Because if they *were* lost, and they had to be rescued, and his mother found out about it—death would be better than the years of harassment that would result.

"The sun's great, isn't it?"

Reclining near Felicia on the foredeck, Robin Chatsworth flashed a dazzling smile at Jon, then puckered up and offered him a cute long-distance kiss. It warmed him in a way entirely different from the tropic sunshine, thinking what those lips could do when they were given half a chance, and he was glad that Robin had agreed to come along on this vacation cruise. If they were going to be lost at sea, perhaps cast up on some deserted isle like Gilligan and the rest, at least Jon knew that he wouldn't be bored. If they were stranded long enough, in fact, that they ran out of pills and condoms, Robin could console him with that special talent he had taught her in the front seat of his BMW, directing her and coaching her with tender loving care until she got it just exactly right.

God bless slow learners, Jon Fitzgivens thought. He had begun to stiffen, threatening to make an exhibition in his own tight swimming trunks, and started looking for another topic to distract him.

Something grim, like being lost at sea.

Oh, yeah. That did the trick just fine.

It was the fourth day of a cruise that was supposed to last two weeks, courtesy of their respective wealthy parents, but now Jon caught himself wondering if they would all be around when the sea voyage came to an end. He pictured the *Salomé* adrift, crewless, like one of the ghost ships you heard so much about in these waters.

Goddamn Bermuda Triangle, for Christ's sake! It had titillated Jon when he was ten or twelve years old, reading sensational paperbacks and watching old reruns of Leonard Nimoy *In Search Of* the answer, but age, experience and advancing cynicism had taught him that most disasters—the ''mysterious'' included—could be traced to human frailty: negligence, malfeasance, some deliberate act or oversight.

Why else was he investing all this time and sweat at Harvard Law, if no one was responsible for anything? Whom would he sue, on behalf of wealthy clients, if the world was run by Fate or some such drivel, guiding fingers from beyond the stars?

No, thank you very much. If there was any order in the world, if he had any kind of choice at all, Jon would prefer to sue the bastards. Litigation made the world go around.

"Is that another boat?"

The question came from Megan, standing to the port side of the wheelhouse, one knee raised invitingly to brace her foot against the railing, buttocks taut and round beneath the pastel fabric of her swimsuit bottom. Jon was wishing she had worn a thong to match Felicia's, feeling his tumescence coming back, when he glanced forward, following her index finger, and picked out a speck on the horizon.

"Where?" asked Tommy, still not seeing it.

"At one o'clock," Jon told him, also pointing now.

"I don't—oh, right. Looks like a boat."

"I'd say it was a safe bet," Barry added from the sidelines. "Or perhaps we've found a sea serpent."

Megan glanced back at him and winked, suggesting that he had the only serpent that intrigued her—for the moment, anyway. They had been dating, off and on, for something like a year, but in the "off" times, she was not adverse to sampling other men—including Tommy Gilpin, if the campus scuttlebutt was accurate.

"It is a boat!" said Robin. "Maybe they can tell us where we are."

Their captain glared at her for that, but Robin missed it, and Felicia cast a look at Tommy that reminded him he shouldn't look a gift horse in the mouth—at least not if he expected to come within hailing distance of any bodily orifice not his own for the remainder of the cruise.

"We'll check it out," he muttered, barely audible, and cranked the wheel enough to turn the *Salomé* head-on toward that alluring speck.

"I HAVE A VESSEL EAST, sou'east," the lookout called back from the bow pulpit of the sailboat *Ravager*. The vessel's name had once been something else, but that was long ago, and cunning hands had helped her true name to emerge across the stern, in crimson letters.

Billy Teach left his first mate to man the cockpit, moving forward to the lookout's side. "Show me," he said.

The lookout pointed, handing him the glass and guiding it until a sleek yacht filled the eyepiece. There were two half-naked women lying on the fore-deck—lookers, both of them—and three or four more bodies clustered aft. Teach wasn't sure exactly, and he knew there might be more below, but he wasn't concerned about the numbers. Cunning, skill, determination, firepower. He had it all.

"Looks sweet," the lookout said, his unsolicited opinion grating briefly on the captain's nerves, but Billy let it go. The man was right, in any case.

"Good work," he said. And then, to no one in particular, "Let's take 'em!"

With a ragged cheer, his men scrambled nimbly to their assigned positions, trimming the sails and tacking the *Ravager* toward their new target, still barely a flyspeck in the distance for those without spyglasses.

"Remember how we do it, lads!" Teach bellowed at them from the rail, no fear his voice would carry to the target vessel yet. "We can't lose this plum, when she's so rich and ripe for plucking!"

Several of his men were grinning broadly, laughing as they grappled with the lines, but none would miss the dark side of his warning. Any man who botched the mission, now that they had juicy prey in view, would damn well wish that he was dead before his time arrived. Most of the crew had witnessed punishment before, and those who hadn't seen it for themselves had at least heard the stories, grim enough to keep them on their toes and minding their respective tasks.

The *Ravager* had diesel engines down below, but

Billy Teach preferred to travel with the wind whenever possible. It was the way things ought to be, out on the open water, with no throbbing racket down below, no stench from the exhaust pipes. He could lose himself at sea—or find himself, to be more accurate. He could step out of time and live according to his own desires, the way some men had always done, without regard for man-made rules and regulations.

If their prey attempted to outrun them, Billy was prepared to use the diesels in a heartbeat, rather than allow the sweet prize to escape. But it would be a disappointment, all the same—less pure, somehow, than if the wind alone conveyed them to their destination, saw them through their conquest of the unsuspecting pleasure craft and took them safely home again.

As for the weapons, now, that was a different thing entirely. Billy Teach would have enjoyed the use of cutlasses and dirks, subduing rowdy prisoners with a belaying pin, but times had changed, and you could never tell what kind of hardware tourists would be packing in this day and age. Between shark fishermen, drug runners, oil prospectors and the nervous Nellies who imagined they were still back in Miami or New York, there was at least a fifty-fifty chance that any given pleasure craft was armed.

"Bring up the sixty and my twelve," Teach told his second mate.

"Aye, sir."

The whip-thin redhead scrambled to obey. Brief moments later, he was back, handing Teach the black Benelli M-1 Super 90 semiautomatic shotgun they had looted from a Haitian fishing boat some two years back. As for himself, the mate cradled a modified M-60 machine gun, its barrel shortened and fitted with a forward pistol grip, the ammo belt neatly folded into a side-mounted box on the left. Cosmetic modifications aside, it would still spew 7.62 mm rounds at a cyclic rate of some 600 rounds per minute, fast and deadly enough to sweep the deck of any target vessel Billy Teach was likely to select.

The other members of his crew were armed, as well, with knives and handguns of their choice, but they were under standing orders not to fire unless their captain gave the word. Teach didn't mind a bit of bloodshed on his raids—it was traditional, in fact—but in the ideal situation, he decided who should live and who should die. Unless they were embroiled in mortal combat with a well-armed foe, he would not leave that choice to lowly deckhands and the like.

"Remember to stay out of sight with that until I give the word," Teach told his mate. It was unnecessary—might even have been insulting to a man with sharper wits—but he was answered with a brisk "Aye, Captain" and a nod for emphasis.

The *Ravager* was running with the wind now, and

Billy Teach lingered at the toe rail, enjoying the breeze and salt spray in his face. He held the shotgun down against his leg. There was no need for a bracing hand against the toe rail. Billy Teach had grown up on the ocean, or in such proximity that he could hear and smell it in his sleep. He had developed sea legs long before most boys his age had learned to run a football down the field for no damn reason he could ever understand. What kind of sport was that, when you could spend your best days on the water, hunting other men?

And women, aye. Best not forget the women he had glimpsed aboard their target. From what Billy Teach had seen, this lot would more than make up for the one who got away.

There had been some concern about the female prisoner's escape, initially, but Teach had managed to convince himself that she was dead. A city girl and landlubber like that, what chance did she have on the open water, miles and miles from anywhere, without provisions or a hint of how to navigate?

No chance at all.

The sharks and 'cuda would have done for her by now, if she had not been caught up in a squall and simply drowned, or died from thirst and hunger in the open boat she stole. There had been talk of going after her, but it had seemed too risky in the long run. Better to let nature take its course, and if by some bizarre fluke she was found alive—what of it? How could she direct the law to a location she had only seen but briefly, in the early-morning light, as she was fleeing for her life, without a chart or any instruments to guide her?

The wind was brisk behind them, and they had already closed the distance to their target by half. When Teach raised the spyglass again, he saw that their intended prey had sighted them, as well. The two young women on the foredeck had their tops on now, both sitting up and staring back at him, an eerie sense that they could somehow see him, read his mind.

Well, let them. Even witchy magic wouldn't save them now.

There was a third young woman, equally attractive, standing near the wheelhouse, where three men were clustered, one piloting the yacht, his two companions arguing. Not with each other, it appeared, but with the tall man at the wheel. Teach had no skill at reading lips and couldn't tell what they were saying, but he wondered if they were alarmed at the appearance of another vessel here and now. He hoped they wouldn't run for it, but if they did...

When they were still two hundred yards distant from the yacht, Teach faced the stern and called out to a couple of his crewmen standing in the push pit, "Hoist the flag! Let's show these lubbers who we are!"

"SO WHAT THE HELL IS THIS shit?" Tommy Gilpin muttered.

"What?" Jon asked, peering at the console first, as if expecting trouble with the gauges, finally lifting his eyes to scope the sailboat that was closing on their port side, forward, running with the wind.

Jon saw what Tommy had and echoed him. "What is that?"

Barry pointed with the neck of his Corona bottle and remarked, "Looks like a flag to me."

Now, that pissed off Tommy. He knew it was a flag, for Christ's sake. The thing that bugged him was what kind of flag.

"It's black," said Jon. "What kind of flag is that? Does anybody know? Is that some kind of quarantine alert?"

"It's not all black," said Tommy, glaring at the sailboat as it drew inexorably closer. He could see some kind of white insignia, dead center on the flapping midnight field, but it was still too far away for him to make it out. "Get the binoculars."

Barry retrieved them, but he didn't offer them to Tommy. Leaning forward as he scanned the sailboat, shoulders hunched, he momentarily reminded Tommy Gilpin of a character in some effete yacht-racing movie, take your pick, dressed to the nines but casual enough to make a stranger think he didn't really care about the way he looked.

As for himself, now, he felt nothing but the most

appropriate, well-reasoned confidence in his ability
to cope with any situation that arose. Star quarter-
back in high school and at Princeton, now the second
in his class at Harvard Law, with only a pathetic
egghead nerd in front of him, he—

"Jesus, it's a skull and watcha-callit!" Barry said.
"Those bones, you know?"

"A skull and crossbones?" Jon suggested.

"Right. Now, what the hell—"

"A pirate flag," said Tommy. "Shit! We need to
make a run for it."

"You kidding me?" The grin was vintage Barry.
"Hell, it has to be some kind of joke!"

"I don't think so," said Megan, sidling close to
Barry, waiting for his arm to loop across her naked
shoulders.

"Hey, now, babe—"

"You don't think what?" Felicia asked, coming
to join them in the wheelhouse, Robin close behind
her.

"Someone on that boat just raised a goddamn
Jolly Roger," Tommy told them both.

"A what?"

"A pirate flag, okay? You never saw one on TV?
I don't have time to lead a seminar in history right
now, if that's all right. We need to get the hell away
from here, as fast as possible."

"Listen to yourself, would you? A damn Jolly
Roger? And you're gonna take it seriously?"

"Yeah, I am," Tommy snapped at Barry, hating him in a heartbeat with an intensity he never would have believed possible. Sure, old Bare was a pain in the ass sometimes—most of the time, in fact—but he was also the life of most parties. This time, however, Tommy Gilpin had a sneaking hunch that his second-best friend's laid-back attitude just might get them killed.

He brought the wheel around and opened up the throttle, feeling the *Salomé*'s big screws biting water, accelerating off the mark. She was supposed to have a cruising speed in the vicinity of twenty knots—around twenty-three miles per hour in plain English—but he hadn't tested her for speed and had no way of knowing if the maximum, assuming she delivered, would be good enough.

Some precious time was wasted as he veered off course, doubly lost now that he was running for his life, abandoning a heading that had been uncertain in the first place. Where the hell was land? How far away? The compass on his console told him they were running eastward now, which should have put the Windward Islands somewhere dead ahead, but would he miss them? Would they even get that far, before the *Salomé* was overtaken?

He looked back, and what he saw told him the Jolly Roger was no joke.

Felicia came to the same realization. "Tommy,

God, they're chasing us!'' The edge of panic in her voice had the effect of fingernails on slate.

''We're maxed out on the speed,'' he told his five companions. What should they do? What could they do?

Even Barry finally had a clue. He had stopped smiling. ''We'd better find some weapons.''

''Right!'' Jon's voice was dripping scorn. ''Did you pack the grenades, or was that my job?''

''Anything, all right?'' snapped Tommy. ''Knives, the flare gun, anything at all.''

''It could still just be a stupid joke,'' Robin insisted. ''They're just trying to scare us.'' From the tremor in her voice, she didn't half believe it.

''Then we'll laugh, before we kick somebody's ass,'' said Tommy at the wheel. ''Meanwhile, it stands to reason if they raid a boat out here, they won't want any witnesses, so do like Barry said and find some weapons! Now!''

They scattered to obey, but even Tommy didn't believe they'd have much luck. He had a jackknife with a four-inch blade, and they could use the flare gun, maybe try to set the pirate's sails on fire, some shit like that, but what else did they have? Some kitchen knives, of course. A hammer and some wrenches they could use as makeshift bludgeons, a couple of screwdrivers for stabbing, if they ran out of steak knives. There were no guns aboard: the leasing agent had been adamant on that score, and none of them owned firearms anyway. What were you supposed to shoot at sea, for Christ's sake, on a summer holiday?

He hoped they could outrun the sailboat, prayed the wind would fail, but damn near every craft that he had ever seen or heard of had an engine in reserve these days. It might not be a powerhouse, but just enough to help the wind along and give their pursuer the kick in the ass he required to overtake them, bring himself within hailing range.

Or within shooting range.

Tommy Gilpin reasoned that if these guys had unfriendly intentions, they'd have no shortage of guns. While he hated giving up without a fight, he didn't relish the thought of going down with the ship that much, either.

At the moment, he was only worried that he might not have a choice.

THE SAILBOAT WAS LOSING headway as her prey— the name of *Salomé* was painted on the transom in electric blue—poured on the diesel, churning up a wake that smelled in equal parts of salt and burning fuel. At this pace there was a chance they could lose her still, and Billy Teach wasn't about to let that happen.

"Crank up the engine," he commanded, and his first mate nodded, then turned a key protruding from the console. For a moment, Teach imagined that the engine down below would fail him, that it would be out of fuel or suffering from shoddy maintenance, but then it rumbled to life, the sailboat shuddering before it caught a swift kick in the ass and started surging forward, gaining speed beyond the simple power of the wind.

A couple of the crewmen whooped and cheered, but they didn't allow the moment to distract them from their duties. While the *Ravager* was under sail, they still had work to do, lines to attend, and a mistake could slow them, cost them the race, although it would not stop them altogether once the engine was engaged. Teach didn't have to warn them of the consequences for the man who made that happen, not while he was pacing up and down the foredeck with a shotgun at his side.

''We're closing!'' bawled the lookout, but Teach didn't need a blow-by-blow report to tell him that. The gap between the *Ravager* and the *Salomé* had already been cut by half, and it was shrinking by the moment. In another ten or fifteen minutes, if the wind held, they would close the distance to effective hailing range.

His worry, at the moment, was the radio on the *Salomé*. Unless the yachters were a bunch of total idiots, they had to have a Mayday signal on the air by now, reporting their location and the nature of their jeopardy. His first concern was that some other passing vessel might respond to the alarm—perhaps a government patrol boat, or a tough commercial fisherman with able hands and guns on board. In either case, it could mean trying to outrun the hounds, at best, and giving up their prize...or fighting to the death, at worst.

Whatever happened, Teach wouldn't surrender the *Ravager*. His crew would never dip their colors to the enemy, as long as he was still alive and in command. Far better to go down with all guns blazing, on the open sea, than to be hanged or wind up in a cage for life.

But, then again, perhaps no one would hear the Mayday call. Or when they heard the call the authorities might laugh it off. Pirates were a real danger on the seas, to this very day, but a sailing vessel? Flying the skull and crossbones? It was difficult to take seriously—although Teach took himself very seriously indeed.

Even if rescuers did come, it was unlikely they would arrive in time at the *Salomé*'s coordinates. For what Teach had in mind, he wouldn't need all afternoon.

They were no more than thirty fathoms distant from the stern of the *Salomé* when Teach called for the bullhorn they had taken from a shrimper off Grenada. It was red and white, but someone from his crew had scratched a clumsy skull and crossbones on the side. He pointed it toward the *Salomé* and squeezed the trigger, spoke into the mouthpiece—

and heard nothing but his own voice, speaking in a normal tone.

Teach double-checked the on-off switch and tried again, without result. The batteries were dead. Disgusted with another failure of technology, he turned and flung the bullhorn toward the sailboat's stern, no longer watching as it skipped across the deck and fetched up short against the taffrail.

"Close it up!" he shouted at the first mate behind the wheel. "We've got no bloody time to waste!"

He knew the engine had to be laboring, and yet it found another ounce of speed at his command—or maybe he was favored by the wind, old Neptune pitching in to bless their hunt. Five minutes more, and the *Ravager* had pulled abreast of the *Salomé*, matching her speed, the frightened-looking passengers aboard the yacht regarding Billy Teach's crew with something close to abject terror.

Maybe, he decided, they weren't as stupid as he thought.

Teach leaned against the starboard rail, with the Benelli muzzle-down against his leg, his second mate and the machine gun well behind him, hidden from the anxious eyes on the *Salomé*. He raised one hand, not fool enough to let the shotgun go, and strained to make the tourists hear him over throbbing engine sounds, the rush of sea and wind.

"Switch off your engines," he instructed them. "We need to come aboard."

The nearly naked women huddled close together at the stern, while their companions muttered back and forth, debating strategy. A moment later, Billy Teach was startled when the tall man at the wheel of the *Salomé* stuck out one arm, his fingers wrapped around the dark grips of the largest pistol Teach had ever seen. It took a heartbeat for the pirate to decide it was a Very pistol, and by then the flare was airborne, sizzling toward the *Ravager,* trailing green smoke.

It struck the mainsail more or less dead center, flashed and burned right through the canvas, barely slowing as it disappeared to port and dropped into the sea. It left a smoking hole, with bright flames nibbling around the edges, threatening to spread. In the *Salomé*'s cockpit, the pilot had his pistol broken open and was fumbling with a second flare.

''Secure that sail and douse the fire!'' Teach barked at anyone in a position to obey. Before he even finished speaking, he had stepped back from the starboard rail a pace and raised the shotgun to his shoulder, bracing for the recoil as he found and framed the yacht's bold captain in his sights.

The 12-gauge kicked against his shoulder once, twice, bright red cartridges skittering over the deck. He saw the buckshot pellets strike, some peppering the *Salomé*'s console, others chipping paint, enough striking the pilot to slam him over backward like a rag doll, dropping where he stood.

And still, no one aboard the yacht made any move to switch off the engines. Teach glanced back at his second mate and nodded toward their prize. The mate stepped forward, leveled his M-60 from the waist and hosed the sleek yacht's cabin with a burst of twenty-five or thirty rounds. The racket was hellacious, but he didn't envy those on the receiving end, where bullets shattered glass from portholes, chewed through wooden bulkheads, sent the *Salomé*'s survivors scrambling for a safe place on the deck.

"Enough!"

The mate stepped back, smoke wafting from his weapon's muzzle, and Teach resumed his place at the rail. "Again, I tell you, switch off the engines! We're boarding, one way or another! You decide how it will be, and do it now!"

One of the two men still unwounded crept into the yacht's wheelhouse, reached up for the ignition key and turned it off. The diesels grumbled and went silent, while the *Salomé* began to drift. The *Ravager* would have continued on her way and left the yacht behind, except that Teach was barking orders to his men.

"Strike sails and give me half speed on that engine, damn your eyes! Close up to starboard, now! I need a boarding party." He jabbed an index finger at the mate with the machine gun. "You, Tom. Jess and Verlan. Patch makes five. That should be all we need. The rest of you, sit tight and keep an eye skinned for patrol craft. Deacon, don't neglect that radio!''

The *Ravager* swung close to the *Salomé*, a deft hand on the tiller keeping them from a collision, while Billy Teach and his second mate covered the cringing survivors. Another moment, and the lines were fast, the two vessels secured.

"With me!'' Teach shouted to his men, then threw himself across the starboard rail.

MEGAN RICHARDS TOLD herself it had to be some kind of nightmare—that she had to still be below-decks, dozing after she and Barry finished making love—but still she could wake. She had already pinched her plump thigh hard enough to leave a bruise, and all she had to show for it was niggling pain, forgotten as she stood and stared at Tommy Gilpin, gasping in a pool of blood that spilled across the deck.

At least he wasn't dead, not yet, but Megan didn't need a medical degree to know that he was fading fast. The whole front of his muscle shirt was soaked with blood, torn where the bullets had ripped through his chest and stomach, with another bloody wound in his left thigh. He seemed to be unconscious, more or less, but he kept moaning as if he were struggling to regain awareness.

Barry was trembling when she took his hand, and while he almost flinched from her before he caught himself, she hung on for dear life. A part of Megan instantly despised him for the show of weakness, even though she couldn't really blame him, not with Tommy stretched out at their feet and men with guns lined up in front of them. Still, there was a part of Megan that was glad she had decided to break up with Barry after this vacation, once the all-expense-paid cruise was over.

Now, she had to wonder whether she would ever get the chance.

Five men with guns, and more back on the sailboat that had overtaken them. She didn't know much about weapons, but she recognized the big machine gun one of them was carrying, the shotgun that their leader held. The rest had pistols, one kind or another, most of them with sheathed knives on their belts.

It was their clothes that Megan found peculiar, mostly so far out of style that she remembered nothing like them from her twenty fashion-conscious years. No, that was wrong: a couple of the men were wearing faded Levi's jeans, patched and tattered, but the rest wore pants that looked like something they had sewn at home, so baggy they were almost shapeless, one or two of them without apparent pockets. A couple of the hijackers were bare chested; the other three wore faded shirts that didn't seem to fit them properly, as if they had been picked at random from Salvation Army bins, without regard to size or style. Three of the five wore bright bandannas tied around their heads, and one wore a black eye patch.

My God, Megan thought, they think they're pirates! It would be ludicrous if it hadn't been so terrifying. The men were advancing on the wheelhouse where she stood, together with her friends. The leader stared at Tommy for a moment, finally nodded to a couple of his men—Eye Patch included—as he said, "Get rid of him."

The pirates didn't argue. They stepped forward, hoisted Tommy by his arms, paid no attention to his moaning as they dragged him toward the nearest railing. Jon Fitzgivens made a move, as if to stop them, but he froze as the machine gun's muzzle poked against his chest.

"You'll get your turn," the raiding party's leader said. "Don't rush it, boy."

She didn't watch as Tommy went over the side, but there was no way to escape his strangled cry, the splash he made on impact with the water. Megan knew that sharks would smell the blood—or did they taste it?—and she prayed that he would drown, or anyway lose consciousness, before that happened.

"Tasty wenches," said the man with the machine gun, eyeing each of them in turn. Megan felt naked in her swimsuit, even though it didn't show as much of her as Robin's or Felicia's, with the bottoms that were barely there. Her fear of being murdered by these strangers instantly gave way to a sensation even more oppressive, dreading the fate worse than death.

"Right tasty," said the leader of the boarding party. "I believe we've got three winners here, and no mistake. But first, we need to get rid of the losers."

"Lemme do it," said Eye Patch.

"Not so fast," their leader said. "We have rules, after all."

The comment struck her as absurd, and Megan swallowed laughter that could only be a symptom of hysteria. What kind of rules could anybody have for kidnapping and killing perfect strangers?

Hell, nobody's perfect, Megan thought, and choked on laughter that time, tried to make it sound as if she were simply coughing up some phlegm.

The leader of the pirates spent a moment scowling at her, then turned back to Jon and Barry. "Either one of you a swimmer?" he inquired.

The two law students glanced at each other, wide-eyed, certain they were in the presence of a madman. Barry raised his hand, like a third-grader yearning for the washroom, and replied, "I swim."

"Me, too," Jon echoed.

"Excellent!" The leader of the pirates beamed. "We'll have a race, then. You'll both dive off the gunwale—" he pointed to the stern "—and swim your damnedest for, oh, let's say half a minute, shall we? If you're out of range by then, we let you go. Sound fair enough?''

"You're crazy!" Barry blurted out, unthinking.

"Please yourself."

The shotgun was already leveled at his face as Barry raised both hands and cried, "No, wait! We'll swim!"

"They'll swim," the leader said, and one of his companions giggled. "That's the spirit, lads. You may get lucky, though I'm damned if I'll bet on you. Did I mention that we need your vessel? And these sweet young things, of course, to cheer us on our lonesome journey home."

"You'll never get away with this," Jon said, but he was moving toward the taffrail, Barry trudging at his side.

"Who really gets away with anything?" the pirate leader said. "Come Judgment Day, I reckon every man jack on the bloody planet will have much to answer for. This afternoon, though, you two are the ones who've got a long swim home ahead of you."

Megan was weeping softly, couldn't watch as Jon and Barry went over the side. She heard the splashes, started counting seconds in her mind—one Mississippi, two—and guessed that it was only ten or fifteen seconds after they had jumped, before the firing squad cut loose.

She may have screamed but wasn't sure. Felicia's knees gave way, and she was cringing on the deck, hands covering her ears, Robin kneeling beside her, when the shooting stopped. Megan refused to face the gunmen, kept her eyes closed, but she heard them coming for her, felt a rough arm slide around her naked shoulders, foul breath in her face.

"Now, then," the pirate leader said, "why don't the three of you get down below and have a little rest while we get under way? You'll need your strength tonight, and no mistake."

6

The *Melody* was thirty-five feet long and she should have been called a cabin cruiser, but the term was too crude for a thing of beauty such as she.

Someone with unlimited funds had commissioned her. Whoever that someone was had grown up with money. You had to be very accustomed to large amounts of money to use it in such an understated fashion.

She was an odd combination. Extremely lightweight, high-tensile-strength aeronautic-grade composite alloys were inside. On the outside were hand-forged decorative rails and hand-laid teak planking. Her bridge had enough computer processing power to run a small nation, but the steering could also be performed on the two-hundred-year-old wheel from a British ship that had run the Indian trade routes. Inside, the carpets were handwoven rugs from Turkey, Iran, China and Peru. Entire walls featured original painted murals and contemporary tapestries.

The DEA had removed whatever could be removed after they confiscated her from her third or fourth owner. It was the *Lucky Lady* then, and her owner was a yuppie smuggler based at Cocoa Beach who made his last run up from Cartagena in the spring of 1995. His load was worth an estimated fifteen million dollars on the street, but someone near and dear had ratted on him for a payoff in the low five figures. Agents of the DEA were waiting to collect the *Lucky Lady,* with her owner and his cargo, when he docked at Lauderdale. The boat was confiscated, the cocaine incinerated, and the skipper wound up doing seventeen to thirty-five at Leavenworth, when he refused to "help" himself by rolling over on his source.

That way, at least, he stayed alive, while the *Melody* received a new name, several coats of paint and went to work for Uncle Sam. The DEA imagined she was theirs, but the *Melody* was moonlighting this weekend on behalf of CURE.

"I've never been much good with boats," said Remo when he saw the cabin cruiser for the first time, docked at Charleston.

"Skills are learned. You do not fear the water."

It was not a question; Remo did not bother answering the old man.

The man was indeed ancient. Chiun, Reigning Master Emeritus of Sinanju, was more than a century old, although Remo would have generously allowed that he didn't appear a day over ninety-seven. He was short and slight, a collection of thin bones under pale parchment skin that seemed so thinned by the ages you could see the blood vessels beneath. The ancient little man was Korean, with a head that was nearly devoid of hair except for yellowing wisps over his ears and on his chin. The skin around his eyes was lined and wrinkled, but the eyes themselves were like glimmering emeralds. They might have been the eyes of a child.

Though Remo Williams himself had the title of Reigning Master of Sinanju, the truth was that Chiun still did quite a bit of reigning.

Chiun was right. Remo didn't fear the water, salt or fresh. Nor did he fear the sea wolves they were hunting—if in fact they actually existed. Still, Remo would have preferred to do his manhunting on land, where he wasn't confined to the cabin cruiser's decks. And he wasn't looking forward to spending several days confined in the boat with an occasionally disagreeable Chiun.

"Be careful!" Chiun barked as Remo set the last of eight trunks on the floor in the vast stateroom Chiun had selected for himself.

"I'm always careful. Besides, I think you forgot to pack anything in this one. It feels empty."

"Leave it alone!" Chiun snapped. "Get out! Go on!"

"Chill, Chiun." Remo left, but not before adding, "Why in the hell do you need eight trunkfuls of stuff?"

By sundown they were ready to depart. Remo could probably have stalled until after the next morning's breakfast of rice, but he saw no point. If they were going, they had best be on their way. He could see his way around Charleston harbor just about as well at night as he could during the day, so it was no more of a challenge in the semidarkness, even for a navigator of his minimal accomplishments. Chiun was standing several feet away on the aft end of the craft, but Remo still heard the old Korean rolling his eyes in disdain.

When they were on the open water and the sun was gone, Chiun turned away from the black water. "I am amazed at your seamanship," he said simply.

Remo didn't reply. For a long time Chiun stood there.

Finally Remo sighed. "Okay, why are you amazed at my seamanship?"

"There are two large rocks in Charleston harbor. It took skillful sailing to bang us against both of them," Chiun explained.

"Stuff it, Little Father."

When they were well at sea, Remo picked out a southward course and kept the lighted coastline on his right, referring to the compass mounted on his console when he felt the need. The cockpit was above decks, situated on the cabin roof beneath an open canopy. Chiun was in the cabin, testing the reception on the *Melody*'s twelve-inch RCA television.

From the sound of his muttering, it was none too promising. Remo would have thought he'd be able to find some sort of programming to suit his tastes, which of late had run to Spanish-language soap operas.

It was four hundred miles from Charleston to Miami, as the seagull flew. Remo topped off the fuel tanks at Easy Eddie's, on Miami Beach. Two hundred more to Nassau, and they put in for the night, Remo intent on following his orders to present a fair facsimile of wealthy tourists on vacation. Shiftless travelers wouldn't be rushing on from one point to the next without a fair amount of shopping, lazing in the sun and soaking up the "local color."

That was pushing it with Chiun along. The Reigning Master Emeritus of Sinanju bore no more resemblance to an average upscale tourist than he did to Li'l Abner, and his patience for such joys as sightseeing or window-shopping was minute. Chiun could draw almost as much attention simply by walking through a basic gift shop as he would by demolishing the place by hand. On the other hand, if he wanted to, he could walk unnoticed into the office of Nassau's prime minister.

Chiun's unique appearance might, in fact, serve their cause. Remo wanted to look helpless without putting on a Rob Me sign, and traveling with Chiun could be the next-best thing. A city boy alone, unarmed, was no real threat to anyone, but team him with an elderly Korean in expensive silk garb, who appeared to have one bony foot across the threshold of Death's door, and the potential odds for easy pickings blasted through the roof.

These so-called pirates didn't operate from Nassau, but they might have spotters in the city, and Remo used the time to role-play as long as his patience allowed. He managed to pack a lot of ugly-American-type behavior into that twenty-minute stint. He bought and wore a loud shirt over his white T-shirt and made a point of spending too much cash on a few trinkets when he could have talked the vendors down to half the asking price. He bought a bottle of Corona and wobbled around with it for a while, pretending to chug some occasionally. He got noticed by the regular street trash, but as far as he could tell nobody showed special interest, and he made his trip back to the *Melody* without so much as a mugging.

"Like the shirt?" he asked Chiun, who regarded him suspiciously from the deck.

"It is better than the undergarment that is your typical attire," the old Korean said. "If you must wear something brightly colored, why not wear a proper kimono instead of that garish thing? And why do you smell like a brewery?"

"Relax," Remo said. "I haven't gone on a bender or anything. I just carried around a bottle for a while. I didn't even spill any on my hands."

"You still reek of it," Chiun pronounced, adding extra wrinkles to his nose to demonstrate how disagreeable the odor was.

THE RUN TO CAICOS TOOK another day, twelve hours on the water, putting them in port by dusk. Along the way, Remo had kept a lookout for suspicious boats on the horizon, while Chiun remained below, inviting painful and humiliating death to visit all of those involved in manufacturing the yacht's televisions and satellite receiver that vexed him endlessly.

They weren't attacked by pirates.

On Caicos, Remo slipped into his tourist role again and played it to the hilt. He hoped. They would be closer to the pirates now, if there were any pirates to be found, and he hoped they had scouts in port looking for easy marks for future looting. If they had him marked, however, the sea raiders gave no sign.

In the morning Remo dawdled on departure, wasting time to make it seem as if he had a hangover. Chiun came on deck briefly, eyeing his performance like an off-off-Broadway director.

"Why have you not been attacked by the pirates yet?" Chiun demanded.

"Hey, I'm trying," Remo protested. "What do you want me to do? Rent a megaphone and start yelling for them to come and get me?"

"This voyage is tiring."

"Huh. Tiring," Remo said. "Seems to me that I'm the one doing all the work."

"I mean it is monotonous," Chiun clarified condescendingly.

"Yeah. I bet." Remo didn't buy that, either. In fact, he had a sneaking suspicion that Chiun was enjoying this little trip. He was a little too enthusiastic about the *Melody*. He hoped the little Korean didn't get any ideas about moving out of their Connecticut duplex. He didn't want to live on something that floated.

Late morning found them heading south-southeast, for Puerta Plata. They were getting closer to their target zone. The pirate's nest. Remo hoped the pirates came and got them quick before Chiun started thinking about yachting catalogs.

"YOU LIKE 'EM, EH?" Billy Teach asked.

"I would have liked them better if I'd had first pick," said Thomas Kidd, making no effort to disguise the irritation in his tone.

"Um, well, that is…"

Kidd pinned his first lieutenant with a glare that had been known to make men soil themselves. It wasn't that he snarled or threatened; rather, Kidd had learned through years of practice to project pure venom through his eyes, the grim set of his mouth, so that the object of his anger knew exactly what the stone-faced buccaneer was thinking. You could see death in those slate-gray eyes, and it wasn't a quick death, never clean.

When he had made his point, Kidd turned to face the three young wenches once again. His cold expression altered slightly, not quite softening. It was a matter of degree, and those unused to dealing with him may have missed the change entirely. That was quite all right with Kidd, since he wasn't concerned about the nature of his first impression on three female hostages.

The wenches had been naked when Teach brought them from the *Ravager* to Kidd's land quarters— corrugated metal and a sheet of rotting plywood for the walls, a thatched roof overhead and dirt beneath his feet. Kidd had immediately ordered clothing for the three, and one of Teach's raiding party had gone off to fetch the mismatched remnants they were wearing now: two pairs of cutoff jeans, one pair of gaudy boxer shorts, a paisley halter top and two men's shirts. None of the garments fit, and none of them was clean, but dressing had allowed the three young prisoners to face him squarely, rather than with downcast eyes.

There would be time enough to strip them once again, pass them around, when they had learned the rules. Kidd was a firm believer in the notion that you followed certain steps to see a job done properly the first time, deviating only at your peril.

He wasn't afraid of the three wenches. That would

have been ridiculous. What troubled Thomas Kidd was that his second in command had not been able to restrain his crew from having at them on the journey back to Île de Mort. That lack of discipline was dangerous to all concerned. Suppose they had been short of lookouts on the trip back, for example, and patrol boats took them by surprise while three or four of them were busy with the women down below? More to the point, suppose the notion got around that Kidd's strict orders could be flaunted with impunity? What then?

Still looking at the women, Kidd addressed himself to Billy Teach. "Who gave the order for the sharing out?" he asked.

Teach swallowed the obstruction that had suddenly appeared in his throat, half-choking him. "Th-there was no order, Captain," he replied.

"I see." Worse yet. Teach had allowed his crew to run amok, when there was sailing and potential fighting to be done. "In that case, who was first to touch the wenches, in defiance of my rule?"

A sidelong glance at Billy Teach showed Kidd that his lieutenant had begun to sweat. It was uncomfortably warm inside Kidd's hut, but Teach had long since grown accustomed to the temperature on Île de Mort. This sweat sprang from his nerves, the knowledge that his captain was preparing an example, Billy praying to forgotten gods that he would not be chosen as a lesson to the brotherhood.

"Answer!" Kidd snapped, and Billy jumped as if someone had poked a hot dirk in his arse.

"It's hard to say, Captain." The words came out as if Teach had to squeeze them from between clenched teeth. Both hands were fisted at his sides, not reaching for the pistol in his belt. If it came down to that, Teach knew he wasn't fast enough to win the draw.

"In other words," Kidd said, "you weren't paying attention to your crew."

"It isn't that," Teach said defensively. "We had a second vessel to be manned, and we were heading back."

"Which means you needed every man jack of your company at work or watching out for trouble, yes?" the captain said.

"Aye, sir." Reluctantly, but there was no escaping it. Kidd saw his first lieutenant's shoulders sag, the grim weight of responsibility descending on him. It would take only a little extra pressure to crush him flat.

"There's an example to be made," Kidd said.

"Aye, sir." From the expression on his face, his tone of voice, Teach had almost resigned himself to death.

"I want the first man who made sport with one of these," Kidd said. "If it's a tie, pick one at random. I don't care how he's selected. You've got fifteen minutes to produce a man for punishment, or you stand in his place.''

Teach didn't dare to smile, but he was visibly relieved. ''Aye, sir!'' he snapped and waved one hand in what would pass for a salute if he were drunk and suffering from palsy. Then he rushed from the hut to choose a crewman who would be his scapegoat for the latest breach of discipline.

''I won't apologize for what has happened to you,'' Thomas Kidd informed his three nubile prisoners. ''It would have happened anyway and will again before you're done. I wager one or two of you may even find you have a taste for it, if you can just relax. Most wenches do, I've found.''

The three were staring at him now, as if he had emerged from underneath a mossy rock, some kind of slimy grub that had no place in daylight. Kidd wasn't offended by their attitude, since they were new to hostage life. They would be broken in due time and learn their proper place.

''I'm choosing an example for the men because they violated discipline, you understand?'' The wenches stared at him with blank, uncomprehending eyes, arms wrapped around themselves as if they felt a chilly draft inside the hut. ''Orders must be obeyed at any cost. If I allow my crewmen to defy me, we'd have anarchy in no time.''

Billy Teach was back within five minutes, standing

in the doorway to Kidd's quarters. "Found him, sir!" Kidd's second in command announced.

That hadn't taken long. For Billy's sake, Kidd hoped the sacrificial goat had been selected fairly, and that he wasn't a man with many friends among the brotherhood. Otherwise, Teach still might find a dirk between his ribs one night, when he was least expecting it, and Kidd would have to find himself a new lieutenant to command his troops.

"Outside," Kidd told the women, shooing them ahead of him as he rose from his makeshift throne— the fighting chair removed from a sport-fishing boat and mounted on a stump, dead center in his hut. Teach led the way, Kidd trailing as his rank dictated, to the center of the camp, where every member of the scurvy brotherhood except for posted sentries had turned out to witness the punishment.

Two pirates flanked the chosen one, each gripping one of his tanned, tattooed arms. The watchdog on his left had drawn a bowie knife and held it ready at his side; the other had a long-barreled revolver pressed against the doomed man's ribs.

No mutiny so far, at least. Kidd let himself relax a bit and get into the spirit of the thing.

He recognized the chosen man, of course. The brotherhood wasn't so large that any of his subjects were unknown to him by sight. The long scar down the man's left cheek was a result of brawling in the camp itself—a quarrel over looted whiskey, if memory served. Kidd knew the man as Fetch, but he could not have conjured up a Christian name to go with that if his own life depended on it.

"You are summoned to observe the punishment for violation of our laws," Kidd told the crowd. As he began to speak, the muttering among them ceased entirely, and you could have heard a palm frond whisper to the ground. "What is the rule on sharing up of booty?"

"Fair and square on the return to port!" one of his pirates answered, echoed by another handful in the ranks before the noise died down.

"That's right!" Kidd said. "But this one chose to take his piece before you others even had a fair look at the goods. By his example, others were encouraged to do likewise. Some here would have had first crack at these—" he turned and waved a hand toward the three wenches, huddled to his left "—but now you've lost that chance."

An angry murmuring arose and made its way around the clutch of pirates, back to where Kidd stood. He waited, letting those who had remained ashore that day check out the women in their baggy, borrowed clothes, imagining the sight of them undressed, the feel of them before another's grimy hands had blazed the trail.

"What punishment is fit for one who breaks our law?" Kidd asked his men.

"Castration!" one of them called back, the captive crewman losing several shades of tan at that.

"Let him be drawn and quartered!" cried another.

"Keelhauled!"

"Death!"

The latter vote caught on, became a chant, the pirates warming to it, seeming generally happy to condemn their fellow sea wolf without specifying how he ought to die.

"So say you all?" Kidd asked them, shouting to be heard above the din.

A rousing cheer came back at him, and now the prisoner began to struggle, trying to escape his guards, to no avail. The pirate on his right swung the revolver hard against his skull and dropped the doomed man to his knees, blood trickling from a small wound on his scalp.

"Then death it is!" Kidd told the cheering crowd, their racket multiplied by his assurance that they would have blood for supper.

Stepping forward, Kidd removed the big Colt semiautomatic pistol from its holster on his hip. He had relieved a red-faced Yankee yachtsman of the pistol three years earlier, before he cut the bastard's throat and fed him to the sharks off Martinique. Since then, the Colt had served him well on raids at sea, and twice before in matters relative to discipline.

There was no need to aim at point-blank range, but Kidd still took his time. There was a certain ritual to be fulfilled, including one last look into the dead man's eyes before he pulled the Colt's trigger, opening a keyhole in the pirate's forehead, scattering raw brains behind him in the dust.

"I swear—"

The echo of a gunshot snuffed out the dead man's protest, and a cheer went up from those assembled on the sidelines. Kidd stepped back and holstered his pistol, making sure he had the safety on.

"Fish food," he said. "So finish all who break our laws."

His men were cheering as the captain turned and walked back to his hut, Teach and the women falling in behind.

PUERTA PLATA TRANSLATED into *Silver Port.* Remo had no idea who gave the northern coastal town its name, or why, but he was guessing that the only silver seen in Puerta Plata during recent years had come from tourists.

Some tourist dollars came to the Dominican Republic, thanks to several big beach resorts. Still, most of the tourist dollars went to the Bahamas, St. Kitts, Jamaica and the upstart Union Island, which was suddenly the Caribbean tourist destination of choice, stealing business from all the others. Hispaniola sweltered in the sun and took leftovers.

Santo Domingo was the capital and main seaport of the Dominican Republic, which was notably more prosperous than Haiti, its impoverished neighbor on the west side of the island. That wasn't saying much.

Hispaniola had been Christopher Columbus's first landfall in the New World, and Santo Domingo, founded four years later, was the oldest European city in the Western Hemisphere. France, Spain and the United States had jockeyed for control of the island over some 250 years, until Haiti and the Dominican Republic won their respective independence in the 1930s. Three decades of brutal dictatorship under Rafael Trujillo ended with the strongman's assassination in 1961, and the subsequent popular election of a president led to years of turmoil, finally suppressed, for good or ill, by a return of the United States Marines. "Stability" had reigned since 1966, but there were still complaints of fraudulent elections, and most of the republic's eight million citizens still scraped by on a yearly income that averaged three thousand U.S. dollars.

"Not exactly where you'd go to find wealthy tourists," Remo said, trying to ignore the seaport smell.

"So why are we here?" Chiun asked.

"This is where Richard and Kelly Armitage made their last known stop, and Smith thinks this is where they picked up the strange and mysterious Enrique," Remo said. "It's all we've got to go on."

"White man corrupts the black man, then complains of his corruption," Chiun declared. The *Melody* was entering Puerta Plata's crowded anchorage.

"Black man accepts corruption from the white and then bemoans his fate as persecution. It is all so…Western."

"I know for a fact that Koreans breed with Chinese and Japanese—hell, even Native Americans," Remo answered, watching Chiun and preparing to duck behind the console even as he spoke. "Look how good that turns out."

The Master Emeritus of Sinanju heaved a mighty sigh, frail-looking shoulders lifting with the effort. Never mind that those same shoulders had the power to clean and jerk a hippopotamus or a stretch limousine; there was a kind of resignation—even sadness—in the simple gesture.

"Even the most perfect race has deviants and traitors," Chiun replied. "There are always those who seek accommodation with an enemy, in place of offering resistance as they should. Your Arnold Benedict is an example."

"Not my Arnold Benedict," said Remo. "Anyway, you've got the names reversed. His name was Benedict Arnold, at least according to a *Brady Bunch* episode I saw once." That wasn't quite true. Remo remembered learning about Benedict Arnold in history class. In fact, he remembered a lot more than he gave himself credit for.

"Ah, yes," Chiun said. "The Western custom of reversing names, instead of stating them in proper order. I forget sometimes."

Now that was a bald-faced lie. Chiun forgot nothing, not in all their years together. Chiun was old, and he had already been old when Remo first began to study with him. Forgetfulness, like physical infirmity, was one of several dodges that Chiun employed to mask his physical and mental powers from the world at large. But he wasn't hiding anything from Remo. Remo hoped.

A minimob of street urchins was waiting for them as Remo nosed the *Melody* into a berth. Deft, dark hands caught the stout line he pitched, and it was made fast to the dock. Another handful of coins scattered the ragged, half-dressed children. Remo turned to find the Master Emeritus of Sinanju watching him, a little frown wrinkle between his eyes.

"You're going into town," Chiun said. From his tone, he wasn't asking.

"It's the reason we came down here," Remo said. "You're staying on the boat?"

It was a pointless question, and instead of answering, Chiun spent a moment studying Remo's baggy "tourist" shirt, cut from a fabric printed in outrageous floral patterns. It was the twin of the shirt he had worn in Nassau, then trashed rather than wash. Remo didn't think he looked all that touristy, actually, but he wasn't all that interested in undercover work anyway. Putting on the shirt over his everywhere, all-season Chinos and T-shirt was as much effort as he was willing to put into his disguise.

Chiun made a muffled clucking sound and shook his head in evident disgust. "You are a white man, after all," he said. "Your transformation into a long gizzard is too easy, too natural."

It was Remo's turn to frown. "You mean lounge lizard?" he replied.

"It's all the same," Chiun said. "A worthless leech by any other name—"

"Would smell as sweet, I know," interrupted Remo in the interest of a swift departure. "Anyway, I'm taking off. Want anything from town?"

"I want to be away from town," said Chiun.

"So, keep your fingers crossed. I get a bite the first time out, we could be on our way tomorrow."

"I hope TV reception is improved in this forsaken place," Chiun said, then took himself below.

7

All harbors smell essentially the same, even if some are worse than others. There is the bracing aroma of the sea, with undertones of rotting seaweed, fish left too long in the sun, the pungent tang of gasoline and motor oil, exhaust and diesel fumes. If there are seafood restaurants close by, their grills and garbage bins add unique smells to assault the senses, luring and repelling new arrivals all at once.

A visitor who wanted to see and smell the city proper had to proceed beyond the waterfront, search out the avenues and byways where the natives spent their daily lives. In Puerta Plata, torn between the tourist trade and simply getting by, that meant a mixture of boutiques, dive shops, trendy cafés and travel agencies with simple restaurants and markets, general stores that catered to the working fishermen and captains who maintained their boats as much through sweat and sheer determination as by any great influx of cash. There were small banks, a neglected library and a maritime museum that had apparently been closed for renovation several years before, with little or no progress logged since then.

Remo was looking for a group of ruthless sea wolves, men who wouldn't shrink from murder, rape or God knew what in the pursuit of pleasure, profit, self-advancement. It wasn't an attitude that anyone in modern-day society would call unique. It was evident every night on television, every morning in the headlines. Only some of the peculiar trappings, as described by Kelly Bauer Armitage, made this group of destructive human animals stand out.

Assuming she was rational, Remo amended. If her pirate story was a product of delusion, post-traumatic stress, whatever, he could well be wasting his precious time.

Still, Smitty and Mark Howard seemed to think there was something to this. Remo was their contracted Reigning Master of Sinanju, and he did what he was told, without ever a word of complaint.

He worked his way inland from the waterfront, paying only cursory attention to the dives that lured rough-and-tumble fishermen or seamen. Such establishments might harbor pirates, it was true, but they wouldn't have drawn the likes of Richard Armitage or his wife, Kelly. Wherever the naive Americans had met their enemies, Remo would bet it hadn't been on the docks.

Where, then?

He made his way through narrow, crowded streets,

feeling the eyes of the locals watching him. They would mark him as a gringo with more cash than common sense, he hoped. It was possible that someone would attempt to mug him, but Remo wasn't concerned about a confrontation on the street. He could dispose of any such straightforward opposition swiftly.

Just now, his mind was fixed on other predators, the kind with sense enough to plan ahead, check out a stranger and discover that he had an extremely high-priced boat tied up at the marina. Someone who might try to win his confidence, suggest that his vacation would proceed more smoothly with a native guide, for instance, or some local boys to serve as crew aboard the luxurious *Melody*.

Of course, such offers might be perfectly legitimate, no more than an attempt to make ends meet by picking up a little extra cash. Remo would have to trust his intuition. Maybe he'd get lucky and a guy would have a peg leg or an eye patch or a parrot on his shoulder.

The first nightclub he tried was the Flamingo, three blocks inland from the waterfront. It was a stylish place, as such things were appraised in struggling Third World ports of call. A twenty-something hostess met him just inside the door, established that he was alone and led him to a booth against one wall, then left him with a thousand-candlepower smile that could have suntanned an albino. Moments later, he was talking to a cocktail waitress in a low-cut peasant blouse and ruffled skirt. She made a point of bending over Remo's table as she took his order for a fruity rum concoction he had never heard off, offering her cleavage almost as a side dish—or an appetizer for delights to come, if he was only man enough to ask.

Instead, he grimaced and let it pass. His drink arrived, and Remo pretended to sip. He listened to the music, made a show of working on his drink until he felt that he had adequately scoped the clientele, deciding there were no apparent buccaneers in sight.

The first club was a warm-up. At his second stop, a flashy place called La Deliciosa, Remo waved off the hostess and found an empty bar stool, ordering another cocktail that was basically chopped fruit deluged in rum. Once more, he pretended to drink it through a stingy straw and, when he was sure no one was looking, reached over the bar and dumped most of the contents in the bartender's sink. The bartender returned a moment later, and Remo tried to engage him in casual conversation.

A purple plastic name tag on the barkeep's shirt declared that he was Pedro, and although he seemed willing enough to talk, a combination of poor English and deficient knowledge kept him from imparting any useful information. Pedro didn't know where local guides or temporary crewmen could be hired, he had only the vaguest knowledge of sport fishing in the area and Remo's passing reference to pirate treasure left the young man with a blank expression on his face, as if he had been asked to give a speech on quantum physics.

Remo had already had enough undercover baloney for one day. He wondered if it was too early to phone Smitty and tell him the trip was a washout.

Then he sensed someone approaching him from behind.

"Excuse me? Sir?"

The voice was native-born American, with traces of New England clinging stubbornly to life beneath a Southern accent picked up in adulthood. Remo swiveled on his stool and faced a trim man in his middle sixties, iron-gray hair receding from a high, aristocratic forehead that was deeply tanned, like the remainder of his face, from years of regular exposure to the tropic sun. The stranger's blue eyes had a sparkle to them as they peered through steel-rimmed spectacles, and his lips curled in a smile that was both tentative and self-assured.

"Forgive me for intruding, please," the stranger said, "but I could not help overhearing that you're interested in pirates."

"Well..."

"I suppose you'd say the subject is a kind of personal obsession. May I join you, Mr....?"

"Rubble. Remo Rubble. Sure. Have a seat."

"Ethan Humphrey," said the older man, immediately shifting to the empty stool on Remo's left. His handshake was not limp, exactly, but there was no hidden strength behind it. Remo pegged him as a bookworm, maybe retired from teaching or some other sedentary occupation, probably a bachelor, spending his retirement on what passed for an adventure in his relatively cloistered life. He reminded Remo of Harold W. Smith.

"I can't decide if you're from Maine or Massachusetts," Remo said.

His new acquaintance blinked, taken off guard, then cracked a smile. "Oh, yes, I see. The accent, yes? It's Massachusetts, actually, although I thought I'd lost it during fifteen years of teaching at the University of Florida, in Gainesville."

"Teaching what?" asked Remo.

"History, of course—whence springs my interest in the buccaneers of the Caribbean. You're interested in treasure, I believe you said?"

"Well, not commercially," said Remo, "but I'm down here on vacation, checking out the islands, mostly killing time. I thought it might be interesting to spice the trip up with a look around the seamy side of history, you know?"

"Indeed I do," said Humphrey, with a smile that put expensive dentures on display. "And you've come to the right place, I assure you. Not Puerta Plata specifically, but Hispaniola and environs. Do you know much about pirates, Mr. Rubble?"

Remo flashed a sheepish smile and shook his head. "A little *Treasure Island* and some Errol Flynn wraps it up," he said, feigning embarrassment.

"In that case," Humphrey told him, "you're in for a treat. The West Indies were notorious as a haven for pirates in the seventeenth and eighteenth centuries, you know. John Avery had the protection of the British governor in the Bahamas, raiding French and Spanish shipping from Martinique all the way to Madagascar and the Red Sea, circa 1695, before he disappeared out east. His crew was ultimately hanged in England, when they tried to do without official blessings, but the captain simply vanished. Howell Davis was another buccaneer who sailed from Martinique, but came to grief when he abandoned piracy to join the slave trade. There were even female pirates, though you seldom read about them in the common histories. Anne Bonney and Mary Read both sailed with Calico Jack Rackham, fighting tooth and nail beside male members of the crew when there were galleons to be looted, but women's lib only went so far. When they were tried for piracy in 1720, both women claimed that they were pregnant, which officially precluded them from being hanged."

"Fascinating," Remo said, although it was only interesting. Barely.

"Of course, no buccaneer who ever plied these waters could compare with Morgan," Humphrey said, continuing his impromptu lecture. "In 1670, Sir

Henry led an outlaw fleet consisting of thirty-six ships and some two thousand men, raiding from Jamaica all the way to Central America, where he sacked the Spanish garrison at Panama and installed himself as the warlord in residence. That bit of banditry got him knighted in England and earned him a posting as lieutenant governor of Jamaica.''

"So crime does pay," said Remo.

"Oh, indeed it does, my friend, in certain circumstances." Humphrey flashed the dentures again, then flagged down Pedro to order a refill on his vodka Collins.

"What about today?" Remo asked. "Are there any pirates still around the neighborhood?"

"Today?" The ex-professor seemed amused. "I shouldn't think so, Mr. Rubble. We're discussing history, you understand, and none too recent history, at that. There are such activities in the present day, of course...."

"That's what I mean," said Remo, stopping short of slurring words that would have made him incoherent. "Anythin' can happen, and it usually does."

"That's from Walt Disney, I believe," said Ethan Humphrey.

"What's the difference?" Remo challenged. "Just as long as you know what I'm talkin' 'bout."

"I seem to follow you so far," said Humphrey, leaning closer, hanging on his every word.

"An' all I'm sayin' is, that if the pirates used to

make a killing in the old days, wha's to stop 'em doing the same thing right now?''

''Well.'' Humphrey frowned and cleared his throat, as if preparing to impart a lecture. ''There are more laws, of course, where few or none existed in the past. Technology has changed, allowing naval units and the Coast Guard to pursue potential miscreants from distances that would have made a roundup hopeless in the old days. As for the killing side of modern-day technology, you have a range of craft and weapons that would slaughter any old-style pirates in the area today.''

''That's just supposing that they hung on to the old ways, am I right?'' asked Remo.

''It would be scandalous!'' Humphrey proclaimed, as if Remo had dared suggest his favorite daughter might turn out to be a mindless slut. In fact, he didn't seem embarrassed by the notion of surviving pirate bands, but rather by the notion that they might adopt newfangled methods for themselves, in place of raiding as their great-great-great-grandfathers had conducted their attacks two centuries before.

''So say these free spirits did exist,'' said Remo. ''How would, say, a freelance journalist with cash to spend get hold of them and make arrangements for an article, perhaps a full-length book?''

''You're taking much for granted,'' Ethan Humphrey answered, showing off the store-bought pearly whites. "Naturally, I'll see what I can do, but don't expect too much in way of miracles."

"I never do," said Remo, sounding far more sober than when he had spoken just a moment earlier. "I also need a travel agency, trustworthy and reliable, to recommend a native crewman for the next leg of our journey."

"Native crewman?" Humphrey struck a pose right on the stool, pretending that he had to scan his brain for an idea.

In fact, if Remo's instinct was on target, Humphrey was about to set him up with a potential nest of con men, maybe worse.

"There is a certain travel agency," the transplanted New Englander went on. "Trade Winds, the owner calls it. Nothing terribly original, but they arrange for guided tours, pilots, crewmen, anything you need to make your island getaway a memorable experience."

"Sounds perfect," Remo said. "Where do I find them?"

"Bay Street," Ethan Humphrey said. "Are you familiar with the town at all?"

"Just what I've seen since we got in, about an hour ago."

"When you say we...?"

"I have a traveling companion," Remo said. "He's been with my family for years."

"Faithful retainer, eh?"

"Yes," Remo smiled. "Faithful retainer. Exactly."

"I understand, of course." The pearly dentures flashed again. "It does you credit, bringing the old boy along to see the sights on your vacation. There's no Mrs. Rubble, then, if I may be so bold?"

"Not currently," said Remo.

"Ah. Two men out on their own, then, challenging the sea."

"Well..."

"It's the finest way there is to travel." Humphrey leaned in on his elbows, dropping his voice to an almost conspiratorial tone. "Women simply muck up these adventures, don't you find?"

Remo was waiting for the older man's hand to find his thigh and was relieved when Humphrey kept his paws to himself. Apparently, his rapt enthusiasm was restricted to the bounding main.

"I really couldn't tell you," Remo replied. "This is my first time out at sea, I guess you'd say. I mean, I used to take the family sailboat out from Montauk sometimes, in the summers, but it's been a long, long time."

"You never lose the feel, though, do you?" Humphrey didn't wait for a response to his own question. "Being on the water is like dreaming, flying, giving yourself up to magic that's been drawing men away from land since time began."

"You're some enthusiast," said Remo.

Humphrey may have blushed behind the tan, but

it was difficult to tell. "Forgive me, please, if I sound maudlin. I'm afraid the sea has always been my one great love. It's difficult for landlubbers to understand, I know. As for myself, I heard the calling early on, but it has only been the past few years, since my retirement from the halls of academia, that I've been able to indulge myself."

"You live here?" asked Remo.

"What, in Puerta Plata?" Humphrey had to think about it for a moment, as if he could not remember his address. "I've been here for a year—or is it eighteen months? No matter. I go where the sea winds blow me, as the spirit moves."

"Some life," said Remo, wondering how much of it was total bullshit.

"Yes," the older man said, beaming back at him, "it is. I'm working on a book about those days. My magnum opus, you might say. There's never been a definitive study of the Caribbean pirates before, the way they lived and died, the reasons why they chose an outlaw life."

"About that travel agent," Remo said, "if you could let me have the address..."

"Of course," said Humphrey, coming back as if Remo had summoned him from dreamland. "It's at number 20 Bay Street." He rattled off the directions and was disappointed when Remo called it a night, claiming he needed to be up early.

"Of course, I understand," Humphrey said, giving

Remo a final glimpse of false teeth. "Good sailing, then."

Outside, the night was cooling down. Streetlights were few and far between, but Remo did not mind darkness. Even if he hadn't been able to expand his pupils to make catlike use of the ambient light, a handy Sinanju skill, he still would have been able to find his way back to the harbor by following his nose and keeping to the streets that ran downhill. The handful of pedestrians ignored him as he made his way toward the waterfront.

As Remo walked, he thought about his conversation with Ethan Humphrey, the old man's fascination with pirates and their lawless lifestyle. It was a little odd, but not freaky-odd, Remo decided. A professor of history who kept up with his hobby in retirement, finding a way to blend study with relaxation in a pleasant tropical climate—it didn't seem so peculiar. Still...

The muffled scream distracted him. Remo went in search of it. He might save a damsel in distress and that would be his good deed for the year, or it might be a trap, some kind of setup. He hadn't been subtle in his questions, here or in the other ports of call where they had briefly stopped along the way. There was at least an outside possibility that someone, possibly the very men he sought, would try to take him out and end this unpleasant undercover work.

Please be a trap, please be a trap, he thought as he stepped into the brooding shadows of an alley, the source of the scream.

8

The alley looked and smelled like any of a thousand others Remo had explored as a teenager, as a Newark cop, or during his years with CURE. Bare dirt and gravel under foot. A reek of garbage that had nearly liquefied when no one bothered to collect it. Scuttling, feral sounds of rats or scrawny kittens as they foraged in the trash for something edible. This night, though, this alley held the muffled sobbing of a terrified woman and the gruff, excited voices of her tormentors.

Remo made no conscious attempt to camouflage his approach, but some of his earliest training with Chiun had taught him to move with effortless silence. His soon-to-be adversaries huddled in the blackness at the far end of the alley. Remo counted four of them by their voices. It was a lengthy dead-end alley, Remo saw, with no escape for their intended victim—or for them, now that he stood behind them, cutting off their only access to the street. The alley made as good a killing pen as he had ever seen.

Three of the men were Remo's height or shorter,

average for the Caribbean mixed breed they repre-
sented, while the fourth and nearest to his left stood
six foot five or better. Remo guessed the hulking
mugger's altitude had marked him as a freak from
adolescence, opening him up to taunts and ridicule
that would have led him into fights and taught him
to rely upon his strength and size for settling arguments.

All four were dressed in peasant shirts and baggy
trousers. Mr. Big displayed patches on his rump. One
of the men, on Remo's right, had picked up a Malcolm X cap somewhere; he wore it backward, at an
angle, the curled bill half covering his neck, the
faded X resembling a target on the back of his skull.

Remo caught a glimpse of their victim, and that's
when he wanted to start shouting profanities. The
woman cornered in the stinking alleyway was Stacy
Armitage.

In fact, Remo wasn't tremendously surprised, just
ticked off. Their conversation back in Maryland had
left him thinking that she was the ambitious type,
likely to make an attempt to solve the mystery herself, and now here she was, ass deep in alligators,
waiting for a sympathetic knight to come along and
rescue her.

Of course, that wasn't fair. From what Remo
saw—the blouse torn open to expose one breast, the
dark smudge of a bruise on Stacy's cheek—she
hadn't counted on the rough reception she was get-

ting in Puerta Plata. She *probably* hadn't set him up for this, he decided. Even so, there was a moment when he thought of leaving her to sort things out herself—enjoy the benefits of amateur sleuthing with limited resources and no one to back her up in the event that she encountered trouble.

A couple of the thugs were talking back and forth in Spanish, chuckling at some not-so-private joke, and all were keeping their eyes on the woman.

Remo didn't bother to dredge up his bare minimum of Spanish, all of it learned from constant repetition from Chiun's Mexican soaps. He didn't even know what it meant. Probably, "and now, a word from our sponsors." So instead he said, in English, "Is this a private game, or can anybody play?"

The four thugs spun in unison, as if they choreographed it.

"Nice footwork," Remo said. "But it's so sad to see how far the Four Tops have fallen since their years as pop music superstars."

The Four Tops stopped being surprised almost immediately and started being angry. Stacy Armitage showed a mixture of relief, desperation and stark surprise in her features. Remo became grudgingly convinced she hadn't been expecting him—or anyone—to come along and save her from the evil-smelling gang.

The tallest attacker was first to find his voice. Whatever he said was unintelligible, but Remo had no difficulty with the tone. It was a warning, a threat, telling Remo that the girl belonged to him and his buddies and possibly suggesting Remo should get wise and run away.

"Don't speak the lingo, sorry," Remo told them. "All sounds the same to me, you want to know the truth."

"Joo got big prublem, gringo," said the weasel in the backward cap.

Remo addressed the English-speaker. "Are you being anti-Semitic? Can't we stop the hate? You know I was going to cut you guys some slack and let you walk, but now you've gone and pissed me off."

The muggers glanced at one another, three of them apparently confused, their faces registering anger as the fourth translated Remo's words. Stacy Armitage clutched her open blouse and watched Remo with a dazed expression, convinced that he would soon be dead.

"Lass chince, gringo," said the interpreter. He drew a switchblade from the right-rear pocket of his baggy pants and snapped it open, long blade gleaming even in the darkness of the alleyway. As Remo stood and watched, the other three pulled weapons of their own: another knife, a razor and a length of rusty chain for Mr. Big.

"You losers shouldn't play with toys like that,"

said Remo, smiling as the muggers started to en-
circle him.

Considering the crude enveloping maneuver,
Remo half expected them to rush him all at once, but
it was Mr. Big who made the first move on his own.
He swung the chain at Remo's head, as if delivering
a roundhouse punch, the steel links hissing in the
night air.

Instead of shattering the skull he aimed for,
though, the big man's flail sliced empty air. Remo
simply stepped aside and let the chain swing by
harmlessly. He waited just long enough for Mr. Big
to realize he had missed entirely, then retaliated with
a swift kick to the big man's knee.

There was an ugly cracking sound, immediately
followed by a scream as Mr. Big lurched backward,
hopping on his one good leg. The chain was totally
forgotten as he lost his balance, long arms flailing,
and collapsed into a pile of garbage spilling from a
capsized trash can. As he fell, the giant's own chain
whipped around and struck him in the face, adding
insult to injury.

Remo's trio of lice-ridden adversaries hesitated,
each man glancing briefly at his companions as their
hulking comrade fell. Mr. Big's rapid defeat might
have prompted them to run, except that Remo barred
their only exit to the street.

"C'mon, c'mon, c'mon!" Remo complained.
"Let's just get this over with, huh?"

Remo Williams, Reigning Master of Sinanju, was far less distracted and impatient than he seemed. His senses provided him information from all directions and his awareness was high, like the awareness of a hunting big cat. He knew that Stacy Armitage was moving, for example, seeking out a corner of the dead-end alleyway and searching for a weapon, anything that she could use in self-defense if Remo failed to drop his three opponents. At the same time, he was also conscious of the wounded mugger to his left, moaning in pain as one hand clutched his thigh, the other still wrapped up in chain.

Mr. X advanced with his switchblade held in front of him, lips drawn back from his teeth as he cursed Remo in a steady stream of gutter Spanish.

Remo didn't even try to translate, gliding forward to surprise the blade man. The blade man was very surprised indeed. One second he was facing an unarmed skinny white tourist. The next second his knife was gone, his wrist was broken and the wall on one side of the alley was rushing at him at a hundred miles per hour. He bounced off it, more bones breaking inside his body, and before he could fall he found himself facing the skinny white guy again. The pain of the broken wrist was just screaming into his brain as he felt the white guy take his head in his hands. There was a brief flash of rapid movement, then there was blackness.

When Mr. X collapsed, the faded cap was facing

forward and it was the blade man's head that was reversed, facing directly backward on a broken neck.

That was enough for the two men still on their feet. They wanted out of there, but Remo didn't plan to let them go so easily. He stood his ground and waited, knowing they would either have to rush him or—

The dark man with the knife turned and made a rush at Stacy Armitage, but the rush didn't get too far. Remo had lost patience with this gang of dull blades and stepped in fast, giving the would-be hostage taker a quick nudge in the back. The knife man flew into the brick wall near Stacy Armitage with a liquid thump. Not hard enough to kill him, but the knife man's good looks got squashed into pulp, which he would discover when the pain would bring him screaming back to consciousness hours later.

Mr. Big chose that moment to drag himself erect, one hand clutching the filthy wall behind him, his good leg taking his weight. It had to have hurt like hell, but he was grimly silent as he made his move. Remo faced off the razor man long enough for Mr. Big to get himself up, then moved in fast on the razor man. Too fast for the razor man to even see, and then the razor man was flying—for a fraction of a second he was actually airborne.

The two muggers came together with stunning force, damaged each other irreparably, then fell away from each other like two sides of a lightning-split tree trunk.

Stacy Armitage couldn't quite believe all she had witnessed in the past few seconds. Suddenly her attackers were neutralized. No longer crying, she stared at Remo as if she couldn't believe her eyes.

"Are they all dead?" she asked finally.

"Not that guy," said Remo, pointing at the wall kisser. "These two I don't know."

Stacy raised one shaking hand at the man in the Malcolm X cap.

"You broke his neck."

"Oh, yeah, that guy is dead, definitely. Let's go."

She almost flinched when Remo reached to take her hand, but at the final moment she gave in and let herself be led away. The alley was two blocks behind them, and they were proceeding toward the waterfront, before she found her voice again.

"I can't believe you killed them, just like that," she said.

"They made the rules," said Remo. "You were in some trouble with those four, as I recall."

"I never said that I was sorry," Stacy told him. "I just can't believe it was so easy. Who are you?"

"We've been through that already," Remo said.

"You're not like any federal agent that I ever heard of," Stacy said.

"Why, thank you! That was a compliment, right?"

"An observation," she replied. "Don't let it swell your head or anything."

"I'll do my best," he said. "Stop here."

Stacy Armitage found the fingers on her arm were an irresistible force. She stopped because she didn't have any choice. They were standing in a dark place between what few lights there were on the streets.

She felt Remo's hands on her body, but she didn't have time to consider the possibility that he had taken her from the would-be rapists so he could ravage her himself. The man touched her in various places, quickly and methodically.

"Anything hurt, aside from the bruise?"

"No," she responded. "I don't think so."

"You'll live," Remo pronounced, and they started walking again. "What are you doing here?"

"As if you didn't know." Her tone was bitter.

Remo knew there was a lot more to come. He gave her a look in the darkness, which was all he needed to do.

"I know you and a bunch of other Feds said my brother's case was being taken care of," Stacy blurted. "I know. Except that wasn't good enough, okay? I couldn't just sit back and wait to read about it in the papers, or to have some stuffed shirt come around six months from now and say it's over, but the details have been classified. I need to see it through. Is that so hard to understand?"

"You almost saw it through tonight," said Remo. "How'd you meet those four gorillas, anyway?"

"I've been in town two days," she said. "Flew down from Jacksonville on Thursday afternoon. The Coast Guard wouldn't give me any information, and the local cops are worse than useless. I've been asking questions, checking out the kind of places where your basic pirates might hang out, if they had time to kill."

No pun intended, Remo thought, but kept it to himself. "So, let me guess," he said. "One of those characters suggested that he might have useful information he'd be willing to let go of, for a price?"

"The Spike Lee fan," she said. "I know he suckered me, okay? Don't say it."

"And he took you to the alley, where his friends were waiting?"

"Pretty much," she said. "I still thought I could talk my way out, maybe buy them off, but they had something else in mind. They would have...I mean, if you hadn't shown up when you did...well, thanks."

"No problem," Remo said. "Unless, of course, somebody in the dives where you were hanging out remembers seeing you with Mr. X. The locals may not care who dropped those four, but if they do, and tongues start wagging, you could have a whole new set of problems on your hands."

"The cops would never think I killed those four back there," she said.

"Which makes it my problem," said Remo, "if you spill your guts."

"I wouldn't tell them anything," she said defiantly.

"You say that now," said Remo, "but this isn't Washington or New York City. The police have different rules down here, and Daddy wouldn't be much help."

"He doesn't even know I'm here," said Stacy.

"But you wouldn't hesitate to call him, would you, if you wound up in a jam?"

She glared at Remo and refused to answer him, changing the subject. "Have you found out anything so far?"

"It's too soon," Remo said. "I keep getting distracted."

"Right. And I suppose that's my fault?" Even as she asked the question, though, Stacy sounded remorseful.

They had reached the waterfront, and Remo led her toward the pier where the *Melody* was berthed. Stacy took one look at the gleaming cabin cruiser, frowned and said, "So this is how you're doing it? You plan to use yourself for bait?"

"Unless somebody else keeps luring the sharks away," said Remo. "Come aboard."

Chiun was in the main saloon, belowdecks, watching television. The selection had to have been abysmal, as they found him staring at an infomercial for an exercise device designed for toning stomach muscles, called the Ab Solution. Remo grimaced at a blond hard body with a thousand-candlepower smile and eyes that looked as if she was coming down from six or seven weeks on speed. The old Korean sat motionless in front of the plasma screen, surrounded by darkness, so motionless he might have been stuffed.

"Is that the best we have to offer, Little Father?" Remo asked Chiun.

"A moment ago this channel was showing a fine Argentinean drama," the old Korean said. "The moment you and the harlot stepped aboard, the signal went haywire and my lovely story of intrigue and romance was replaced with this!"

"You don't need an Ab Solution, Little Father," Remo chided. "Chiun, this is Stacy Armitage. Her father is the senator who turned the screws on you-know-who, who turned the screws on Upstairs."

Chiun never moved a muscle, but the TV abruptly went black. Stacy seemed to see the faintest reflection of a very lined face in the surface of the plasma screen, then the screen blazed back to life. The wizened Korean face was wiped out by a gleaming, muscular woman doing exercises. Even she looked uncomfortable using the Ab Solution, but every rep brought her large breasts, bulging out of their bikini top, looming into the camera lens. Her boobs filled the huge screen, forty-times life-sized.

"Shall I record it for you?" Chiun asked.

"No, thanks."

"The senator's trolloping offspring doesn't quite measure up, does she?" Chiun asked in Korean.

"That's enough." Remo steered Stacy out of the media room.

"He's a friendly old fart," Stacy said in a whisper.

"You caught him at a bad time," Remo said. "He wants his MTV. *M* as in Mexican."

"Listen, do you think those guys tonight were…well, you know?"

"Good citizens? The welcoming committee? Talent scouts? I'd vote for none of the above," said Remo.

"Dammit, this is serious. I need to know if they were in on what happened to Richard."

"It's a little late to ask them now," said Remo, "but I doubt it."

"Why?" she asked.

"It's just a hunch," he answered, "but they didn't have that pirate feel about them. Not a peg leg in the bunch, for openers. No parrots on their shoulders that I noticed."

"Very funny, Mr. Rubble."

"Call me Remo. If I had to guess, I'd say those four were city boys who didn't spend a lot of time at sea. In fact, I don't think they cared much for drinking water, much less sailing on it. What you did is set yourself up to be robbed and raped by some gorillas who had time to kill. In fact, I wouldn't be surprised to hear they'd pulled that kind of thing before. But hijacking a ship at sea?'' He shook his head. ''It doesn't wash.''

''Unfortunately, I believe you're right,'' she said.

''So, now that you've experienced the wild life, may I take it you'll be going home?''

''Did I say that?''

''Not yet,'' said Remo, ''but I keep hoping for some evidence of common sense.''

Her cheeks flushed pink at that, but Stacy swallowed the sarcastic answer that immediately came to mind. ''My brother's dead,'' she told him, ''and I want to find the men responsible. What's wrong with that?''

''In theory, nothing,'' Remo answered, ''but in practice…well, you've seen how it plays out. You need some basic skills to go along with the enthusiasm, or you're just a sitting target.''

''You could teach me,'' Stacy said, ''and I can help you, too. You'll make a more inviting target with a woman on board ship.''

''I'm guessing that you never had much problem with false modesty,'' said Remo.

''None at all,'' she answered, smiling for the first time in their brief acquaintance. ''And you know I'm right. Admit it.''

"Either way, it makes no difference," Remo said. "Do you have any other siblings, Stacy?"

"What?" She was confused by Remo's change of tack. "No, there was just my brother. What's that got to do with anything?"

"In case you didn't know, your father is the man behind this operation," Remo said. "He called in some markers with the big cheese and got things rolling. I don't imagine he'd approve my using you for bait. What do you think?"

"So you're afraid of him? That's it?"

"I have a job to do. Right now, you're in the way."

"I won't go back," she said. "You can't make me."

"Oh, really?" Remo let her see a twisted, mirthless smile.

The silence stretched between them long enough for Stacy to replay the alley scene in her mind and watch him kill four would-be rapists. Her voice was softer, carrying a tad less self-assurance when she said, "You wouldn't."

"Damage you?" He shook his head. "But I'll be glad to put you on the next flight to Miami, maybe call and have your father send down an escort. That should embarrass him enough to get him off his ass and make him take care of the problem. In the meantime, though, the men who killed your brother will have that much extra time for covering their tracks."

"You send me back, and I won't stay," she said. "I swear to God, I'll be right back here in another day or two. I don't care what my father says or does. I won't give up until I find the men who murdered Richard."

"And then what?" asked Remo.

Stacy held his eyes with hers. "I want to see them die. That's your department, I believe."

"If I decide to let you stay," said Remo, trying to ignore the little clucking sound Chiun was making in the media room, now two rooms away, "we have some ground rules going in. The first time you break one of them, I bounce your preppie ass back to D.C. Agreed?"

"Let's hear the rules," she said, then smiled.

9

Remo and Stacy Armitage were window-shopping on Bay Street when Trade Winds Travel opened for business at 9:30 a.m. Remo felt rested and relaxed, despite Chiun's displeasure with Remo's decision to allow Stacy to travel with them.

"He doesn't like me, does he?" Stacy had asked over a breakfast of steamed rice.

"Chiun takes some getting used to," Remo said.

"That's okay. So do I."

Remo hadn't replied to that. Whatever happened, one way or another, he knew Stacy wouldn't be around that long.

The sole proprietor of Trade Winds Travel was a forty-something Englishman whose baked-in tan made him resemble a Hawaiian islander, until he opened his mouth. Long years of living in the tropics had done nothing to disguise the Cockney accent that betrayed his origins. His sun-bleached hair was showing threads of silver at the temples and receding slightly from a pointed widow's peak. The body underneath his lightweight cotton suit seemed fit enough, though he would never be mistaken for an athlete.

"Here, come in, come in!" he said as Remo followed Stacy through the office door, a cowbell clanking overhead. "What can I do for you this morning, aye?"

"Your poster advertises guided tours," Stacy said.

"That it does. You've got a sharp eye there, if I may say so. Howard Morgan, at your service."

"Remo Rubble, my wife, Stacy," Remo told him.

"Charmed," Morgan said. "Actually, we have several different packages available. If you require a boat—"

"We have our own," Stacy informed him, sounding just snotty enough for a well-bred child of privilege.

The travel agent fairly beamed. "That's all the better, then," he said. "Reduces overhead, you understand. In that case, I can fix you up with special maps, brochures and booklets for an independent cruise, if you want privacy. Guides are available on almost any island you may care to visit, and I can retain their services on your behalf, as well. We have them ready, that way, when you reach your port of call."

"No private guides?" asked Remo, sounding disappointed.

"Well, of course we—"

"And the extra crewman, darling," Stacy added. "Don't forget, you're on vacation."

"Right you are," said Remo, thinking that it would have sounded better on a polo field or at a posh New England country club.

"We rather wanted to relax," he told the travel agent. "It's our second honeymoon, you understand."

"Of course," said Morgan. "Say no more. If all you're wanting is a man to navigate and help with basic sailing chores, and not a chef or anything like that…"

"Sounds perfect," Remo said, giving Stacy a squeeze for emphasis.

"Sounds marvy," she concurred. "In fact, we have a friend back home who hired a guide in Puerta Plata, several weeks ago. A young man named… Enrique something, I believe it was. He simply can't stop jabbering about their trip and all the things they saw. Our friend, I mean. I don't suppose…?"

The travel agent's face was blank. "Well, I can try, of course, mum. But I have to tell you that Enrique is a fairly common name in these parts, much like Henry in the States."

In fact, it was Henry, in Spanish, but Remo saw no point in showing off his meager knowledge of the language. "It's not important," he told Morgan.

"I'm sure anyone you have on staff would be quite satisfactory."

"We aim to please, sir. Tha's a fact. When did you wish to start?"

"As soon as possible," Stacy said. "Hopefully today. Tomorrow at the latest."

"I'd best get started calling, then. On live-aboards, your average local costs twenty-five to thirty U.S. dollars for a day, with the arrangements worked out in advance. Have you considered how long you'll be visiting the islands?"

"Oh," Stacy said, "a week or two. No one's expecting us at home until the Dickens party on the twenty-ninth."

"Well, then, I'll see what I can do. I'm sure that we can find you someone suitable, perhaps by early afternoon."

"Outstanding," Remo said.

"Terrific," Stacy echoed.

"It's traditional to barter prices with these islanders, but I can do that for you, if you like."

"Sounds good to me," Remo added.

"Me, too," said Stacy Armitage.

"In that case," Morgan said, beaming, "I'll get to work right now and hope to be in touch with you, say, noonish?"

"Noonish would be lovely," said Remo. He knew the moment it came out that it didn't sound quite natural. Note to self, he thought. Don't use the word *lovely* when undercover. Or ever again, for that matter.

The travel agent blinked, but kept his own broad grin, and waved in parting as they left his office.

"Smart-ass!" Stacy muttered, as they crossed the busy street.

"You mean I wasn't marvy?" Remo pulled a sad expression.

"He's dirt, Remo," Stacy said. "Couldn't you smell it on him?"

"That's your basic island hygiene, I'm afraid. *Mañana* for the shower, if you get my drift."

"Terrific. Now I'm working with a stand-up comic."

"You're not working, Stacy," he reminded her. "You're just along for the ride."

"Oh, really? Do you think you could have hooked old Howard, if you didn't have your 'wife' along to keep you company?"

"We'll never know," said Remo. "But the little woman needs to mind her manners, or we may be headed for a quick divorce."

THE HARDEST PART FOR Howard Morgan still came down to setting up the raids. He loved the money; that went without saying, or he never would have started in the first place. He had even managed to develop a facility for blocking out its source, once the deed was done and he had banked the cash. By that time, with a few stiff rum-and-colas underneath his belt, Morgan could tell himself that it was simply business, nothing that should prey upon his mind.

It was a different story when he actually met the victims, though. He had to deal with them as human beings when they stood before him, face-to-face, conversing in the queen's own English. There was nothing to be done about it, then, but to put on a stalwart face and do the job that he was being paid—and very handsomely, at that—to carry off without complaints or needless questions.

Even so, the faces haunted him sometimes.

It helped that they were always rich beyond his wildest dreams, a trait that helped set them apart from normal human beings in the travel agent's mind. And it was better yet when they came off as bloody snobs who didn't give a damn about the common man, as long as they were able to enjoy their luxuries without restraint. Rich Yanks, at that, most of them. The Americans were worst of all when they had extra money in their hands, unable to resist the urge to lord it over those less fortunate. Loud shirts and too much jewelry, cleavage that owed more to surgery and silicone than Mother Nature. Bloody idiots, the lot of them.

Good riddance, Morgan told himself.

And still, he hesitated when it came to picking up the telephone.

It got a little easier each time, of course, and that

was somewhat troubling in itself. The sense of guilt
was almost welcome, when he started working with
Kidd and Teach. The pangs of conscience had let
Morgan tell himself that he was just as much a victim
as the rotters who were vanishing at sea. He suffered
just as much as they did—more, in fact, because it
was his fate to live with guilt and spend his blood
money on women, cigarettes and liquor that would
surely do him in one day.

But nowadays, the guilt was fading fast, depriving
Morgan of his rationale, the taste of martyrdom that
made it possible for him to face his mirror in the
morning. Lately, it disturbed him that he didn't think
about the dead as much as he once had; they didn't
haunt his dreams compulsively, but only dropped in
on the odd occasion, like a bout of indigestion after
he had eaten too much curry down at Singh's café.

He sat with one hand on the telephone and thought
back to the very start of it. He had been gambling
heavily in those days—one bad habit he had managed to get rid of, more or less—and had run up a
monstrous debt with certain gentlemen of leisure
who were known to settle their accounts with vio-
lence when the money they were owed was not available. The night they came for him, Morgan expected
them to break his fingers, possibly his legs, as well.
He doubted they would kill him, though he couldn't
rule it out entirely. Even so, he had been stunned
when one of them—the slugger, Berto something—

had informed him that his debt was paid, and that he would be hearing from his nameless benefactor soon.

Relief had metamorphosed into panic three days later, when a man who introduced himself as Thomas Kidd walked into the Trade Winds office, introduced himself as Morgan's brand-new business partner and proceeded to describe the scheme that would enrich them both. Kidd was essentially a pirate—hence the name, which Morgan took, and still believed, to be a "clever" alias—who had grown tired of cruising aimlessly among the Windward Islands and decided he would benefit from working with an agent who could tell him when fat targets were abroad, and where they could be found. Morgan assumed that he wasn't alone in serving Kidd, that there were others like himself in different ports of call, arranging "guided tours" and sending wealthy yachtsmen to their fate.

It helped, as well, to think that there were others doing what he did, sharing his guilt. Somehow, Morgan believed it would be worse by far if he alone served Captain Kidd. How could he ever hope for absolution if he was the only one involved?

No matter. He was in too deep to back out now. It would have meant abandoning his home and business, the bizarre but comfortable life he had constructed for himself since he had moved from Kingston, six years earlier, and settled in at Puerta Plata. Unlike Berto and his fellow sportsmen, Kidd and company would not be satisfied to rough him up, if Morgan tried to go back on his bargain. They would kill him instantly, without remorse; of that fact, Morgan had not the slightest doubt.

He had considered fleeing, simply cleaning out his bank account and running for his life, but there was still the niggling question of exactly where to go. Morgan was pushing fifty, and his best years were decidedly behind him. In his heart, he knew it was too late for him to start again, rebuild himself from the ground up, as he had done so many times before. This time was all or nothing, simple logic telling him that it could come to no good end.

The good news was that Kidd had always paid him promptly, and in full. Sometimes, he even got a bonus, when the targets he set up were fat enough. Whatever else Kidd and his buccaneers might be, Morgan could never fault them on their generosity.

It was bizarre, in fact, the way Kidd and the handful of his men whom Morgan had been "privileged" to meet behaved themselves. He knew that they were thieves and killers—more than likely rapists, too, if not a great deal worse—but there was still a kind of Old World pride and honesty about them. On the rare occasions when he spoke to Kidd these days, Morgan couldn't help feeling that he had to have stumbled through a time warp and been dropped into the middle of another century. The way Kidd talked, the way his mind worked, it was like a glimpse back into history, when sea wolves plied the blue Caribbean at will, and free men rarely worried much about the long arm of the law.

Morgan dialed the contact number he had memorized. He wasn't meant to know who picked up on the other end, but he had done a little homework on his own and come up with the name, regardless. It was always the same voice that answered, with its Yankee twang.

"Hello?" Somehow it always came out sounding like a question, as if Morgan's contact never quite believed the telephone had summoned him away from whatever he did to pass the time.

"It's me," the travel agent said. No names were ever given on the phone. It was a simple matter of security. "I've got another customer, if you have anyone available."

"How soon?" his contact asked.

"This afternoon, if possible."

"I'll see what I can do."

The line went dead, and Morgan cradled the receiver, letting out a sigh. Already he could feel himself beginning to unwind. He told himself that it was out of his hands now; there was nothing he could do to change the fate of Mr. Remo Rubble and his pretty little wife.

And for a moment, Howard Morgan almost managed to believe it.

THE WORST PART, MEGAN Richards told herself, was
that you really could get used to anything. It made
her vaguely ill to think that way, but there was simply no denying it.

A mere four days had passed—or was it five?—
since she had been aboard the *Salomé* with Barry and
the others, lost at sea, and they had seen another boat
on the horizon. Four days, maybe five, since Tommy
Gilpin told them that the captain of the "rescue
boat" had raised a Jolly Roger flag, and men with
guns had stormed aboard the yacht, to send her whole
life spinning on a crazy detour into Hell.

When she thought about it, even sitting in the
filthy hut, with nothing but an oversize man's shirt
to cover her, it still seemed like some kind of crazy
dream. A bad trip, maybe, from the crummy acid you
could pick up on the streets of Cambridge, guaranteed to turn your head around, but all bets off when
it came down to quality.

I wish I had a couple tabs of that right now, she
thought, but even as the whim took shape in Megan's
mind, she knew that she would need her wits about
her in the hours and days ahead, if she intended to
survive.

Survive. The word itself was a joke to her now.

She didn't have a clue where they were being held,
except that they were obviously on an island where
their captors had no fear of being taken by surprise
or running into the police. It was the kind of place

where anything could happen—had happened—and no one in the outside world would ever know.

At first, Meg had supposed her kidnappers—she still had trouble thinking of the men as pirates—had some plan to hold her and the other girls for ransom, but the days kept passing, and no one had yet seen fit to ask their names. That was her first clue that the nightmare could go on indefinitely, while the three of them survived.

And that had been her short life's first true moment of despair.

Meg's knowledge—that she had been snatched from privileged youth into a life of slavery, pain, humiliation—might have driven her insane, but she surprised herself by calling on a deep reserve of inner strength she had not known she possessed. The others were reacting in their own strange ways, Felicia slipping into something like a catatonic state, while Robin wept and muttered to herself. Four days, five at the most, and Meg could not have sworn that either one of them was still completely sane.

Whatever they were feeling, though, she guessed that precious little of it had to do with grieving for their dead boyfriends. Megan hadn't seen Barry die, but knew that he was gone. She had been shocked and hurt, of course, made no attempt to hold back bitter tears, but that part of her grieving had been relatively brief. Before the *Salomé* had left his riddled corpse a hundred yards behind, Meg was already looking out for number one.

So much for love. She had suspected that the way she felt for Barry Ward was mostly about sex, mixed up with some kind of infatuation, and the past few days had proved her right. If Meg had truly loved him, surely she would think about him more than once or twice a day, in passing. Even then, she found the image of his smiling face had started to recede, grow vague and hazy in her mind. He was a fading memory, their summer fling no more important now than Meg's first day at school, her senior prom, the first time she went "all the way."

For ten or fifteen seconds, she was moved to wonder what that said about her as a person. How could she have shared her bed with Barry, done so many things with him and let him do so many things to her, and still dismiss him from her mind so quickly when his life was snuffed out by a gang of thugs? The answer was self-evident, so simple that it nearly made her laugh out loud. Disaster had a way of making you grow up. It took you to the deep end of the pool and tossed you in, sometimes with cinder blocks chained to your feet, and you could either fight your way back to the surface or relax and drown.

Meg had discovered that she was a fighter, and the knowledge startled her as much as anything that she had ever learned.

Of course, she had to choose her battles carefully

if she was going to survive. The first two times that men had come for her, she lashed out at them furiously—kicking, scratching, spitting, cursing them with words she had not even realized she knew—but it was all in vain. They beat her down and took her anyway. It was a futile effort, and she quickly learned to stand apart from what was happening, detach herself and get it over with. Immediate survival took priority, ahead of anger, self-respect, fear of disease. Her mind was focused on the next few hours, the next few days. Whatever happened after that was so far in the future that it felt like science fiction.

"What time is it?" Felicia asked. It was the first time she had spoken in a day or more, and Megan took it as a hopeful sign.

"They took our watches, stupid!" Robin hissed. "You know that. They took everything!"

"It's morning," Megan said, resisting an impulse to snap at Robin, tell her to shut up if she couldn't control herself. If they couldn't help one another in the present crisis, there was truly no hope left.

"What time?" Felicia said again.

"For God's sake—"

"Quiet, Robin!" Meg was both surprised and pleased when Robin shut her mouth and turned away.

To poor Felicia she replied, "It's getting on toward ten o'clock, I'd guess. They haven't started setting up for lunch yet."

When Felicia nodded, it was like a puppet, or like

one of those spring-loaded toys you sometimes saw in the rear windows of old people's cars, heads bobbing up and down. Except the plastic heads were always grinning, and Felicia still looked numb, a blank expression on her face.

"Thank you," she said.

"You're welcome." Megan waited for a moment, letting the surrealistic moment pass, before she spoke again. "You know," she said, "the only way we're ever getting out of here is if we put our heads together and work out some kind of plan."

"Get out?" Robin pronounced the words as if they had been uttered in some foreign tongue. "You must be crazy, Meg. They'll never let us go. They're having too much fun."

"I didn't plan on asking their permission," Megan said.

"Oh, right! There's only thirty-five or forty of them, all with guns and knives and… Jesus, Meg, you wanna get us killed?"

Meg answered with a question of her own. "You call this living, Robin?"

"I'll help," said Felicia, speaking in a voice more like her own than Meg had heard her use since they were captured on the *Salomé*, almost a week before. "Just tell me what to do."

"Robin?"

"Shit, you're right. This isn't living. What's the plan?"

"First thing," Meg said, "we have to find ourselves some weapons. After that..."

THE TWO COMBATANTS CAME together with a clash of steel, grim, sweaty faces close enough to smell each other's rancid breath if they hadn't been focused single-mindedly on spilling blood. Each pirate used his free hand, clutching at the sword arm of his adversary, seeking an advantage in the struggle that could easily result in sudden death.

Szandor was taller, heavier, Flick was lean and quick, making the two of them a nearly even match. It would have been a different tale if they were wrestling, even boxing, but the blades they wielded were the perfect equalizers. The briefest lapse by either duelist could leave him stretched out in a pool of blood.

It did not have to end in death, of course. A point of honor could be made by simple bloodletting, provided that both parties to the duel agreed. Considering the adversaries, though—both men with fiery, brutal tempers, prone to quarreling at the best of times—it seemed to Thomas Kidd that one of them had to surely die this morning.

That meant one less crewman for their raiding, one less pair of hands to help around the camp, but Captain Kidd, for all of his authority, couldn't prevent a righteous duel from being played out to the death if the combatants were agreed. It was a sacred point of law among the buccaneers, and he could violate it only at the risk of sacrificing his command.

The present quarrel, predictably, was over women—or, to be precise, one woman in particular. Both Flick and Szandor coveted the tall blonde taken from their latest prize, and while the wench was technically available to any man who paid the captain's price, an argument had broken out as to which buccaneer she favored of the two. It seemed a bit ridiculous to Kidd, grown men imagining a slave girl truly cared a whit for either one of them, but stranger things had happened in the world. Besides, he knew that logic had no place where lust held sway among the sort of men who followed him.

The challenge had been mutual, duly received and answered. Captain Kidd was not empowered to prevent the duel, although he might postpone it temporarily, in the event all hands were needed for a raid, or to defend their island stronghold. In the present circumstances, though, he would invite a mutiny if he denied the duelists their rights or kept his men of a diverting show.

Kidd had a ringside seat for the engagement, lounging in his high-backed wicker throne, the cutlass that was both a weapon and his badge of office resting on his knees. There were no rules in such a fight, per se, except that no one else could interfere to help either combatant. If another member of his scurvy crew so much as raised a hand in aid of either

Flick or Szandor, it would be Kidd's task—indeed, his oath-bound duty—to step in and cut down the bastard.

There was small chance of that occurring, though, when most of the assembled buccaneers had placed bets on one swordsman or the other, and the few not wagering were glad enough to simply cheer on the fighters. It wasn't often that they had a full-fledged duel in camp—six months since the last one, if his memory was accurate—and everyone enjoyed the show.

Last time, prompted by an argument about some missing loot, the winner had been satisfied to draw first blood and let it go at that. Kidd had an inkling that this morning's duelists wouldn't be so easily deterred from murder, and while he was loath to lose an able-bodied crewman, the matter was out of his hands. As captain of the brotherhood, the best that he could do was to sit back and enjoy the show, keep one eye peeled for cheaters and assume that either Flick or Szandor would survive.

The captain's final thought had barely taken shape, when Szandor gave a mighty shout and threw himself at Flick, his sword thrust out in front of him to skewer the smaller man. Flick saw it coming, though, and sidestepped just in time to save himself. His own blade flashed toward Szandor's face, then dipped aside before his enemy could parry, swooping down to gash the taller pirate's thigh.

Szandor recoiled, now limping, and his roar of fury had become a howl of pain. Blood spurted from his wound, but it wasn't a mortal blow, the artery undamaged. Still, it slowed him and made his footwork clumsy, as his cunning adversary had to have planned.

There were no time-outs and no substitutions in a duel of honor. If a man was wounded, he could either keep on fighting, or throw down his weapon and beg mercy from his adversary. Sometimes, he who scored first blood was satisfied to see his enemy in pain, and let it go at that. This morning, though, Szandor didn't throw down his sword, and Flick displayed no evidence of magnanimity.

The fight went on, and now Kidd knew, beyond a shadow of a doubt, that it would be a battle to the death.

One leg of Szandor's torn and faded denim pants was soaked with blood from thigh to ankle, yet he kept on fighting, lurching after Flick like some demented creature from the pit, too stubborn and too hateful to admit defeat or give his enemy the satisfaction of knowing that he hurt. In fact, while he was slowed by the wounded leg, his slashing thrusts still demonstrated the same power that had made him one of Kidd's most deadly fighters. Flick would be in trouble yet if he allowed himself to fall beneath that flashing blade.

There was a scowl of concentration on the smaller

pirate's face as he continued fighting, dancing rings around Szandor in an attempt to wear out his adversary. Sadly for Flick, it seemed that Szandor had attained that place on the plateau of suffering where pain no longer made a difference. His movements might be clumsy, but they showed no evidence of flagging, even as fresh blood continued pulsing from the deep gash on his thigh.

The wound was killing him, Kidd knew, but Szandor seemed determined not to fall before he settled with his sprightly foe. He aimed a roundhouse swing at Flick's bald head, a move so telegraphed that a blind man could have seen it coming, but when Flick attempted to sidestep the slash, Szandor reversed himself with stunning speed and rammed his long blade home between the smaller pirate's ribs.

Flick stiffened, biting off a scream, and brought up his free hand to seize the blade where it protruded from his abdomen. Szandor was trying to withdraw his sword and strike again, to finish it, but Flick would not release the blade, in spite of fresh blood spilling from between his lacerated fingers. Stepping closer to his enemy, he seemed to drive the long blade even deeper, through his vitals, in his grim determination to strike back.

Szandor gave up, released his sword and was about to step back out of range, but he had stalled too long. Flick's sword came whistling down with all the little pirate's weight behind it, biting deep into the flesh of Szandor's shoulder where his neck joined with his trunk. A startled grunt escaped from Szandor's lips, immediately followed by a jet of crimson blood that struck Flick in the face and dribbled down his chest.

As Kidd and company looked on, the two men fell together, slumping to their knees, like lovers locked in an embrace, before they toppled over sideways, linked by the sharp blades that pierced their flesh. Both clung to life for several moments longer, but there was no power on the island that could save them now, no medicine or magic that could heal those massive wounds.

A groan went up around the killing ground, as disappointed gamblers realized all bets were off. Both men were dead, their deaths so nearly simultaneous that no one could have named a winner if his life depended on it.

Two men gone, and while the bout had been exhilarating, Kidd could not help thinking that he had no ready means of filling vacancies these days. Of course, they ran across the odd rogue every now and then who jumped at a chance to join the band, but they were few and far between. Most killers with that kind of nerve were operating on their own, freelance, or working for the syndicates that smuggled weapons, drugs and men among the islands, or to the United States.

Kidd was about to rise up from his throne when

Billy Teach stepped up beside him, resting a hand on his shoulder. Kidd turned to face his first lieutenant, scowling at the hand until it was removed.

"Beggin' your pardon, Cap'n, but we've got another prize comin' our way."

"Says who?"

"Our man in Puerta Plata. Morgan."

"Well," Kidd said, "he hasn't failed us yet. We'd best be getting ready to receive more guests."

"Aye, sir."

"And, Billy?"

"Sir?"

Kidd nodded to the corpses stretched out on the ground within a few short paces of his chair. "Have someone haul that rubbish out beyond the reef, will you? Sharks have to eat, the same as anybody else."

10

The sailor's name was not Enrique. Standing on the pier beside the *Melody,* Howard Morgan introduced the slender, twenty-something man as Pablo Altamira, and it hardly seemed worth Remo's time to ask for ID to verify the name. Remo didn't overlook the stylized tattoo of a sailboat on the web of skin between the young man's thumb and forefinger.

Among Latino gangs of the Caribbean and South America, he knew, that symbol indicated that its bearer was involved in smuggling, typically of drugs.

So far, so good.

Tattoos aside, it would have taken psychic powers to peg Pablo as a bad guy at first glance. He had movie-star looks and wore his hair long, tied back in a ponytail that hung below his collar. Perfect teeth flashed in a smile as he was introduced to Remo first, then Stacy and finally Chiun. The old Korean, for his part, merely glared at them all from the helm, like an unpleasant sea captain forced out of retirement.

Their so-called guide was casual but stylish in a

chambray shirt, new Levi's jeans and a pair of spotless deck shoes worn without the benefit of socks.

"Pablo knows all the islands hereabouts," Morgan was telling them, while his companion smiled and nodded in agreement. "You've my word that he'll show you things the average tourist never sees."

"I'm counting on it," Remo said. "How much?"

"A very modest twenty-five per day, U.S.," said Morgan.

"Very modest," Pablo echoed.

"It's a deal," said Remo. "When can we get under way?"

"Immediately, if not sooner," the travel agent answered.

"Great. Let's do it, then."

Remo endured another flaccid handshake, slipping Morgan a fifty-dollar tip that put some extra wattage in his smile. "Most generous, I'm sure," the travel agent said. "If I can ever help you with your travel needs again, don't hesitate to call."

"We'll definitely be in touch," said Remo, who read the insincerity in Morgan's behavior like he read the white letters on a red stop sign.

Pablo stood with them and watched as Morgan made his way back down the pier. When he was beyond recall, the newest member of their crew turned on another gleaming smile and nodded toward the *Melody.*

"Shall we be going, then, señor?" he asked.

"Suits me," said Remo, turning to include his "wife" in the exchange. "You ready, darling?"

"As I'll ever be," said Stacy Armitage.

Remo spent several minutes showing Pablo around the *Melody,* from her controls to such essentials as the galley, heads and sleeping quarters. The new member of their crew said little, but Remo had the feeling that he was sizing things up, taking the measure of the multimillion-dollar cabin cruiser and her passengers.

Toward what end?

It was a gamble, trusting Howard Morgan to produce a member of the pirate gang. Hell, Remo wasn't even sure there was a pirate gang, at this point, in the sense of one cohesive group that watched the ports and preyed on boats repeatedly. For all he knew, the death of Richard Armitage and the abduction of his wife could just as easily have been a one-time thing, or perpetrated by a loose-knit group that roved among the many islands of the blue Caribbean, killing time here and there between raids, living off the proceeds of their latest depredation until cash ran short again.

Still, there was the tattoo on Pablo Altamira's hand if that meant anything. Not much, Remo decided, as he thought about the countless Latin gang members in North and South America who sported tattoos on their hands. More to the point, while wanna-bes would seldom go so far as getting a tattoo, the marks

were seen on many ex-gang members who had left
a life of crime behind them, but who never had the
inclination or the cash to have the brands removed.

So, he had nothing yet, except a young man without references beyond one dipsy travel agent, who
was on the payroll now, for good or ill. If he turned
out to be a spotter for the hypothetical buccaneers,
so much the better. And if not...well, hiring him
would mean that they had blown their chance to act
as bait.

It troubled Remo that so much hinged upon his
chance meeting with Ethan Humphrey in a bar, some
fourteen hours earlier. The old man was eccentric,
granted, but his personal enthusiasm for the sea ro-
vers of yesteryear didn't mean he was presently involved in hijacking or worse. If that were true, then
it would naturally follow that dragons were slain at
Renaissance festivals, while Civil War "recreation"
groups would be marching on Atlanta and Gettys-
burg, armed to the teeth.

Pablo met Chiun, after a fashion, in one of the
main cabins, where Chiun had staked himself out,
staring at the grainy image on a twenty-inch wall-
mounted LCD television screen. He wasn't squinting—Remo, in his whole life, had not known a man
of any age with keener eyes—but Chiun was leaning
forward slightly, hands braced on his knees, as he sat
in a modified lotus position.

"What's on, Little Father?" Remo asked him.

"Butt Master," Chiun replied, his tone somehow combining fascination and disgust.

Remo stepped closer, peering at the screen. Three shapely women dressed in leotards stood with their backs to the camera, bent forward at the waist, as if to moon their audience. Their thighs were working, in and out, some kind of bellows action, as if each of them were holding an accordion between her knees. Instead, as Remo finally made out, their legs were clutching strange devices that resembled giant, twisted paper clips.

"Didn't Suzanne Autumns sell those things years ago?" Remo asked. "Isn't she the one who got bonked in the brain when one of her models lost control of the thing and it flew out from between her thighs?"

A moment later Suzanne Autumns herself appeared on-screen, looking twenty years older than she had ten years ago—and not much prettier. A Farrah-style hairdo, as outdated as her acting career, couldn't fully disguise the surgery scars on Autumns's scalp. "Now with rubber Thigh-Grip-Ers, so they're safer than ever!" she recited from a cue card.

"She talks like she has marbles in her mouth," Remo said.

"Butt Master is still better than Pec Man," Chiun informed him solemnly.

"He's right, señor," said Pablo, chiming in for the first time without a pointed invitation to speak. "I've seen the Pec Man ads. They suck big time. And they have Lady Pec Man, too. The things those women do with—''

"I believe we get the picture, Pablo. Thanks for sharing."

If the young man took offense at being interrupted, it did not show on his smiling face. "When shall we start?" he asked Remo.

"Sooner the better," Remo told him. "Right, Chiun?"

The Master Emeritus of Sinanju frowned and said, "Tell him to take us where we'll get decent reception."

Pablo appeared to know his business when it came to casting off and piloting the cabin cruiser out of port. In fact, there wasn't much to handling the cruiser, with its GPS positioning, automated piloting and other electronics that Remo had been instructed not to fiddle with. In fact, he had been keeping the thing under manual control since they took her out. Pablo engaged the electronics as a matter of course and soon had them on their way. Remo glanced at the controls, found all the blips and messages benign enough, as far as he could tell, and left him to it. If the course was not correct, he'd know, electronics or no.

The act of taking on a crewman for a boat the size of the *Melody* was more to give the passengers some extra leisure time than to preserve their lives at sea.

Some would have called the new addition to their crew a status symbol. Remo preferred to think of him as an investment in success.

The first day out from Puerta Plata they sailed east by southeast, roughly following the coastline, barely keeping it in sight, until they reached the Mong Passage and nosed due south. They had a distant glimpse of Puerto Rico, green on the horizon to their east, or left, but Pablo or his electronics seemed to know where he was going as they passed by the U.S. territory and sailed on, turning east again only when they were well into the Caribbean proper, the vast Atlantic safely behind them.

"Señor Morgan tells me joo are interested in pirates, *sí?*"

"Could be," said Remo. "You know about that kind of thing?"

"Oh, *sí,*" said Pablo. "Anyone who grows up round this place knows pirate stories."

Remo noted that the young man didn't mention knowing pirates, and he wasn't sure if that should be a disappointment or relief. He experienced another moment of regret for letting Stacy Armitage aboard the *Melody,* but he suppressed it quickly, concentrating on the job at hand. That was when he noticed the scampering of small feet coming up to the bridge. Either the *Melody* had vermin or...

"You can show us where the pirates of old did

their business?'' Chiun squeaked as his head popped into view and he scampered up top.

It seemed to Remo that their pilot's grin was brighter than it should have been as he replied. ''Oh, *sí,* señor. This time *mañana,* next day at the latest, joo. see where the pirates lived. I think joo not be disappointed.'' Was there something in his voice, his eyes, besides the goofy smile? Or was Remo looking for some evidence of guilt and finding it where none in fact existed?

Before the summer afternoon began to fade, Stacy had already passed judgment on the new addition to their crew. ''He's dirty,'' she told Remo as they sunbathed on the forward deck. ''I feel it. Everywhere I go, he's watching me.''

Remo considered the bikini bottoms she was barely wearing and the bikini top she had discarded entirely, and couldn't resist a smile. Her normal clothing flattered her, of course, but it didn't do justice to the supple body hidden underneath. A blind man would have dropped his pencils on the street corner if Stacy Armitage had passed by close enough for him to smell her sun-warmed, nearly naked skin.

''He has good taste,'' Remo said.

''I'm being serious,'' she told him. ''He may not be the one who set my brother up, but I don't trust him.''

Remo had to ask. ''Who do you trust?''

''Right now? Myself.'' She stared at Remo from

behind big sunglasses, perhaps attempting to discover if his feelings had been wounded. When he gave no outward sign of injury, she frowned, whether from disappointment or concern, he couldn't say.

"That isn't fair, I guess," she said. "I should trust you."

"Don't be so hasty," Remo said, eyes closed against the sun's glare. "I've been looking at you, too."

She let that pass, but there was just a beat of silence, hesitancy, before she spoke again. "What do you think of him?"

He almost mentioned the tattoo on Pablo's hand, but let it slide. She was keyed up already, and he saw no point in goading her. If she was right about the new addition to their crew, it would be risky pouring any more fuel on the fire of her suspicion. She might say something, do something, that would divert the young man from his plan, either by scuttling it or striking prematurely. On the other hand, if Pablo was entirely innocent, Stacy might scare him off with some rash word or deed.

"I think we need to keep an eye on him," Remo stated, "but discreetly. If he has his own agenda, we don't want to spook him, right?"

"I'd like to crack his skull and toss him overboard," she said through clenched teeth, smiling at him all the while.

"That's my department," he reminded her, "and

it would ruin any chance we have of finding out if he's connected to the men who killed your brother. Am I right?''

She was about to make a face at him but caught herself, glanced back toward Pablo in the wheelhouse, keeping up her smile. "He's watching me again," said Stacy.

"Good. That ought to keep him suitably distracted for a while, in case he has some kind of mischief on his mind."

"My God, it's true! You men are all alike, with only one thing on your minds."

"I'd say that depends," said Remo.

"Oh? On what?"

"The man, the moment and the inspiration," he replied.

Her voice turned coy, surprising Remo with the change, under the circumstances. "Would you say that I'm inspiring?" Stacy asked.

"I never thought about it," Remo declared, while pointedly avoiding even the suggestion of a glance in her direction.

"Is that right?" He couldn't tell from Stacy's tone if she was getting angry now, or simply teasing him.

"We're here on business," he reminded her. "Distractions could be fatal."

Remo felt her glaring at him after he had closed his eyes. The heat that radiated from her now had more to do with anger than the tropic sun above, or

any fleeting passion that she may have felt. He felt
an undeniable attraction to the woman lying nearly
naked at his side, but Remo was at this point in his
life enjoying the company of a woman who didn't
get all aroused by the mere presence of his body
chemistry.

It was an odd side effect of his Sinanju training.
At first he thought it was the greatest thing in the
world how women responded to him. They went
gaga. They got all loopy. It got old pretty fast, having
any woman you wanted.

Eventually he learned that eating shark meat
dampened the effect. That created its own set of
problems. Like Chiun behaving as if he had the
world's worst BO and the fact that he wasn't all that
fond of shark. Later Remo gained some control of
the effect himself, but it came and went. It was one
of those Sinanju skills that he never quite got full
control of.

"How come you aren't getting burned?" Stacy
demanded.

Remo shrugged. "I've got Native American blood.
They don't burn as easy."

"Because of their skin pigmentation, which you
don't show evidence of," she accused.

"I don't know, then."

He smiled at Stacy's muttering, as she rolled over
on her stomach, offering her well-oiled backside to
the sun. Once again, Remo found himself hoping that

Pablo Altamira was one of the pirates they sought. Preoccupation with a raid to come might keep the young Dominican from making any moves on "Mrs. Rubble" that would ultimately lead to trouble on board the *Melody*.

The last thing Remo needed at the moment was a mutiny inspired by hormones. He had enough to think about, with Chiun still out of sorts about the lack of soap operas and whatever other bugs were up his Emeritus butt these days.

Their first night out of Puerta Plata, Remo sat with Chiun and Stacy at the table in the dining room, which could seat twelve, while Pablo took first watch. Chiun had done the cooking. Stacy seemed a little disappointed by the mound of rice and steamed fish on her plate.

"Everything all right?" asked Remo when his plate was nearly clean and Stacy had begun to eat with visible reluctance.

"Fine," she said. "I'm just not used to so much health food all at once."

"Americans eat garbage," Chiun declared, his chopsticks moving deftly, cleaning up the last few morsels from his plate. "Red meat and entrails. All things fried in pig's fat. Too much sugar, chocolate, grease—all poison to the body. No surprise that you are fat."

Stacy recoiled, as if Chiun had slapped her face or called her by a filthy name. She wore a low-cut cocktail dress that fit her like a second skin, and Remo noticed with amusement that she sucked in her stomach, perhaps unconsciously, as she replied to Chiun.

"You think I'm fat?" She sounded horrified.

"I speak of Americans in general," Chiun said offhandedly. "White women feel they need huge breasts and buttocks to attract a man. Of course, white men encourage same, with their attraction to obesity."

"Obesity?"

Stacy resembled an incipient stroke victim. Remo knew better than to step in now. He ate his rice.

"White women are beset by too much leisure time," Chiun said, continuing his lecture to a red-faced audience of one. "Watch too much television. Eat too many bonbons, cupcakes, dildos."

"Dildos?"

"He means Ding Dongs," Remo interjected.

Chiun made a dismissive gesture with his chopsticks. "Ding Dongs, dildos, it is all the same."

"That's not exactly—"

"Of course, my son is the perfect example of the crude white male."

"Your son?" Stacy squinted at Remo. "He's really your father?"

"Not biologically," Remo explained.

"I'm surprised he is taken with you," Chiun rambled on. "You're one of the rare white women whose proportions have not been exaggerated through surgery or gluttony. Usually Remo likes his women to be balloon breasted.''

''Congratulations, you've just been complimented,'' Remo said.

''That was a compliment?''

''As good as Chiun gives.''

''Of course, the other extreme is just as repulsive,'' Chiun said. ''Those emaciated, bloodless females who feel the way to attract a man is to look like a starving mongrel waif. I cannot understand where this attraction comes from. Starvation is not enticing. In fact, the starvation of the villagers of Sinanju—''

''Little Father?'' Remo said.

''So does this character think I'm fat or not?''

There was a dead silence. Remo said, ''She's talking about you, Chiun.''

''I am not a character. I am Chiun. Young woman, you are reasonably proportioned for your race.''

''Thank you,'' Stacy Armitage said, satisfied.

''But your hips are too narrow,'' Chiun added.

''My hips are just fine!''

''They will constrict your birth canal.''

''What?'' She almost screeched.

''I assume you plan to coerce Remo into giving you his seed, but I must warn you that his offspring will give you a difficult birthing.''

Stacy sputtered. No words would come. She

looked at Remo for help, and he became very interested in the bland scraps of steamed fish on his plate.

"I am out of here!" she blurted finally.

"One look at Remo's grotesquely huge skull should be warning aplenty," Chiun pointed out helpfully. "Would you attempt to pass an offspring with a head proportioned like his?"

She made a final furious sound and slammed the hand-hewed oak door behind her.

"Terrific," Remo muttered. "You couldn't have saved that for another time?"

"She clearly was not being too observant, or she would have come to this realization on her own. Your head is quite the monstrosity, my son."

"You might consider cutting her some slack, if not me," Remo said. "I'll go and try to calm her down. Pablo needs his dinner, while you're at it."

"So, I am a servant's servant now?"

Remo knew it was hopeless. Rising from the alcove where he sat, he followed Stacy topside, found her standing at the starboard rail, arms crossed, lips set in a thin, angry slash.

"You all right?" Remo asked.

"Obviously not," she snapped. "I'm lazy and obese from sitting on my ass all day and eating dildos. Not to mention my inadequate birth canal."

"Chiun has trouble with the language sometimes," Remo lied.

"Is that my problem?" Stacy asked him. "Is there

any reason you can think of why I ought to take the heat because he has a thing about white women?''

''Welcome to my world. He dislikes whites in general,'' said Remo. ''In fact, he dislikes virtually all races, creeds and nationalities.''

''Except Koreans?''

''He pretty much despises Koreans, too, although less than everybody else.''

''Does he even like his own villagers?''

''Not so much.''

Stacy turned to face him, leaning on the rail provocatively. ''So, as one persecuted honky to another, do you think I'm obese?''

''What difference does it make?'' asked Remo suspiciously.

She frowned, a pouty look that had a feel of having been rehearsed about it. ''Hey, we're man and wife, remember? Even if it's just for little Pablo's sake. A husband ought to show some interest, don't you think?''

She glanced up toward the flying bridge, then back at Remo.

''Strictly for the mission?'' Remo asked her.

''Absolutely.''

''Well, in that case...'' Remo leaned in close enough that he could smell a hint of peppermint on Stacy's breath and wondered where it came from. ''Why don't you go on ahead,'' he urged. ''I want to have a word with Pablo.''

''Don't be long.''

He watched her go and had a fair idea what he was passing up. Already having second thoughts, he didn't intend to complicate the situation by engaging in a shipboard romance or even just a lusty romp.

He went aft, climbed the ladder to the flying bridge and met their pilot with a smile. "My turn," he said. "You've earned a good night's sleep."

"If you are sure?"

"I'm sure," said Remo. "See you in the morning."

Was there something devious behind the young man's smile as he made way for Remo at the console, or was that simply imagination working overtime? Remo could not be sure, but he was positive about one thing: if there were pirates waiting for them in the darkness, up ahead, he didn't want the new man at the helm.

Besides, he had schemes of his own to carry out. Carefully, so as not to touch any of the helm electronics, he lifted the satellite phone and dialed home. Dialing home consisted of leaning on the 1 key until somebody answered.

"Basique Boutique."

Remo honestly couldn't tell if it was a male voice or a female voice. It sure did lilt a lot. He said, "Give me Smith."

"We have a Judith working tomorrow." Remo realized that he was, in fact, talking to a computer. "Also a Maximillian."

"I want Smith."

"Well, actually, there's a new stylist starting tomorrow. Not sure of his name. You realize we're closed now, don't you?"

"If I don't get Smith, Harold W., in the next five seconds I'll call up Armitage, Senator Chester, and let him handle this problem."

"Remo, it's me," Smith said, coming on the line abruptly.

"Hey, Smitty, I don't appreciate having my chain jerked by your fruity little mainframes."

"It's a new system, Remo. Just be a little patient. It's not always easy to get a positive voice ID, especially on the poor audio signal a telephone provides."

"Is this screening really necessary?"

"My old methods of screening out bad calls just aren't as effective as they used to be," Smith explained curtly. "If I could convince you to learn a few basic code numbers—"

"Forget it," Remo sniped. "Where's the ferry?"

"On its way. Let's see. ETA twenty minutes."

"Who's handling the pickup?" Remo asked.

"DEA."

"They know the plan?"

"Yes, they were fully briefed."

"I'd rather not go swimming this evening if they screw it up."

"They won't."

"Twenty minutes," Remo said.

"Make it nineteen," Smith answered tartly.

REMO DIDN'T WEAR A WATCH. He didn't need to. He had a clock in his head and it kept perfect time.

He went belowdecks, moving silently. Not a floorboard creaked. He paused outside the economy berth belonging to Pablo Altamira and listened to the breathing of the man inside. Pablo was asleep.

Then he went to the luxury stateroom where Stacy Armitage waited. She was in her vast, circular bed wearing only the ivory satin topsheet and a perky smile.

"I thought you wouldn't come," she said. He could read the arousal in the pattern of her breathing, in the dilation of her pupils.

He sat on the bed alongside her. She dropped the sheet. Remo nodded sadly and said, "Unfortunately, I won't."

She was confused for just a moment, then he touched her neck. She slumped over, unconscious, breathing peacefully. It took him minutes to stuff her limp limbs back into sweatpants, sandals and an oversize T-shirt from a Puerta Plata souvenir shop. It featured a large toucan lounging on a beach towel and drinking a tropical drink from a pineapple. It was emblazoned with the message, "I changed my attitude in Puerta Plata!"

"Not really, you didn't," Remo said to the sleeping daughter of a U.S. senator, who simply didn't know when to leave well enough alone.

He draped her over one shoulder and toted her

onto the deck. He heard Pablo still sleeping, but knew he had someone waiting for him outside.

"Oh, Remo, are these the tactics to which you are reduced to procure female companionship?" Chiun asked, shaking his head sadly.

"I wish. I'll have you know she was ready for a hay roll. Instead I put her to sleep and got her dressed without any hanky-panky."

"Because?"

"She was responding to the pheromones or whatever, just like all the others. No, thanks."

"Maybe it wasn't your Sinanju essence. Maybe she was attracted to you, Remo Williams." Chiun followed him down the length of the *Melody*.

"Come off it, Chiun."

"Unlikely, I know, but still possible. Stranger things have happened. I have seen the most hideous and deformed human beings with mates, so why not you, my son?"

"What, with this big head?"

"It is a comically oversized brainpan, yes, but there must be a woman somewhere who can overlook this trait. Perhaps the trollop sprung from the senator's loins was the one."

"I don't think so," Remo said as he yanked out a life raft and pulled the plug, hoisting it off the aft end of the *Melody* as it expanded from a tight rubber wad into an eight-person raft. He handed Chiun the line that held it and leaped down to the raft. He laid the unconscious woman inside it.

"Of course, there are also the ears, which are genuinely repulsive," Chiun mentioned. "And then there are your flabby, slobbering lips. They disgust me, but perhaps a woman in desperate straits would see past them."

"I doubt it," Remo said, half listening to Chiun as he peered into the wake of the *Melody*. The nineteen and a half minutes were up when he saw the strobing light, so distant as to be nothing more than a glimmer on the horizon.

"Let her go," Remo said.

Chiun shrugged and released the line.

Stacy Armitage, sleeping quietly, floated off into the blackness of the Caribbean night.

Remo watched the raft until even his sharp eyes could no longer make out the black shape on the black ocean.

"Wow, is she gonna be pissed," he observed.

"Yes," Chiun agreed. Remo could hear the amusement in his voice.

He returned to the helm and phoned Rye, New York, and found himself talking to Jude, the night-shift manager of Pets? You Bet! Pet Supply Warehouse, "where all rawhide chew toys are on sale for two weeks only!" Of course it was the new CURE call-filtering system. In order to provide the system with a sufficient audio signal from which to make a positive voice print ID, Remo began an in-depth description of what use she should make of her discounted rawhide bones.

"Does your mother hen know that kind of talk comes out of your mouth?" interrupted a familiar voice—but it was not Harold W. Smith's.

"That's nothing compared to some of the creative Korean stuff he says when the TV reception goes bad," Remo answered. "What's the status on our pickup, Junior?"

"Dr. Smith is in contact with the DEA agents, but it hasn't happened yet," reported Mark Howard, CURE's assistant director.

"Is there a problem? There better not be a problem."

"No. They've spotted her. They're just letting her float in. It'll be a few minutes."

"I'll hold."

Five minutes later Howard reported, "They've got her. Safe and sound and sleeping like a baby."

"My advice is that they stay clear when she wakes up," Remo said. "The fish are gonna fly."

THE MORNING WAS PEACEFUL. Remo enjoyed the quiet. Pablo was at the helm and hadn't blinked an eye when told Mrs. Rubble was feeling sick and was staying in her cabin. He'd have to think of a better excuse later if he needed to.

But Pablo started getting agitated later in the morning. He shifted his feet frequently. Remo saw

Pablo scanning the horizon too intently, using the helm binoculars too often.

It was coming soon.

He wasn't surprised when he spotted the speck on the ocean.

Minutes later the speck was much bigger and he turned to Pablo Altamira, back on station at the helm, raising his voice to be heard above the sounds of the sea and their engine. He pointed out the other watercraft. "Can you make out what that is?" he called.

"Not yet," the young Dominican replied. "Too far."

Remo went belowdecks and found Chiun in front of the TV, sending hate rays from his eyes at a TV that alternated a snowstorm of static with a scene of two weeping and impeccably manicured women speaking Spanish.

"We may have company," Remo announced.

"I heard you bellowing. Are they pirates?"

"I don't know yet. You want to have a look?"

"Later," said Chiun.

"Fine," Remo muttered. "This is the worst three-hour tour I've ever been on." As he strolled back on deck he felt a minute shifting in the *Melody*'s course. He glanced at Pablo in the helm seat, thought of saying something to the young Dominican and then decided it was better to keep still. Let the plan play out.

The speck, still better than a mile away, now appeared to be some kind of trawler, neither new nor very well maintained. He spotted one man at the helm, another at the stern, though Remo couldn't tell what he was doing. Neither man was obviously armed, but both had faces turned toward the *Melody*. He waved.

The trawler's helmsman turned, said something to his crewman in the stern, and Remo watched the second man move forward, pausing at the cockpit long enough to reach inside a cabinet and take out something. Remo couldn't have said exactly what it was, but the package resembled a square of folded cloth, partly red and partly black.

The crewman moved toward the stern, where the trawler's stubby flagpole was mounted. Now he separated one part of the bundle in his hands from another, shaking the first one open before he clipped it to the flagpole's halyard, briskly running it aloft. A crimson pennant caught the wind, unfurled and started flapping in the breeze.

Above and behind him, Remo heard Pablo call out, ''They show a red flag. We must help if we can.''

''Right!'' he replied to their pilot. ''Let's go, then.''

The *Melody* was changing course, swiftly and smoothly, with Pablo's sure hands on the wheel. Remo saw the older, smaller boat turning to meet them now, assuming what was nearly a collision course. Her pilot and the crewman in the stern were still the only humans visible on board. Remo reached out over the water, trying to listen past the thrum of the engines and the distortion of the sea.

The distance between the two boats had halved, when the trawler's crewman turned back to the flagpole, swiftly lowered the red distress pennant and raised a square flag in its place. This one was black, except for the grinning skull and crossbones in the center of its field.

"You gotta be kidding me," said Remo to nobody, then turned to get Chiun.

"Stay where you are!"

Pablo Altamira's voice was no real shock to Remo. Neither was the pistol in his hand, its muzzle held rock steady at Remo's chest.

"Can we talk about this?" Remo asked the slim Dominican.

"Indeed we can—and will," said Pablo, grinning brightly now. "My friends will be most happy to discuss the situation with you. In the meantime, though, while we are waiting for them, please do nothing stupid that will make me kill you. *¿Por favor?*"

11

"She don't look all that rich to me," the first mate said.

"Nobody asked you, Wink," Billy Teach replied.

"No, sir."

The first mate's given name was Lester Suff, but that would never do among the rowdy boys. They called him Wink because he had a nervous tic that made his left eye twitch an average of twice a minute, giving him the aspect of a chronic winker. It wasn't a bad nickname, as pirate handles went: less fearsome than a few, less embarrassing than most.

Wink didn't know what he was talking about, either. The cabin cruiser looked tame enough, but Teach could read the signs of her subtle luxury. He saw hand-hewed teak rails on the inner decks, and enough antennas for a small television studio. She wasn't flashy, but the *Melody* was worth big, big bucks.

It had better be, Teach thought. Better be worth the risk.

The word had come from port, their man in Puerta

Plata, and it had been Teach's task to take the trawler out to sea. Most of his crew were concealed below-decks, sweating in the hold and clutching weapons as they struck an intercepting course.

With this crew of merciless rabble, taking the floating puss parlor named the *Melody* would be a piece of cake—unlike the deadly and unexpected encounter of the night before.

They had run into the small, utilitarian craft almost by accident. Teach had been planning to leave it alone, but the men on the small boat had other plans. They had approached Teach's ship. To flee would have invited suspicion—and it turned out, these were very suspicious boaters.

They weren't suspicious anymore.

They were closing on the *Melody* now, their Jolly Roger flapping in the breeze, and Teach's men were lined up on the deck just like a proper firing squad, prepared to spray the yacht with bullets if their man on board couldn't control the passengers.

If anyone had asked for his opinion, Billy Teach would have informed them that he didn't care so much for planting men aboard the boats they meant to raid. His reasons were twofold. First, you couldn't really trust another pirate much beyond your line of sight, and he was always worried that the men they sent ashore to work as plants would turn somehow, betray them to the law, or else go into business for themselves. It hadn't happened so far, but there was a first time for everything, and it made Billy nervous.

The second reason was that he preferred the old ways, coming at your target in a rush, catching him unawares if possible, or else compelling him by brute force to submit. It felt wrong, somehow, when the work was more than half done by a single man on board the target vessel, and the raiders hadn't even stepped aboard yet. Where was the adventure, then? The risk? The rush of spilling blood in combat?

He recognized the need for bloody action as a failing of his own. God knew, Kidd had reminded him of that time and again, telling him that the smart thief was the one who bagged his loot without a struggle, then disposed of witnesses as quickly and efficiently as possible. No fuss, no muss. Each time potential targets were engaged in combat, there was risk to Billy's crew, to Teach himself—and all for what? The path of least resistance was the road of preference for wily buccaneers, and those who lived to see old age would verify that fact.

Teach knew all that, and still he missed the action on an easy raid. Perhaps this time they would get lucky. Maybe someone on the tub they were about to loot would have more balls than brains and try to make a fight of it.

On the other hand, there were incidents like their predawn encounter. Those men had been nosy and stupid, a combination sure to get you killed. And it did get them killed. But the killing had been simple butchery. Very efficient, over within seconds and not very exciting.

Teach kept his fingers crossed and manned the railing as his first mate steered the trawler close enough for them to board the *Melody*. A sickly sweet name that was, but he reckoned the Colombians would change it soon enough if they agreed to buy the cabin cruiser. There was little fear that they would turn it down, given the way Ramirez and his people went through boats on smuggling runs to the United States. Between the Coast Guard, DEA and mainland hijackers, the cocaine barons never seemed to have sufficient vessels to fulfill their needs.

Three men were waiting for Teach at the *Melody*'s starboard railing. One of them he recognized, if only vaguely, as their inside man. His name was Paco something, Billy thought, but it made no real difference. The only thing that mattered was that he had done his job, keeping the others covered, making sure they offered no resistance to the boarding party.

Too bad.

Checking out the other two, Teach had to smile. In fact, it was an effort not to laugh out loud. The taller of the men looked soft, as tourists often did, more suited to a desk job than to a sailing tour of the treacherous Caribbean. Teach would have bet his share of any loot they found aboard the cabin cruiser that her skipper had soft hands, together with a yellow streak that ran the full length of his spine.

It was the *Melody*'s second passenger who made Teach want to crow with laughter as they pulled alongside and prepared to board. He was an ancient Asian, possibly Chinese, whose few remaining strands of hair were baby fine, stirred by a breeze that wafted from the south. He wore some kind of robe that looked as if it were made of silk. Long sleeves almost concealed the old man's hands, but Teach could tell that he was scrawny in the Asian style, a stringy skeleton wrapped up in yellow skin. The man had to be a hundred, and he probably weighed less than that.

Some kind of servant, Teach decided. Probably the cook. It gave him hope if these two landlubbers were rich enough to drag a Chinese cook along with them when they went on vacation. That could mean there was cash aboard the *Melody,* perhaps with some expensive jewelry for dessert.

"Ahoy, there!" he called out to Paco something at the rail.

The young man raised his free hand in a kind of vague salute, keeping his pistol trained on *Melody*'s passengers. "We ready for joo," he replied. "But there's a problem. I cannot find the woman!"

"Can't find the woman?" Teach knew the younger man was supposed to have his wife on board. His blood chilled slightly.

"We'll find her!" Wink shouted.

"Hold, dogs!" Teach commanded, and suddenly an odd stillness fell among the expectant, rambunctious crew. "Describe this woman!" Teach shouted.

"CAN WE KILL THEM NOW?" Chiun asked. He had grudgingly allowed himself to be rousted from the television at gunpoint to join them on deck, and the look he gave Remo spoke volumes. Remo could read those volumes, which mostly described how off-putting this entire charade was, how personally in debt Remo was for Chiun's vast patience with it all and how Chiun would much rather have silently switched Pablo off so he could go on watching his soap opera.

Pablo had seen the same look on the old Korean's face when he ordered him out of the media room, but to Pablo, ignorant of the fact that those who interrupted Chiun's TV watching were typically committing suicide, interpreted it as an expression of fear.

"Be my guest and swim on over," Remo replied, voice low and lips barely moving. Pablo was too busy to notice them speaking. "I think I'll wait until the boat is within jumping range. Just remember to leave enough alive to take us to their secret pirate fort."

"You want me to do all the work," Chiun complained.

Remo wasn't listening to Chiun any longer as the

pirate on the approaching ship shouted to Pablo, "Describe this woman!"

Pablo looked confused, but shouted back a brief list of Stacy Armitage's physical attributes.

The pirate captain then looked worried. He turned to one of the crew and barked, "Bring her up."

"Oh, crap," Remo Williams muttered. He knew what he was going to see next, and Fate didn't disappoint him.

Stacy Armitage, disheveled, frightened and furious, was dragged up from the depths of the trawler.

Chiun sniffed. Remo was more vocal in his frustration.

"Shut up!" Pablo said savagely. He was scared now. "What is going on?" he demanded of the pirate captain.

"We took her off a boat we met up with a few hours ago. She was with two DEA agents," the pirate called.

"Now can we start killing them?" Chiun asked as the pirates tossed padded grappling hooks over the *Melody*'s rail and Pablo took the time to set them fast, still covering his prisoners.

Remo was watching the pirate captain, who placed a pair of his men to guard the senator's daughter, and sent them belowdecks.

"Not yet, Little Father. Not until Stacy is safe."

Chiun gave Remo another look. It said simply, Well, okay, but you are going to owe me big time.

Okay, Remo thought, bringing the babe was a big boo-boo. Chiun was right and he was wrong. But what the hell was he supposed to do, let her wander the streets of Puerta Plata asking the wrong people the wrong questions until she got herself thoroughly killed?

Well, yeah, that probably would have been better than letting her fall into the hands of this freaked-out band of buccaneer wanna-bes.

Self-recrimination was one of the two trains of thought jockeying for dominance in Remo's brain as the pirates boarded the *Melody*. The second was an unquenchable disbelief in what he was seeing. He had never really believed they'd run into a bunch of pirates who really thought they were pirates. It was nuts. But here they were, all decked out in garb that, minus zippers and assorted other trivia, could easily have passed inspection in another century. Half of them were shirtless, while the rest wore shirts sporting bishop sleeves and antique-looking buttons where they closed in front at all. A lot of them left their shirts gaping open like some pretty boy on the cover of an historical romance novel. Their pants were faded, baggy, patched, some held in place with rope strung through the belt loops. Several of the men wore cross belts, supporting a variety of swords or sabers, in addition to the firearms they displayed. Bright-colored scarves were knotted around several necks, and two of the attackers wore bandannas on their heads. One of the boarders wore an eye patch, and the trawler's captain had produced a tricorne hat from somewhere, prior to boarding, and it perched atop his head now, like a kooky badge of rank.

"Permission to come aboard, sir," the pirate captain in the tricorne said, laughing aloud at his own wit. A couple of the others chuckled, too, but it was plainly more from courtesy than any real appreciation of the joke. Most of the boarding party had seemed intent on stripping Stacy with their eyes, or else examining the *Melody* for any sign of loot.

"Permission granted," Remo said, playing the game.

"Ah, courtesy." The pirate leader smiled. "We don't be seein' much of that these days."

"Life's hard," said Remo.

"That's the ever-lovin' truth, and gettin' harder all the time," the pirate said. "William Teach, at your service. I'll be takin' command of your vessel today."

It was a bad sign that the leader of the boarding party gave his name, Remo knew. It meant that Teach didn't anticipate survivors testifying in a court of law against him. Even though that knowledge came as no surprise to Remo, still it emphasized the desperate nature of his mission, and the peril facing Stacy, should anything go wrong beyond that point.

"I don't suppose you'd entertain objections?"

Remo asked. It was pushing his luck, but he felt better, stalling for time.

"Oh, aye," said William Teach. "I'll entertain whatever you've a mind to offer, but I doubt that it will do you or the missus any good. If she's really your missus, which I doubt. Name?"

"I'm Remo Rubble. You've already met my wife, Stacy. And Chiun, a family friend." He let his voice turn hard as he glanced back toward Pablo Altamira. "You know our guide, I take it."

"That's the dyin' truth," Teach said, and laughed again. "Young Paco there's a friend o' mine."

"Pablo," the young Dominican corrected Teach.

"Whatever." Teach didn't so much as spare a glance for the offended gunman.

"Under the circumstances," Remo said, "he won't mind if I hold up payment for his services."

Teach brayed another laugh, enjoying Remo's wit. "Hold up his payment! That's a corker, it is. But you're right as rain, sir. You'll be payin' me this trip. I'll see young Paco taken care of, right and proper."

"That's a load off my mind," Remo told the pirate, managing a smile. "Why not let my wife join us?"

"No more games," Teach said, but he was still smiling. "You DEA?"

"No, but the DEA asked us to keep an eye out for suspicious activity while we were on our cruise," Remo said, coming up with a cover story on the spot.

"See, we have all this special stuff in the helm. Computers and what have you. Paid an extra half million just for the electronics. I guess the DEA's stuff isn't as good, so they said as long as we were cruising around maybe we could keep an electronic record of ship activity."

"That doesn't explain why we found the missus in a DEA boat before dawn this morning," Teach prodded.

"They radioed last night that they thought a big drug run was going on in the vicinity and offered to take Stacy to safety. Since she was debarking in a couple of days anyway, we took them up on the offer. Where are the DEA agents?"

Teach nodded vaguely at the vast Caribbean. The meaning was clear. The DEA agents were feeding the fishes. Teach's smile was taunting now. "Not a very likely story, Mr....Remo, was it? Now, what kinda name is that, if I may ask?"

"Unlucky," Remo said.

The pirate laughed again. "Truer words were never spoke, my friend. Unlucky's what you are, all right, but as it happens, I've been feeling generous all day. How would it be if I said you could choose the way you'll die?"

"I'd pick old age."

"Well said!" Teach answered, chuckling. "But that method isn't on the menu, I'm afraid. Suppose

I tell you what's available, and you pick what you like.''

''Whatever.''

''We could try keelhauling, but I don't recommend it to the friendly sort. There's still beheading, and the firing squad, of course. Old standbys, if you will. I'd offer you a duel, but that's too time-consuming, I'm afraid. If you're a sporting man, you just might want to walk the plank.''

''And have you shoot me in the water?'' Remo asked.

Teach placed one hand over his heart and raised the other, with a shiny pistol in it, to the sky. ''My word of honor as a gentleman,'' he said without apparent irony. ''We'll leave you sink or swim, as Fate would have it.''

''What about my wife?'' asked Remo. ''And Chiun?''

''Your 'wife' goes with us, o' course, just in case your friends happen to catch up to us, which they will not,'' said Teach. ''We're not as cruel as that, to kill a sweet young thing who's barely gotten started on the road of life. She'll not be lonely in her widowhood, I promise you. As for the Chinaman, I haven't made my mind up yet. He wouldn't cook, by any chance?''

Remo was sure Chiun was going to start doing some killing before the entire word ''Chinaman'' was uttered, but the old master stood stock-still, hands in his sleeves, face impassive. Remo couldn't begin to calculate the favors he was going to owe Chiun.

"This really is your lucky day," said Remo, holding on to his peculiar smile. "He makes the best damn Chinese food you ever tasted."

"I suppose it wouldn't hurt to try him out, then," Teach replied. "Not promisin' you anything, o' course, if he don't pull his weight."

"I understand," said Remo. "Every man for himself."

"That's it in a nutshell," Teach agreed. "Now, as to walkin' that there plank, we haven't really got a plank, as such. It's more a matter of you jumpin' o'er the rail, you see."

"Just diving in?"

"Simple as that," Teach said.

"And you won't shoot me, once I'm in?" asked Remo.

"I already give my word on that," Teach answered, frowning. "You're not tryin' to insult me, are you?"

"Not at all," said Remo. "I'm just making sure we understand each other."

"Fair enough, then. Off you go."

Remo strolled past Chiun and muttered briefly in Korean. "Keep them from killing her. Please. I'll catch up soon."

''There is very little an old Chinese cook can hope to accomplish,'' Chiun protested.

''Goodbye, old friend,'' Remo said formally, in English, for show. ''For me, Little Father,'' he added in Korean.

''I'll do what I can,'' Chiun sniffed.

Cripes, Remo thought. He was going to be doing all the cooking for the next six months.

''What'd you say to him?'' Teach asked.

''I asked him to refrain from killing the lot of you before I could catch up,'' Remo said.

Teach chuckled as he and a couple of his crewmen herded him along the deck, their weapons trained on his back. Remo reached the stern rail, stepped up onto it, arms spread for balance and pitched forward, out of sight.

Teach wasn't chuckling now. He actually admired the man, going so stoically to his death. When the pirate on his left prepared to aim and fire his shotgun, Teach thrust out a hand and jarred the man off balance, cursing him.

''I give my word, you scurvy bastard! Make a liar outta me an' I'll be forced to do for you.''

The pirate with the shotgun glowered but didn't protest the insult. Moments later, Teach came back to Chiun, surrounded by the other members of his boarding party.

''Mr. Chin, I hope for your sake that you make some mighty fine chop suey, because that's the currency yer gonna be buying your mortal existence on.''

Chiun, Master Emeritus of Sinanju, said in a squeaky voice, ''I understand, Captain.''

But what he was thinking was, That inconsiderate white son of mine is going to be doing the cooking for the next six months. Maybe longer.

''Where are we going, Captain?'' he asked.

''A true pirate's home,'' said William Teach. ''A tropic island paradise, and no mistake.''

REMO STRUCK THE AZURE surface of the water in an imperfect swan dive, making sure to create a splash. He could have entered the water soundlessly, without a ripple that the eyes of the pirates could see, but he didn't want them getting suspicious.

Plunging deep, he left a trail of bubbles in his wake for some distance, also for show on the surface. He submerged to thirty feet and began releasing only the tiniest carbon dioxide bubbles as he progressed rapidly. When he surfaced he was 150 yards due south of the *Melody* and her companion vessel. Without field glasses, he knew his head would be invisible to anyone on board the boats. He watched the activity. His plan was to board whichever vessel Stacy ended up on and get her safe. There was a sudden fury of activity, men passing between the vessels, and Remo was heading for the trawler when he smelled a distraction.

A slight tang in the water. Human blood. So Teach wasn't so honorable after all. He hadn't shot at Remo, as he promised he wouldn't, but he had taken some steps to insure Remo died in the water, one way or another.

Remo wasn't worried that the blood might be Stacy's. He knew she was a valuable prize and they wouldn't sacrifice her. And he didn't even consider it might be Chiun's. If the pirates tried to slit Chiun's throat, the sea would be scarlet with blood—pirate blood.

The faint smell had the odor of slight decay. It was one or both of the deceased DEA agents, steeped in the ocean to serve as a kind of dinner bell. And it worked.

He spotted a dorsal fin heading in his direction just as the boats were separated and the engines started.

He didn't know what kind it was, but from the rough dimensions of the dorsal fin, he guessed that it was ten or twelve feet long. Too far away for him to get a decent look by ducking underwater, but he knew that any fish that size could be a problem if it caught his scent and felt like having him for brunch. Maybe it would just swim on by.

The dorsal fin became a thin knife in the water. The shark was coming directly at him. The trawler and the *Melody* started moving.

Remo made a swim for it, heading for the trawler with a sudden burst of speed that sent him through the water like a torpedo. The shark didn't know human beings well enough to understand that Remo was moving faster than humans were supposed to. Remo was just another fast-swimming, warm-blooded creature to the shark. It ate them every day.

It veered at Remo, who was coming more or less in its direction anyway. When Remo had his first clear view of the shark, he guessed it was a tiger. There were no stripes readily apparent, but the broad, flat nose sparked memories of something he had seen once, years ago, in an aquarium. The gaping mouth was sickle-shaped and bristling with curved, serrated teeth, located well behind the snout, so that he guessed the fish would have to roll sideways to execute a strike.

The twelve-foot tiger shark changed directions in a heartbeat and did a good job of staying on an intercept course. Its muscular body convulsed to veer its trajectory to match Remo's long-range dodges. He realized he had a choice to make. He could go around the tiger shark or through the tiger shark.

The first option meant the boats would leave without him. Catching up would be iffy. Following their trail would be impossible, eventually, which meant he'd be swimming for the nearest land—not to mention depending on Chiun to handle the situation with Stacy.

The second option meant, well, that he had to deal with a tiger shark.

Remo had no choice at all, really. He hated that. Fate had a bad habit of spinning his life out of control without consulting him first. Fate was a bitch.

Remo Williams swam at the shark.

Streamlined and perfected by several million years of evolution, the eating machine aimed itself directly at Remo's midsection, bearing down upon him like a gap-toothed juggernaut.

Lots of people had wanted to kill Remo over the years, but they usually had motivations other than lunch. He would be damned if he was going to end up being digested by this or any other fish, mammal, bug, whatever. He was distantly aware of the engine noises from the trawler and the *Melody,* moving away from him.

The tiger shark thrust its great body into Remo with a burst of speed and brought down its great jaws.

This wasn't Remo's first encounter with a hungry, huge *elasmobranch,* and he knew just how to dampen its spirits. As he corkscrewed in the water and the shark found its maw unexpectedly empty, Remo jabbed his fist into the exposed dental work. It was a hard, fast strike that shattered several serrated teeth and sent the fragments flying into the thing's mouth.

The tiger shark gyrated away, momentarily frenzied by pain and confusion, but came back around a moment later, moving faster, spurred by its frenzy.

It shot at Remo and snapped at him, but Remo was still too fast. He punched out another handful of shark teeth and when the shark whipped away he grabbed for the gills, digging his fingers like grappling hooks into the fleshy slits just forward of the big pectoral fin. The shark thrashed wildly, and Remo ripped out a handful of flesh along with a square foot of skin and gills. Blood clouded the water.

Smart move, Remo Rubble, he told himself. Do just the right thing to attract a *bunch* of sharks. Over his self-recrimination came a wave of alarm as he realized that the rumble of the boats was now just a tiny vibration in the water as the distance increased. Dammit!

The tiger shark was hurt but not slowed. It veered in a tight circle and came back fast. It was in pain and it was angry—but not as angry as the Reigning Master of Sinanju.

"I've had enough!" he shouted. It wasn't the most intelligent behavior for a Master of Sinanju who was twenty feet below the surface with a big carnivore to contend with, but the shout would have shattered a man's eardrums above water. The tiger shark's head snapped as if it had been sucker-punched, and it fled from Remo Williams.

Remo knew a good thing when he saw it. He made his way to the surface, gulped air and descended as the tiger shark came back at him. This time Remo had full lungs and he let the shark get close enough to touch, then he exploded *"Back off!"*

Your average human being couldn't have even come close to vocalizing so loud and so powerfully, and the wall of sound collided with the shark like a depth charge. It jerked away, stiffened momentarily and hung in the water. It made no motion for seconds, and its twelve-foot-long body began to descend in a lifeless twisting motion. Then it flicked its tail, righted itself and moved weakly away.

Remo spotted another dorsal closing in when he reached the surface. Time to get the hell out of there.

He began to knife through the water, chasing the boats, but keeping an eye out just in case. The sharks might come after him, but their burst of speed could not be sustained like Remo could sustain his speed.

Remo could swim for hours without resting, and swim fast, but not fast enough to catch up to the boats. The *Melody* was immensely overpowered for a pleasure yacht, and for once her engines were actually being used beyond a fraction of their capacity. The trawler was clearly outfitted with a power plant that was faster than your typical fishing vessel might need.

That maniac pirate captain, Teach, had obviously been spooked by his run-in with the DEA and the possibility that the *Melody* was a sting operation. He was getting out of the vicinity fast.

Too fast for Remo.

Well, shit.

The boats shrank to specks that appeared only occasionally over the tops of the waves, and when they were almost gone from his sight they veered in opposite directions. Cap'n Teach was going to confuse any pursuit that might be coming.

Remo kept swimming in the direction the boats had headed originally. He would keep going that way until he hit land. Any land. He wondered how long he would actually last.

Hell, he was warm enough. He could rest when he needed to. He could go for days if necessary. But days might be too long for Stacy Armitage. By this time tomorrow, Remo was grimly aware, she would still be alive, but in all likelihood she would have been subjugated to the entertainment of the pirates.

He had seen what that did to Stacy's sister-in-law. He didn't want it to happen to her, too. He kept swimming.

Then he saw a new speck.

It was a sailboat, gliding toward him, still something like half a mile away. If it held to its present course, he thought that it would pass within a hundred yards or so of his position.

Remo swam to meet it.

12

Despite the brave front she had managed to put on for her abductors, Stacy Armitage was terrified. Her brother's death and the brutal torment suffered by his widow prior to her escape were still too fresh in Stacy's mind for her to cling to any illusions of security. Then the more recent whirlwind events. Just hours ago she awoke on a small boat with a pair of DEA men, put there by that asshole Remo Rubble. They were taking her to safety, they said.

That was twenty minutes before the pirates stopped them, shot them, slipped their bodies in the Caribbean, then sank their boat.

She was even more shocked when she was pulled out of her cell on the pirate trawler to find herself looking at the *Melody*. She saw Pablo, with a gun held on that asshole Remo and the old chauvinist Chiun.

She watched Remo jump to his death.

Chiun was put on the trawler with her, along with the buccaneer named Teach, and half a dozen of his crewmen. The remainder had been left to pilot the

Melody, which ran a hundred yards or so behind the pirate craft. The skull-and-crossbones flag no longer flew above the trawler, which for all intents and purposes appeared to be a normal, run-down fishing boat once more—except that it went like a bat out of hell. The hull vibrated, and she could feel the engines straining to maintain the pace.

Stacy and Chiun were housed belowdecks, out of sight and under guard. They didn't have a pirate with them in the tiny cabin they had been assigned—more like a storage closet, Stacy thought, wrinkling her nose in disgust at the squalid room—but Teach had left a man outside the door, and others passed by, talking to him, at sporadic intervals.

She wondered how much time had passed since they were taken prisoner and Remo had gone overboard, but glancing at her wrist reminded Stacy that the pirates had already relieved her of her watch. It was a birthday gift, from Cartier, and while the watch itself was trivial, all things considered, staring at her bare wrist brought fresh tears to Stacy's eyes. She felt so helpless, and it galled her to have come this far, only to have her quest end in failure.

"Not to worry," said Chiun. It was the first time he had spoken since they came aboard the trawler, and his words took Stacy by surprise. "We have them now."

"Excuse me?"

Chiun edged closer so that he could speak without

the guard outside their cell hearing his words. "These pirates have big trouble," he declared.

"Uh-huh. Just let me get this straight," she said. "We're trapped in here, but they're in trouble?"

"One man's trap may be another's opportunity," said Chiun.

"Confucius?"

The old Korean scowled. "Chiun!" he answered.

"Sorry."

"I could stop these vermin now, of course," Chiun went on, "but that is not the plan."

"The plan?"

"We must discover where they live and breed," said Chiun. "When Remo joins us, we shall know the time is right."

"Remo? But he…I mean…he's gone!"

"Dawdling, probably," Chiun corrected her. "There were sharks in the water when he jumped."

"What?" she gasped, terrified.

"He doubtless deemed it more important to stop to eat one of them before he joined us," Chiun sniffed. "The stink will make you less attracted to him."

Stacy already felt like Alice on the wrong side of the looking glass, but now she was convinced that she had lost her mind. She had heard so many astonishing and insulting statements at one time she didn't know how to sort it all out.

Chiun, she decided, had retreated into fantasy. Poor old man.

"Chiun," she said gently, "Remo is not coming. Remo is dead."

"Oh, no. Although he may try to use that as an excuse for his tardiness—I would not put it past him." Chiun spoke without blinking, his timeless face impassive.

She nodded solemnly. Clearly, the faithful old man had gone into some sort of state of extreme denial. That wasn't going to help them.

"But what if he is dead?" she pressed, but gently.

"Then I will kill them all myself." Chiun shrugged.

Stacy tried to imagine the frail old man in combat, but she couldn't manage it. With Remo, having watched him kill four men, it was a different matter. In Chiun's case, though, it was impossible to picture him engaged in any exercise more strenuous than watching television or preparing rice and fish.

"You let the pirates think that you're Chinese," she said.

Chiun's lips twitched. A grimace or a smile, Stacy could not have said exactly which it was. "Their first mistake," he said.

"Did you know Remo long?" she asked. The question came out of left field, surprising Stacy herself.

"Since he was born again," Chiun replied.

Another riddle. Remo had never impressed her as a religious man, especially after that scene in the alley in Puerta Plata. Still, there were all kinds of true believers, she decided. Pressing her luck, she tried for a follow-up question.

"Was he a fighter when you met him?"

"He was dead before then," the old Korean reminded her.

Stacy tried to find a riddle in his words, but Chiun appeared to mean the statement literally. She didn't pretend to understand what the old Korean meant, but rather tried to change the subject.

"What exactly did he do?" she asked.

Chiun considered that before replying. From a slight frown, Stacy watched his face relax into a calm expression of repose. "He is Reigning Master of Sinanju, more or less. Granted, he has much to learn still, but he makes minor progress, here and there."

"I meant to ask, what does he do for Uncle Sam? You know, the government?"

"Ah," Chiun replied, "the Emperor. Such things are not for woman's ears."

Stacy gave up. She couldn't tell the difference between when Chiun was playing games with her and when he was speaking from the wrong side of the dividing line between reality and delusion. Stacy had no idea as to who or what Sinanju might be, but she knew damn well there was no emperor in the United States. In fact, unless Remo had lied to her in Puerta

Plata, her own father was instrumental, at least in part, for Remo's being on the case. That told her that he served the Feds in some capacity, whether he was a regular or some kind of independent contractor.

None of this was helping her get a handle on when to expect reinforcements from the U.S. to come barging in.

Chiun's lack of doubt in Remo's survival made her doubt what she knew had to be true. How long could a man survive at sea, without a raft, food, water? If there were sharks—although that may have been a part of Chiun's mental instability—they would have finished him off in minutes. She needed something, some hope to sustain her in her present situation, other than Chiun's assurance that he would eliminate the pirates by himself if called upon to do so. Stacy didn't doubt the old man's good intentions, but she didn't trust him as the last line of her personal defense.

If only she could believe that Remo was alive. If only there was some chance for him to appear and save her, save them both, from her private waking nightmare.

She shook it off. The fantasy was too seductive. She couldn't let herself slip into a fantasy world, too, if she wanted to have any hope of escape.

AN AUDIENCE WAS WAITING on the beach for the *Melody* when she entered the shaded cove on Île de

Mort. Kidd had refrained from going down himself, with the excuse that he had other business pending, but he really meant to take a smidge of pride away from Teach, before the youngster's britches got too small and Billy Boy got tempted to go shopping for a larger size. Something in captain's colors, for example.

It was trivial, as insults went, but Kidd was hoping he would get his point across. He valued Billy Teach, but not enough to jeopardize his own position as the leader of the pirate clan. Before he would allow a full-scale challenge—one that Kidd wasn't absolutely certain he could win—he would arrange an accident for Billy, maybe have him lost at sea, and choose another second in command while they were mourning the incalculable loss.

The "work" Kidd had to do while Billy brought his prize in was in fact another session with the slender brunette from their last raid, when the boarding party had come back with three girls. Kidd had already tested each of them in turn, as was a captain's right, but there was something in the sultry brunette's attitude, defiance simmering behind a mask of bland submission, that excited him almost as much as spilling blood. She was his favorite, and Kidd regretted that she probably would last a few more weeks at most.

He let the brunette please him, told her what to do, keeping a knife and riding crop within arm's reach, in case she tried to take advantage of her placement, kneeling in the space between his thighs. A captive woman had gone off on Wink, one time, and nearly ruined him. The twitching of his eye had been dramatically exaggerated after that, and there were some in the community who said that eyelid was the only part of Wink that twitched anymore.

Not this one, though. Kidd was too cautious for her, even in the final moments, when he felt himself begin to reach his peak. Kidd was particularly watchful then, when she would think him helpless. Curiously, vigilance enhanced the moment for him, rather than detracting from it, since his eyes saw every detail of her sweaty face, himself, the place where they were joined.

The wench was finished, slumped back on all fours, when Captain Kidd heard footsteps drawing closer to his quarters. Rising stiffly from his throne chair, one leg half-asleep, he pulled up his baggy trousers and buckled them in place. The cross belt that he wore across his chest was sweat-stained, like his clothing, but the cutlass it supported had been polished till the blade shone like a mirror. It was razor-sharp, that blade, and Kidd would gladly demonstrate on visitors if anyone provoked his wrath.

The kneeling woman scuttled off to one side, crablike, when rough knuckles rapped on Kidd's front door. She found a shady corner, huddled there, as if she somehow hoped to make herself invisible.

"Enter!" Kidd said, his tone imperious, but no more than his rank deserved. The door swung open on its badly rusted hinges. Billy Teach was the first man across the threshold, leading two fresh captives, who immediately seized Kidd's full attention.

The red-haired woman was striking in her own right, slightly older and vastly more attractive than the three young women Teach had found last time, aboard the star-crossed *Salomé*. She was a full-fledged woman, rather than a pretty girl, and Kidd was drawn to her immediately, craving her, despite his just-finished tussle with the slim brunette.

The second prisoner was something else entirely. He was old, for one thing, and an Asian at that, and dressed in a robe that made Kidd's best pirate garb look subdued. Kidd would have been surprised to learn that he weighed ninety pounds. Almost completely bald on top, with yellowing fringes of white hair that hung delicately over his ears. There was something in his eyes that almost bordered on amusement, but he kept the main brunt of his feeling tucked away. At least he wasn't stupid, Kidd decided, or a coward begging for his life.

"Why that one?" Kidd asked Billy Teach, nodding to the old man.

"Guy said he cooks great Chinese food."

"Which guy would that be, Billy?"

"Skipper of the good ship *Melody*," his second in command fired back, without a moment's hesitation.

"He's no longer with us here, alas. A swimming accident."

Kidd smiled. At least Teach had not brought all three of them back to the camp on Île de Mort. The woman would be useful in more ways than one, perhaps an item he could sell to the commercial flesh dealers, once he had sampled her himself. As for the ancient Chinaman, if he could cook and clean, so much the better. Captain Kidd would let him live while he was capable of doing women's work, and when his time ran out...well, there were always hungry fish in the lagoon.

"So far, so good," Kidd told his first lieutenant. "How's the tub?"

"A classy one," Teach replied. "Bet her retail value makes her one of our best ever. Don't know what we'll get for her, though. I reckon the Colombians will take it off our hands, but they won't appreciate her fine appointments."

"Let's check it out," the captain said, already moving toward the exit from his quarters, passing close before the redhead and the wizened Asian. "And leave the woman here," he added. "Under guard."

A frown at that from Billy Boy, and that was fine. He didn't have to relish every order from the captain, just as long as they were carried out immediately, to the letter.

And God help him on the day he failed in that.

THE SAILBOAT SLOWED WHEN it spotted him. There was a figure in the bow—a man, bare chested, heavy-set—who pointed toward him with one hairy arm and waved the sailboat's skipper onward with the other.

Moments later, Remo's would-be savior plucked a life preserver from the deck, between his feet, and tossed it overboard. The outsized doughnut trailed a nylon line behind it as it splashed down on the surface at about the same moment Remo was hauling himself over the rail and onto the deck.

The hairy lookout was slack jawed for a second, then got his wits together. "Are you all right, pal?"

"Getting better by the second," Remo said.

"How long you been swimming around out here?" The spotter's lanky sidekick demanded.

"Couple of hours."

"Huh," the taller of the two men said. "You damn lucky we came along. You damn lucky Dink's got good eyes."

The lookout, Dink, was staring hard at Remo. "Two hours?"

"My boat went down," said Remo, improvising on the spot. "Some kind of engine trouble. I don't know exactly what it was. First thing I knew about it was a little smoke, and then the damn thing blew. I swear she went down five minutes flat. I barely got over the side."

"Explosion, huh?" the tall man said, still sounding skeptical. "We didn't hear a thing or see no smoke."

"It was a couple of hours ago, like I said," Remo said. "I'm not sure that I could have lasted if you hadn't come along."

"Nobody lasts out here, without a deck beneath 'em," Dink replied. "What kinda boat was that? What did you call 'er?"

"*Trudy,*" Remo said, answering the final question first. "A cigarette."

"Where from?" the tall man asked.

"St. Croix. Took off this morning, but I must've lost my way."

"Don't read the compass all that well, I take it?" There was clear suspicion in Dink's voice this time.

"Apparently," said Remo. "Maybe there was something wrong with it."

"You shoulda checked it out before you out to sea," the tall man groused. "Damn foolishness to take a chance with your equipment thataway."

"You're right, I guess. Of course, it wasn't really mine. I borrowed *Trudy* from a friend of mine, back in Miami."

"He'll be tickled pink to hear this news," said Dink.

Remo considered Dr. Harold Smith, then thought of Chiun and Stacy, riding with the pirates toward an unknown destination. "Yeah, I wouldn't be surprised," he said. "Speaking of news, where are we putting in for the report?"

"I reckon Fort-de-France would be the closest," Dink replied. "Right, Titch?"

"That's it," the tall man said, still frowning.

"Fort-de-France it is," Dink said. "We best be haulin' ass."

13

Howard Morgan smiled obsequiously, turning on the well-oiled charm for Mr. Burston Sykes, of Bristol, Connecticut, and his young, blond wife. She was so young, in fact, that Morgan would have pegged her as the fat man's daughter if Sykes had not made a point of introducing her otherwise. The wedding ring on Mrs. Sykes's hand was new, the solitaire diamond on her engagement ring an easy four carats.

That spelled money, and Morgan didn't care if Ellie Sykes was Burston's daughter, as long as some of the fat American's dollars found their way into Morgan's pocket. The American was big in textiles, or so he said. Probably meant he ran sweatshops in Third World nations, but the source of his money was likewise a matter of total indifference to Morgan. The travel agent always focused on the bottom line— meaning his bottom line, the profit he could turn from any given deal.

In this case, Burston Sykes and his child bride were talking package tour, the kind of deal that would turn a handsome profit for the owner-operator of Trade Winds Travel. It meant a boat and crew, provisions, berths and tours on sundry islands—all paid in advance, with a sweet commission for Morgan himself.

It was the best deal he had closed that month—the best legitimate transaction, anyway—and Morgan was already calculating how to spend the money as he finished touching up the deal on paper. He was dotting i's and crossing t's while his clients sat beneath the lazy ceiling fan and sweated through their clothes.

"Damn hot in here," Burston Sykes said. "Why don't you spring for air-conditioning?" he groused.

"Bit pricey in the islands, don't you know? We have to make ends meet," Morgan said, striving just a little harder to preserve the phony smile. "Trimmin' expenses does the trick, you know?"

"It's still damn hot," Sykes told him. "Keep your patrons sweating, and you won't have much repeat business. You mark my words."

"Yes, sir, I'll keep that fact in mind." The paperwork was done, and Morgan spun the contract deftly, pushing it across the desk toward Burston Sykes, offering his fountain pen. "Now, if you'll just sign here, right at where X marks the spot…"

The textile magnate looked over the contract, pausing here and there to read the fine print in detail, before he signed and dated it, then passed it back to Morgan. "Done," he said.

"I'll get to work immediately," Morgan said, reserving his brightest smile for the fetching Mrs. Sykes, "as soon as you've filled out that check we spoke about...."

Sykes frowned and reached for his hip pocket, bringing out a checkbook that was probably real alligator hide. He used the pen Morgan had handed him, together with the contract. Despite his evident wealth and the relatively small fee involved, Sykes still showed visible reluctance as he filled out the check, looked it over and handed it to Morgan.

"We done here?" the businessman asked.

"Indeed we are, sir," Morgan answered. "All you and your lovely wife must do, from this point on, is pack your bags and find your way to the marina in the morning. Let's say tennish, shall we?"

"Ten o'clock it is," Sykes said.

"Your vessel is the yacht *Christina*," Morgan said. "She and her crew will be prepared to sail when you arrive."

"I hope so," Sykes informed him, shepherding the missus out of Morgan's office to the street, where afternoon was baking shadows on the sidewalk.

Howard Morgan smiled, folded the check in two and slipped it into his shirt pocket. It was damn good money, and his five percent was still enough to put fresh lobster on his plate for several nights if he was so inclined—or land a fresh piece in his bed, assuming that he felt like shelling out a good deal more.

If nothing else, the Sykes deal meant that he could close down for the day. He would have to, in any case, if he was going to arrange the details of the tour package he had sold. The yacht *Christina* was on call, he knew, together with her captain and a two-man crew, but there was shopping to be done—for food and liquor, any incidentals that a rich man and his wife would likely carry with them on a tour of the Caribbean.

He pushed back in his chair, the casters rasping on the vinyl floor, and rose to hit the kill switch on the coffee urn that occupied one corner of the Trade Winds office. Morgan was a coffee addict, even in the tropic heat, without an air conditioner, and certain clients also favored it above the cold drinks he kept handy in his minifridge.

He was about to flick the switch off when a voice behind him said, "I'll take some if you've got it made."

The sound made Morgan jump, as unexpected as it was, but the surprise paled when he turned and recognized the man who stood before his desk.

"Er...Mr. Remo Rubble, isn't it?"

"That's very good."

The travel agent glanced in the direction of his office door, wondering why the damn cowbell suspended on a leather strap had failed to warn him of a new arrival in the Trade Winds office.

"Back so soon?" he said, cold perspiration forming on his face. "There's nothing wrong, I hope."

The man he knew as Remo Rubble smiled and took a long step closer, smiling as he said, "Howard, I think we need to have a little chat."

"Of course," the worried-looking travel agent said. "Sit down, by all means. Where's the missus, then? What brings you back to Puerta Plata?"

"Just a hunch," said Remo, closing on the cluttered desk with easy strides.

"A hunch?" Morgan repeated. "As regards to what, if I may be so bold?"

"Your pirate buddies," Remo said. "I'm betting you can tell me where they spend their time when they're not looting pleasure craft."

"Pirates?" There was a hitch in Morgan's voice, a subtle paling underneath his tan, but he recovered quickly for a man with no experience of rough interrogations. Or perhaps it was the ignorance of what was coming that allowed him to preserve the calm facade. "I'm sure I don't—"

His first kick drove the desk back, scraping furrows in the vinyl, slamming into Morgan's thighs and pinning the travel agent with his hips against a waist-high counter, where his flailing arm upset the coffee urn.

"God's truth!" Morgan wailed, shoving at the desk with both hands, getting nowhere. Remo had it pinned against him with one foot. The travel agent would need far more power than he had to budge the desk. For emphasis, Remo gave the desk another nudge, the hard edge digging into Morgan's groin and thighs. A wordless squawk of pain escaped his lips, as they were drawn back from tobacco-yellowed teeth.

"Hold on a moment now! You've got this wrong, I tell you! I don't—"

Remo stepped back from the desk, as if considering the papers strewed across its top. Morgan prepared to take advantage of the respite, breaking off the lie he was about to tell and shoving at the desk with both hands to release himself.

Before he found the strength to move it, though, Remo bent forward and one hand slapped the desk-top. The desk acted as if an ax crashed into it. A fissure opened in the wooden desktop, front to back, and Remo had resumed his easy stance before the shattered desk collapsed into a V-shaped ruin, pinning Morgan's feet and spilling papers all around his legs.

"God rot it!" Morgan blurted out, and lost his balance, toppling forward, sprawled across the desk to lie at Remo's feet.

Remo bent down to grab a handful of the travel agent's hair and hoist him upright, holding him so that his toes were barely grazing vinyl. Morgan was surprised by his new altitude, in evident discomfort from his thighs and groin, his feet, and now the pain that lanced his scalp.

"You're obviously quite upset," said Morgan. "I assure you, even so—"

"I'm running out of furniture to break," Remo warned. "If you plan on lying to me any more, you take your chances."

"Surely you don't mean—"

A twist of Remo's hand, and Morgan plummeted to strike the hard floor on his knees. The pain of impact was nothing to the burning of his scalp, however, where a fist-sized clump of hair had given way to raw, red flesh. The missing hair cascaded past his face, as Remo's fingers opened to release it.

"Looks a little thin on top," said Remo. "You should try some Rogaine."

"Jesus 'aitch!" the travel agent swore. "If you'd but let me speak a moment without smashing furniture or ripping out me hair, there may be something I can tell you."

"I've been counting on it," Remo said.

"You mentioned pirates, now," the travel agent muttered, struggling painfully to gain his feet. "Historically, this area—"

Remo grabbed the man by an earlobe. Howard Morgan never would have thought the most sensitive part of his body was his earlobe, so he got a real education in the next few seconds. The pain was excruciating, and it flooded his body from ear to toes.

He was mute with agony, although his mouth opened and closed, tears streamed down his face and his eyeballs rolled up into his head. He began to stutter finally, then a long low howl began to build up as the pain, impossibly, got worse.

Then, as if the heavens had opened up, the pain was gone.

But Mr. Remo Rubble still held on to the earlobe. Morgan's education continued.

"That was pain. This is no pain," Remo said, then tightened his fingers on the earlobe to an almost imperceptible degree. "You choose."

"No pain! Please, no pain!"

"If I want history," Remo said, "I'll stop by the library. The pirates I'm concerned with are alive and well right now, and one of them's your good friend Pablo Altamira."

"Pablo?" Morgan feigned amazement, lowering the red hand from his face. "He had the best of references. I would have trusted that boy with my life."

"Changed your mind, I see," Remo noted with a nod.

The first time he had given Morgan a full five seconds of the pain thing. But he was annoyed by this whole situation. Annoyed by people who dressed and talked like pirates. Annoyed by tiger sharks. Annoyed by Master Chiun the Moody. Annoyed by Stacy Armitage, because she was making him worry about her.

He gave Morgan ten seconds, and Morgan was blubbering and jerking involuntarily.

He gave Morgan ten more seconds, and Morgan was virtually unconscious from the pain.

"I guess at this moment," Remo said when he stopped, "I'm annoyed by you most of all."

Morgan was different now. Not just different temporarily, but altered mentally. He had snapped and broken, and he was never going to get put together again. But he wasn't insane. Remo had stopped just in time.

"Talk," Remo said.

Morgan looked at Remo and did not see death. Death would have been preferable to the mind-expanding suffering he had just endured. He tried to speak and ended up baaing like a sheep.

Remo pinched him on the neck, and Morgan's bodily weakness seemed to recede.

"At your service," Morgan mewed.

"You book tours," said Remo, hoping to save time if he began the tale for Morgan. "Some of them include crewmen like Pablo—or Enrique. You remember him, don't you? He shipped out with Richard and Kelly Armitage, about a month ago. The man's dead, Morgan, but the woman made it out. You hear me? She can testify to your part in the scheme. How do they punish an accessory to piracy and murder here in the Dominican Republic?"

Morgan wasn't afraid of the law. Nothing the Dominican jail could dish out would be as bad as the Earlobe Pinch of Remo Rubble.

"So, tell me about Captain Teach."

The travel agent's face went blank. "God's truth," he said, "I've never heard of him. I do all my communicatin' with a local jobber, and he sets up the contacts. He's an odd bird, too, I'll tell you that, and no mistake."

"His name?"

"Calls himself Ethan Humphrey. Old man, he is, got pirates on the brain. He runs an outfit here in town. The Cutlass Foundation, it's called. Some sort of research outfit, as he claims, but I'm not buyin' it."

"How often do you speak with him?" asked Remo.

"Maybe two or three times in a month," Morgan replies. "It all depends on prospects, see? Humphrey wants folks with money. Women, too, if it's convenient, but he don't want kids along if I can help it. Some of those want crewmen, like you did, sir. Others, I just point 'em where they want to go and get sufficient information for old Humphrey's playmates to identify 'em after, see?"

"It's clear," said Remo. "What about the crewmen you hire out?"

"They come around the day I need 'em," Morgan said, "with Humphrey's password. Never seen the same one twice."

"And you don't know the pirates? You can't tell me where they go to count their loot?"

"My honor, sir."

"In that case," Remo said, smiling, "I don't believe I need you anymore."

Morgan's face twitched. "No more earlobe, I beg of you, kind sir!"

Remo shook his head. "No more earlobe. I promise."

ETHAN HUMPHREY'S POWERBOAT had been christened the *Mulligan Stew* when he purchased it in 1990, and he had never taken time to change the name. It was inconsequential to him, like the color of the paint inside the master cabin. Humphrey cared no more about the vessel's name—or style, for that matter—than he did about the daily weather in Honduras, say, or the cost of bootleg videotapes in Beijing. What mattered was the fact that the *Mulligan Stew* was seaworthy, capable of taking Humphrey where he had to go, among the islands that were home.

The boat had cost him thirty-seven thousand dollars—more than Humphrey had paid for his small bachelor's home, back in Gainesville, when he went to work at U of F. It had wiped out three-quarters of his savings, but it was worth every dime for the freedom it gave him, the means of pursuing his lifelong desire.

Not that Humphrey could pursue that dream alone, of course. He was too old for that, by far. No pirate he, with years of sea raiding behind him, muscles toned from trimming sails, swabbing decks and hand-to-hand combat. He had missed his chance, spent years in school as both student and teacher, before he ever dreamed that the buccaneers he idealized still existed in a modern world of jet planes, nuclear power and the information superhighway. It had come as a complete surprise, the single greatest shock and thrill of Humphrey's life.

He was sailing this day, off to pay a little visit, as it were, but he wasn't sailing by himself. He knew the way by now—Kidd trusted him with that much, after all that he had done for the seagoing brotherhood—but Humphrey's strength and health were not what they had been in younger days. Whenever he went off to visit his new friends, Kidd needed warning in advance, and he would send along a man or two for crew and company.

This morning, waiting for him on the dock, were two of Kidd's men whom Humphrey recognized, although they hadn't previously pulled the escort duty. One was Pascoe, a stocky, balding sea dog in his late thirties, who shaved his scalp in defiance of the bare patch on top. He wore a tattoo of a grinning skull and crossbones on his chest, now covered by a denim work shirt with the sleeves cut off to show his burly, sunburned arms. The other was a skeletal rogue with greasy, shoulder-length hair, who called himself Finch. The long scar down his left cheek crinkled when he spoke and when he smiled—the latter event occasioned only by sporadic references to acts of bloodletting.

"You're late," Finch said, as Humphrey came along the pier. The duffel bag he carried as his only luggage was slung across one shoulder.

"No, I'm not." Humphrey didn't consult his wristwatch, knowing he was right on time. Finch always tried to pick an argument with anyone available, and it was best to put him in his place or simply ignore him. At the moment, Humphrey hoped he had done both.

"Let's get on with this," Pascoe said. "We're burning daylight."

Humphrey recognized the line but couldn't place it. Was it from a John Wayne movie? Never mind. He climbed the gangway, taking his time about it, dispensing with any further pleasantries. The men Kidd sent to chaperon him on these little jaunts weren't chosen for their winning personalities, nor were they meant to keep him entertained. Kidd never said as much, but Humphrey knew that even after all they'd been through, there was still suspicion in the pirate's mind, a fear that Humphrey would betray him somehow, change his mind about their mutual arrangement and lead the authorities to Kidd's lair. In that event, Humphrey knew, his payoff would be a swift death and a tumble overboard to feed the sharks, as befit any traitor.

But that would never happen, Humphrey knew. He had no intention of betraying Kidd or the others. It had never crossed his mind, in fact. Why should it, when the whole arrangement had been his idea to start with? He had dreamed about this moment all his life, without imagining that it could ever really come to pass. It was a fantasy from childhood, carried over into the adult domain with no good reason to suspect that he would ever have a chance to live it out.

How many men his age—or any age, for that matter—were ever privileged to truly realize their dreams? It was a first in his experience, and nothing in his life, he knew, would ever be the same again. He had already passed the point of no return, and there could be no turning back.

Not that he wanted to turn back.

Again, the possibility had never even crossed his mind.

"How long have you been waiting?" Humphrey asked, addressing the question to no one in particular.

"Feels like all damn day," Finch said.

"I make it forty minutes," Pascoe said.

"So, we're ahead of schedule then," Humphrey declared. "Just as well, because there are a few things I forgot."

"Such as?" Pascoe sounded suspicious now.

"Provisions," Humphrey said. In fact, he had forgotten nothing, but he liked to play games with his escorts, sometimes. Even when he yearned to be on Île de Mort—an interesting name; he gave Kidd credit for the choice—it helped for him to have some measure of control.

"Goddamn it!" The disgust was evident in Finch's voice. "Go get the damn things, then."

"It would save time if you could do it," Humphrey said. "You know, since I have things to do on board, before we leave."

"Well, shit! You go," Pascoe said to his younger, long-haired shipmate.

"Why should I—?"

"It would be quicker," Humphrey interrupted them, "if you split up the list. Is that all right?"

Pascoe was visibly suspicious now, while Finch was merely angry over the delay. "You got some kinda list?" he asked, the corners of his mouth turned downward in a scowl.

"Won't take a minute," Humphrey said.

"No funny business while we're gone," the bald rogue cautioned him.

"I wouldn't think of it," Humphrey said honestly.

"All right, let's have it, then."

Humphrey chose wine and cheese, because the shops lay off in opposite directions from the waterfront and would compel his escorts to divide their forces. One more little goad, to keep things interesting, while he got busy stowing items on the boat and made ready to sail.

It was perfect. Humphrey almost felt like a full-fledged pirate captain himself, manipulating rogues who would have cut his throat in any other circumstances. Granted, it was Kidd's authority that stayed their hands, not any strength of Humphrey's, but illusions were like that, devoid of objective reality.

And they still made him smile.

"Don't dawdle now," he told the grumbling buccaneers as they went down the gangway to the pier. "We're burning daylight, yes?"

IT TOOK REMO FAR TOO long to cover the ground—make that water—between Fort-de-France and Puerta Plata, on the northern coast of the Dominican Republic. On arrival, he had made his first stop at a public phone booth, where he found a home listing for Ethan Humphrey, complete with number and a street address.

There was no listing for a Cutlass Foundation in Puerta Plata, but the name alone gave Remo a fair idea of what it would entail. An outward cover for his fascination with the pirates of another century, for starters—and beyond that, what? Was Humphrey working on a book, perhaps, that would establish him as the ultimate expert in his chosen, highly specialized field? Or was something more practical involved, perhaps the distribution of loot taken from

the private craft his friends were raiding throughout
the range of the Lesser Antilles?

No matter.

Remo took the phone-book page with the home
address listing for Ethan Humphrey, showed it to a
cabdriver and soon found himself paying a call on
the former professor at his home. The dwelling was
a smallish bungalow, a quarter-mile inland, located
in a residential district that would pass for middle
class by local standards. There were roses and bou-
gainvillea in the yard, behind a low, white-painted
wooden fence. No lawn to speak of on the tiny lot,
but Remo was more interested in the house. It had
smallish windows, trimmed with lacy curtains, and a
green door that contrasted nicely with the white-
washed stucco walls. The roof was Spanish tile and
well maintained. It could have been an advertisement
from *Travel & Leisure,* a getaway for the man who
had everything and needed a place to hide from it on
certain special occasions.

Remo had himself dropped off a half block away
and didn't approach too closely. His hearing reached
out to the little house and noted the sounds of quick
movement. Somebody in a hurry, assembling some
belongings. Remo forced himself to wait, and
minutes later he saw Ethan Humphrey emerge. Humphrey had a green duffel bag in one hand, and he
paused long enough to lock the door behind him before he moved to the gate and through it, turned left

on the sidewalk and proceeded toward the harbor. Remo fell in step behind him. Humphrey never heard him, never sensed his presence.

Ten minutes later, as they drew closer to the docks, houses gave way to stores. Humphrey knew where he meant to go, and he let nothing slow him, distract him from his course. The jaunty stride, the smile he had been wearing when he left the bungalow, suggested that some kind of pleasure lay in store for him. Remo wondered what it was. His patience was running thin. All he needed was a moment of the pirate lover's time, in which to squeeze him like a toothpaste tube and see what came out.

Humphrey walked down to the marina and moved along one of the piers, out to a smallish cabin cruiser that was clearly years beyond its prime. Remo read the name someone had painted on the transom in italic script.

Mulligan Stew.

Okay, so it didn't have to make sense or fit the old man's personality. Remo doubted whether he had named the boat himself, and who cared if he had? More interesting, by far, were the two men awaiting Humphrey on the deck as he approached.

They didn't look like the role-playing pirates he'd run into that morning. No swords or flintlock pistols were in evidence, no eye patches, peg legs…and yet, there was a certain air about the men that would have marked them down as criminals in Remo's mind, regardless of the circumstances. From ten yards away he eavesdropped on their conversation and was glad he had decided not to trounce Humphrey the minute the old man emerged from his little house.

They were about to embark on a sail to the pirate's island. Finally his lousy luck was starting to reverse itself.

There was some unpleasantness as Humphrey informed the two roughnecks he needed some supplies and convinced them to fetch the items in the interest of time. It was all a lie; Remo heard it in every syllable the old man uttered. Ethan Humphrey got his way, however, and the other two came down the gangway, moved along the pier with angry strides, passed Remo without seeing him and split up to move in opposite directions as they left the waterfront.

Humphrey had the *Mulligan Stew* to himself, but he was clearly in no hurry to leave, certainly not without the shipmates he had taken pains to send on some errand that got their blood up. He wouldn't sail without them; Remo was convinced. Whatever the charade Humphrey was playing, it looked more like something he had thought up to amuse himself.

Laugh while you've got a head to laugh with, Remo thought. You never know when somebody might find a good reason to remove it.

14

Chiun had cooked rice so many thousands of times in his lifetime he could intuit the readiness of the water by breathing the steam and could sense its doneness by the richness of its aroma.

The man assigned to watch him was a toady with no intellect to speak of, surely nothing that would pass for functional imagination. He had watched Chiun build the fire and put the water on, offering no help as Chiun filled a bucket and brought it back from the stream. It gave Chiun the opportunity to moan and stagger slightly, listing to the right as if the pail were nearly too heavy for him to carry.

Chiun was smiling on the inside, and he made another sound, too quiet for the toady to hear: "Heh-heh-heh."

It said much of his present adversaries, Chiun decided, that they could behold a Master of Sinanju and believe that he was powerless. He was enjoying himself, although such clandestine behavior was well beneath his dignity.

There was just one reason he was willing to go

along with it—and it was not because his adopted white son with the bulbous nose asked him to protect Stacy Armitage.

Oh, he would protect her. She would not be tortured or defiled under his watch. But as far as going on a killing spree and sending this bunch of pretenders from centuries past to their deserved graves, that would wait. When Remo came, they could perform the cleaning up. They'd have a better chance of saving all the prisoners on the island with two of them on the job.

But why kill the pirates now? They might serve a purpose still.

If this was the correct island, the place that had been known once as the Island of Many Skulls, it was not a small patch of land. Even a Master of Sinanju would have difficulties finding a treasure that had been buried here—a treasure buried centuries ago. Buried deep. Buried, in fact, by a Master of Sinanju.

If these pirates had some of their history, then maybe they could help him locate the landmarks described in the Sinanju scrolls. The nature of some of those landmarks made it unlikely that they still existed.

Chiun would know soon enough.

He began to add the rice, sifting a handful at a time into the boiling water from a heavy burlap bag the pirates had provided him at his request. The shellfish—peeled and deveined already, piled up in a wooden bowl, within arm's reach—would be the last addition, when the rice was nearly done. Meanwhile, he had time to observe his enemies and find them wanting in the skills that might have saved their worthless lives, once Remo was available to finish them.

It would take time, of course, for Remo to discover where the pirates were. Chiun wasn't precisely sure how that would be accomplished, but he had no doubt that Remo would succeed.

Remo didn't come across as one of great intellect. Or cunning. He wasn't prone to great feats of mental dexterity, or even mediocre ones. Some had even labeled him a simpleton.

But somehow Remo always failed to live up to others' expectations of idiocy. Somehow, like unexpected lightning, the flashes of insight would always come to the young white Reigning Master. Or he would simply worry the thing to death. Or meander aimlessly, so it seemed, into the solution. But the most important thing was that the solution was always reached. Chiun thought that there just might be—and he would never in a thousand generations admit this to Remo or another living soul or even dare notate the thought in the sacred scrolls of Sinanju or even *think* it too loud for fear some wandering mind reader would happen across it and blurt it out—but there just might be a streak of, well, brilliance to be found in there. Somewhere. If you really looked for it.

Chiun took a wooden ladle and began to stir the rice with lazy, counterclockwise strokes, putting a palsied shake into his hand just for added effect. His watchdog lit a hand-rolled cigarette and started puffing clouds of smoke into the air. He was within arm's reach of Chiun, a killing distance, but it wasn't time to start the deadly dance.

But first, the search.

"YOU'VE BEEN HERE HOW long?" Stacy asked.

The woman who had earlier identified herself as Megan Richards glanced at her companions in the dingy, thatch-roofed hut. Felicia Docherty frowned and shrugged while the other, introduced by Megan as Robin Chatsworth, sat still and said nothing.

"Four, five days," said Megan. "I'm not exactly sure. Time runs together here. You'll find out what I mean."

Stacy was hoping that she wouldn't be among the pirates long enough that she lost track of time, but anything was possible. With Remo gone—not dead, she told herself, please, God, just don't let him be dead—there was no way of knowing how or when she would be rescued from her captors.

"And they killed your boyfriends? Christ, I'm sorry."

"Not exactly boyfriends," Megan said. "It was a shame, though."

Megan Richards didn't sound as if it were a shame, but Stacy knew that people dealt with grief in varied ways. Or maybe there had been no more between these women and the dead men than casual sex. Less than that, perhaps, if they had just been "friends." Such things were not unknown.

"And what about your boat?" asked Stacy. "What was it, again?"

"The *Salomé*," Felicia Docherty put in. "Is that some kind of Arab name, or what?"

"I couldn't tell you," Stacy said. "Did you have anybody else on board?"

"Like who? You mean a chaperon?" Megan was close to laughter, but it sounded more like hysteria in the making than any real vestige of humor.

"No," said Stacy. "I was wondering if you had hired a guide, or anyone to help you with the boat along the way."

Meg and Felicia shook their heads as one, while Robin sat and stared. "Nothing like that," Felicia said. "The guys knew all about that stuff, okay? We didn't have the room, besides, and who wants witnesses?"

To what? Stacy was on the verge of asking, but she checked herself. She knew what the young woman meant, and what she had in mind. A college fling was easily forgotten, but it might come back to haunt you if your parents heard about it. From a stranger, for example, who had watched and listened, maybe asking you for money that would keep him quiet in the days and weeks ahead. Trust no one, if you didn't know them going back to grade school.

But it hadn't saved these three. Not even close. Their young men of the moment had been killed, three more lives wasted in addition to God knew how many that had gone before, and from the evidence before her, Stacy knew these three had suffered in captivity. The faded shirts and baggy, twice-patched pants they wore weren't the clothes they had been captured in; she would have bet her life on that. And from the bruises on their skin, the shadows underneath their eyes, the silence Robin held before her like a shield, Stacy was sure the men who stole their clothes had taken much, much more, as well.

"Do you have any idea where we are?" Felicia asked.

"Not really," Stacy said. "They kept us down below after they took the *Melody*."

"That's not much better than the *Salomé*," said Megan. "Jeez, where do they get these names for boats?"

"Who's the old man?" Felicia asked before Stacy had time to answer Megan's question.

Stacy wondered how much she should tell these strangers, and decided there was little they could do to help her, even less that they could do to help Chiun.

"He was my husband's friend," she said, preserving the fiction for what it was worth. "They've known each other from when Remo was a boy."

"Remo?" Felicia said. "What kind of name is that?"

"Armenian," Stacy replied, ad-libbing as she went along. "His great-grandparents came from Eastern Europe."

"Oh. Yeah, right."

"What happened? Can I ask you that?"

"They made him, uh, jump overboard," said Stacy. Even as she spoke the words, they had a kind of unreality about them, as if it were more of Remo's cover, something he had taught her to repeat on cue.

"That's rough," Felicia said. "Same thing they did with Jon and Barry. Did they shoot him, too?"

"Felicia, Jesus!" Megan sounded angry.

"I was just asking, for God's sake!"

"There was no shooting," Stacy said.

"Well, who knows?" said Felicia. "Maybe he's okay, then."

Megan glared at her, making Felicia shrug, but Stacy was already thinking, Yes, maybe he is. Maybe he is all right. And wouldn't that be something?

She would have to keep her fingers crossed, to wait and see. If Remo came, he came. If not…well, there was still Chiun, his promise to destroy the pirates on his own, if it should come to that.

With a start she saw the path her thoughts were taking. Crazy thoughts! Stupid dreams. She was losing touch with reality just as surely as poor old Chiun.

Remo was dead. Chiun was living in a fantasy world. He was a hundred years old—he was *not* going to start kicking pirate ass. If she let herself start believing all this make-believe stuff, she would never be able to think her way out of this situation.

She had to take care of herself.

The thought left her trembling with a sudden graveyard chill.

CAPTAIN THOMAS KIDD had a decision to announce. There were procedures to be followed, certain risks involved, but he had made his mind up on the crucial point, and there would be no turning back. If there were any challenges, then he would have to meet them as he always had before—head-on, with all his might and courage.

It wasn't the easiest decision Kidd had ever made, but he had weighed it carefully, examined all the angles and potential arguments against his choice, before deciding that he should proceed at any cost. The time was right; he wasn't getting any younger, and the notion was entirely logical when viewed from that perspective.

It was time for Captain Kidd to take a wife. A queen, more properly, to help him rule the kingdom he had carved out for himself. In other circumstances, bygone days, there would have been a chance for him to shop around, survey the prospects in the islands—maybe even sail away to Florida and try his luck among the coastal cities—but the modern pirate life had more severe constraints. The captain was required to make do with the stock at hand.

Most times, Kidd would have seen that limitation as an insurmountable impediment to courting, but Fate had a way of sneaking up on him sometimes. He was accustomed to the flow of captive women moving through the camp, few of them lasting long. A year or so had been the maximum for most; they had a tendency to die from tropical diseases, overwork or sheer despondency. A handful killed themselves, and one—the wench Billy Teach had captured aboard the *Solon II*—had actually managed to escape. Most were attractive in their way, some of them stunning, but they lacked a certain quality of majesty.

Until today.

Granted, she could have used a better name. Stacy was not a monarch's name, granted, but Captain Kidd was willing to ignore such minor flaws. It was the way this woman carried herself, defiance flashing from her bold green eyes, refusing to be cowed by her surroundings, even now.

She hated him, of course. That was a given, and he understood the feeling. What else could a kidnapper expect at first? Kidd knew it would take time for her to come around, but once she recognized her destiny, the transformation process could begin.

And there was no time like the present to proceed.

Kidd armed himself and left his quarters, moving purposefully through the compound to a central point, beside the cooking fire. The captive Chinese cook glanced at him in passing, his head jittering from side to side from some sort of disorder of the nervous system, and turned back to his stirring of the large, fire-blackened kettle.

Captain Kidd stopped walking when he reached a kind of minigallows that had been erected near the center of the compound. It stood shoulder high, and where a body might have hung if it had been, full-sized, a twisted triangle of rusty metal was suspended from a chain. Above it, on the crossbar of the wooden structure, lay an old screwdriver with a well-worn wooden handle and a twelve-inch blade.

Kidd took the screwdriver in hand and rapped the blade repeatedly against the rusty iron triangle. The clamor echoed through the pirate camp, bringing men from their huts, from their chores, one or two hobbling back from relieving themselves in the bush.

He waited until most of his men were assembled, roughly surrounding him, jostling one another for position. Several called out questions, which Kidd ignored, giving his rowdy brothers time to quiet down. When they were as silent as Kidd could expect, he raised his voice in order to be heard by everyone.

"I'll waste none of your time," he said by way of introduction to his plan. "The time has come for me to take a wife. A queen, in fact. A woman who will give me sons and raise them in the grand tradition of our brotherhood."

That brought a murmur from the crowd, more than a few of them regarding Kidd with curiosity or frank suspicion. They were skeptical of change, and with good reason, since most alterations in the daily lives of outlaws brought them to a jail cell or a rope. A few of them were also wondering which woman he had chosen for himself, Kidd knew, and calculating how his choice would slash the list of wenches otherwise available to the community at large.

"The woman I've selected is the captive known as Stacy," Kidd announced. "We'll marry in accordance with the laws of our community, and life will go on as before, except with prospects for an heir."

No one among Kidd's audience suggested that the woman might have anything to say about the union; that wasn't an issue in such cases, when a pirate chose himself a mate. Still, some of them were muttering, and Kidd paused, biding his time, waiting to discover if a man with courage would reveal himself among the crew.

"What's that leave for the rest of us?" a harsh

voice challenged Kidd from somewhere in the ranks. He didn't see the man who spoke but thought he recognized the voice.

"Who asks me this?" Kidd scanned the rows of faces, waiting for the one outspoken buccaneer to show himself.

A tall man shouldered through the press to take a stand in front of Kidd, perhaps ten feet away. As Kidd had thought, it was scar-faced Rodrigo, standing with his feet apart, hands fisted on his hips. Kidd knew without having to check that Rodrigo was wearing a dagger sheathed on his belt, behind his right hip, where he could reach it swiftly as the need arose. He was no mean hand with the weapon, either, if memory served.

"I ask it," said Rodrigo. "And I wager that I'm not the only one who's thinkin' it."

Rodrigo glanced around to see if anyone would second him, and while a number of the others stared at Kidd, as if expecting the performance of a special drama for their entertainment, none was forward enough to support him in words.

The shortage of support didn't appear to cow Rodrigo. If anything, he seemed emboldened as he turned once more to face his captain, fists still planted firmly on his hips. Had the pirate's right fist edged closer to his knife?

"It is a captain's right to choose his mate," Kidd

told Rodrigo and the rest. "Who would dispute this time-honored law?"

"I would," Rodrigo said without a moment's hesitation, "if it means a shortage for the rest of us, where nookie is concerned. I, for one, have been going without long enough."

"You've not been idle with the other hostages from what I hear," said Kidd.

Rodrigo frowned and cleared his throat. "That's neither here nor there," he blustered. "Whether these curs will 'fess up to it or not, I'm speaking for the lot of them. We want the redhead shared out with the rest. When we have wenches enough to go around, then it'll be time enough to think about your wedding plans."

Kidd smiled and clasped his hands loosely behind his back. "And is there aught else on your mind?" he asked.

Rodrigo hesitated for a moment, glancing back to left and right once more, then nodded to himself. "There is, indeed," he said. "This business of an heir is something some of us don't hold with absolutely, either. Any pirate's law I ever heard of called for captains to be chosen from the brotherhood, by challenge. When did we start breedin' 'em?"

"A question worthy of reply," Kidd said.

Behind his back, the fingers of his right hand curled around the grip of a .38-caliber revolver, which he wore tucked into the back of his stout leather belt. In one smooth motion, Kidd drew the side arm, thumbing back the hammer, and thrust it out in front of him. The three-inch barrel was on target before Rodrigo knew what was happening, and Kidd squeezed the .38's trigger a heartbeat later.

The bullet struck Rodrigo squarely in the middle of his forehead, flattening on impact and toppling him over backward in the dust. Before the echo of the shot had died away, Kidd had another challenge for his men.

"Who else disputes my right to choose a mate?" he asked in his most reasonable tone.

When there was no reply, Kidd slowly lowered his revolver, turning back in the direction of his quarters. Offering his back to any coward who would take the chance, hoping that he would not be called upon to kill another of his men this afternoon.

Behind him, as he walked away, he heard the ancient Oriental's high-pitched voice. "Clear trash away!" he said. "Wash filthy hands and come to eat!"

The only one who dared speak was a senile old man—that brought a chuckle to the lips of Captain Kidd.

CARLOS RAMIREZ TAPPED the ash from his cigar into an ashtray fashioned from a jaguar's skull. It was illegal to hunt jaguars, since they had been registered as an endangered species, but such laws meant little

to a multibillionaire who earned his living from cocaine.

"Another boat," Ramirez said. "Our friends are
having busy days."

"They take too many risks," Fabian Guzman said.

"Life is a risk," Ramirez said.

"These locos thrive on danger," Guzman argued.
"They are not normal businessmen."

"What's normal?" asked Ramirez. "The Jamai-
cans? The Italians? The Chinese? We have enough
trouble with enemies, amigo. Do not borrow more by
picking quarrels with our friends."

"Suppose they are discovered?" Fabian went on,
insistent. "Do you think that they would hesitate to
tell the Coast Guard or the DEA who buys the boats
they steal?"

"I doubt that they would let themselves be taken,"
said the cocaine lord of Cartagena. "They are loco,
as you say, and hate the law more than you do. Also,
they seem to lead charmed lives. A padre told me
once that God takes care of fools and children."

"They leave witnesses," Guzman replied.

"You mean the women? What is that to us? These
locos need some entertainment on their little island,
no? Is that so terrible? The women are not yours,
amigo."

"I am told they let one get away."

Ramirez took a long pull on his prime Havana
cigar, savoring the taste of it, slowly expelling twin

streams of smoke through his nostrils. He had heard the story, too, about a Yankee woman who was fished out of the ocean, telling tales of pirates and the foul indignities she suffered at their hands, but nothing had been done about it so far. With no positive response from the authorities, Ramirez thought there must be one of two solutions to the riddle. First, the story might be false, one of those rumors that came up from time to time, without apparent origin, and got some people overheated while they sought in vain to track it down. The other possibility was that a woman had escaped the pirates, but that she could give no useful information to the law. She could be dead by now, perhaps deranged from her experience, or simply ignorant of where she had been held.

In any case, Ramirez told himself, no problem.

Unless...

Carlos Ramirez had survived this long in a treacherous business, while others fell around him, because he left nothing to chance. His dealings with the pirates led by Thomas Kidd had amply benefited both sides, and he had no wish to sever the connection if there was a means of keeping it alive. Security came first, however, and he wouldn't sacrifice himself, the empire he had built from his estate outside of Cartagena, in the interest of some loco pirates who weren't even from Colombia.

"What are you thinking?" he inquired of his lieutenant.

"Simply that we must be cautious in our dealings with these people, Carlos. They are not part of our family—they never will be. When I talk to them and look into their eyes, it is like talking to—" Guzman dropped his voice to a whisper, though they were alone "—like talking to Jorge."

Ramirez looked at his lieutenant sharply, surprised at the breach in etiquette. Jorge's name was not to be mentioned.

"I say this," Guzman stated carefully and seriously, "so that you will know what I am thinking. If I am right, then we need to do something about it."

The brief flare of anger subsided, and Ramirez nodded in understanding. Guzman's point was well taken. Jorge, the unmentionable cousin, was a crazy boy, kept in seclusion in a comfortable but hidden and remote private asylum in the jungle. Just him and a few dozen overpaid caretakers. Ramirez and Guzman visited him regularly—every Christmas Eve without fail.

Jorge had insane eyes, and now that Ramirez considered it, he had maybe seen a touch of that in the eyes of the pirates. Just a little, but it was there, masked behind their animal cruelty.

Of course, you had to be crazy to live like they did. Kidd had insisted that they were like the American Amish people, who lived their lives by codes of conduct that the rest of the world forgot centuries ago. They just didn't happen to have the religious rationale that made the Amish look "normal."

There sure was nothing moral or ethical in the pirates' code. They were savage, even by the standards of the Colombian drug trade.

Bloodthirsty and at least slightly unbalanced. Not a good combination. Not the kind of people you necessarily should be putting your trust in.

Yes, he told himself. The loco label said it all.

Still, they were useful in their way. They had supplied Ramirez with an average of ten to fifteen boats per year since he had first begun to deal with Captain Kidd. A handful of the craft were still in use on smuggling runs—repainted now, of course, with brand-new serial numbers guaranteed to pass at least a cursory inspection. The rest were either seized or sunk, some of them auctioned off by U.S. Customs or the DEA under provisions of the federal assets seizure program. It was a point of special, ironic pride to Ramirez that some of those very boats would be repurchased at a discount by his own jobbers, returned yet again to the smuggling trade…and that they would no doubt be seized again at some time in the future.

The more things changed, the more they stayed the same.

Ramirez had trusted Thomas Kidd. Should he continue to trust the man—within the limits of his own ability to trust?

They would never be the best of friends, that much was preordained, but Carlos didn't think the pirate would betray him, either.

Not unless Kidd found a way to profit greatly from the treachery.

In the devious world of Carlos Ramirez, there were only two ways to insure loyalty—fear and favor. Colombians even had a phrase in Spanish that expressed the concept: *plata o plomo.* Silver or lead. If you didn't accept the silver that was offered willingly, you got the lead when you were least expecting it. Sometimes the other members of your family got the lead, as well.

Ramirez wasn't prepared for a war with the pirates of the Windward Islands. They had served him well, so far, without a hitch. It might be useful, even so, if he could find a way to reinforce their loyalty now, before some outside stress or stimulus should put it to the test.

"When are we picking up the latest boat?" Ramirez asked.

"Tomorrow or the next day," Guzman said.

"Make it tomorrow. Send the word."

"Sí, jefe."

Guzman didn't like the order, but he would obey it all the same. It was his nature to be second in command, a follower. That was why Ramirez trusted his lieutenant more than any other living man. He knew that even if poor Fabian should find the courage to rebel against his master, it wouldn't occur to him. He would no sooner try to run the family by himself than he would sprout wings and fly up to Panama City for carnival season.

"When we go, this time," Ramirez added in an offhand tone, "I'm going with you."

"Carlos! Why, for Christ's sake? It could be—"

The cocaine lord raised his hand for silence, and Guzman's mouth snapped shut like a mousetrap. Angry color darkened Guzman's cheeks, but he had nothing more to say without permission from his commander.

"It has been some time since I sat down with Kidd and talked about our common interests," Ramirez said. "It can do no harm to show our partners that we value their participation. I may even feel disposed to pay a bit more for the next few boats, if it seems feasible."

"Carlos—"

"I must look into those eyes again, Fabian." Ramirez took another pull on his cigar, let the smoke leak slowly from between his teeth. "I must see if I see—what you see, then decide what to do."

Guzman understood. He said as much with new determination in his brief nod.

"Go send the word," Ramirez said. "And while

you're at it, get the troops together. I want twenty men for this excursion, well armed."

"*Sí, jefe.* As you say."

Guzman went off to carry out his orders, while Ramirez sat alone and thought about the day to come. A nice excursion to the islands, sun and sea, a bit of an adventure with the pirates waiting for him at the other end. And if his meeting with the pirate leader gave him any cause to think Kidd might betray them, well...

Plomo o plata, sí.

Lead and silver.

They made the bloody world go around.

REMO THOUGHT THE *Mulligan Stew* would never leave. First Ethan Humphrey spent what seemed like hours in his cabin, unpacking his duffel bag and making up his room with the diligence of the true anal retentive.

Finally the buccaneers returned from their respective errands and groused with the master of the vessel over whatever it was that he had sent them off to fetch. Then, at last, they cast off.

Remo watched them go.

When they were about a hundred yards from shore, he ran after them.

Running on water wasn't easy, even for a Master of Sinanju. It involved, simply put, sensing the natural pressure of the water's surface and not allowing

your footsteps to apply pressure in excess of that.
Remo didn't understand it himself, exactly, and
found it was better not to think about it too much.
Just do it. If you wanted to keep dry, it was better
than swimming.

The calm Caribbean helped. He crossed the open
water in a smooth blur of flying feet that touched,
but never quite broke the surface, and landed as
soundless as a feather on the rear diving platform of
the *Mulligan Stew*. And he wasn't wet except for
some droplets clinging to his shoes.

Time to take over.

There was some kind of a racket on the front deck,
a sound of spillage, something broken, followed by
an angry outburst from one of the pirates. Heavy
footsteps came around the back of the deckhouse and
turned into the companionway without noticing
Remo.

Remo followed him inside. It was the man with
long hair, cursing to himself and reaching for a
broom or mop in a closet, and he finally sensed trouble. He turned around fast, but it was too late for
him. Remo took him by the scruff of the neck in a
two-finger pinch that froze him solid.

Remo put the fallen mop in the long-hair's hand,
closed his fingers around it and walked him back
outside. Long Hair mewled.

Remo heard the skinhead muttering, while Ethan

Humphrey told him to relax, that it was nothing to get excited about. A little glass, was all.

"Spilt milk," he heard the ex-professor say, and chuckle to himself.

It seemed that either Skinhead or Long Hair had dropped a pitcher with some kind of fruit drink in it, and fractured glass and pinkish liquid spread across the planking of the deck.

Skinhead's back was to him, Ethan Humphrey facing toward the open hatch as Remo stepped into the light with the silent Long Hair. The old man recognized him at a glance but didn't speak. His lips were working, but no sound was coming out. The bald man, as it happened, was busy staring and cursing at the mess around his feet, oblivious to Humphrey's sudden shock.

And then, the ex-professor found his voice. "My God!" he blurted out. "It's you!"

"Huh?" Skinhead grumbled. "What are you talk—?"

Skinhead stopped when he saw the old man's face, eyes focused behind him. He glanced across one burly shoulder, blinked at Remo in surprise and pivoted to face the stranger, reaching for something on his hip. A knife.

Remo moved in slow motion as far as Skinhead or the old man could tell, but the knife wasn't even out of its leather sheath before Remo took hold of the forearm that was grabbing for it. He bent the forearm, but it wasn't the wrist that turned at right angles suddenly—it was the forearm itself, and that required a lot of bone breaking to accomplish. Remo didn't mind putting out the little bit of extra effort.

Skinhead minded. The bellow that came out of him was extraordinary.

"Hey, hey, hey," Remo said as he pinched Skinhead behind the neck in a fashion similar to Long Hair; this made the bellow stop. "People will think you're a foghorn—you want to screw up shipping traffic from here to Key West?"

"What are you doing here?" Ethan Humphrey demanded.

"First things first," Remo said. "Do we or do we not need Dumb and Dumber to make the trip to the pirate island?"

"Wha-what?" Humphrey asked. "Pirate island?"

"They know where the pirate island is," Remo said matter-of-factly. "Don't you, boys?"

In torment, Skinhead and Long Hair still managed to produce vigorous nods of assent.

"If they can get me there, I'll keep them. Instead of you," Remo said. "Got the picture?"

"I get it," Humphrey said miserably.

"You take me where I need to go, and you just might survive," said Remo, "but you don't have tons of time to think about it. Tick-tock, Dr. Humphrey. Sink or swim."

"I'll take you." Humphrey hung his head.

"Good. Sorry, boys."

He lifted the pair of cutthroats and brought them together violently, shattering their bones and pulverizing their softer parts. What remained was fused into a mass of flesh and seeping blood. Remo heaved it into the water before it started to drip on the deck.

Humphrey was staring at Remo, aghast, as he turned back from the rail. "You...you...killed him!" the professor stammered.

"I didn't check pulses but, yeah, I'm pretty sure dead is what they are," Remo asked.

"I'm to be next, I suppose?"

"Well, that depends on you."

"Excuse me?" Humphrey seemed confused.

15

"Excuse me?"

"You're surprised," the man named Kidd responded. "Certainly, I understand how you must feel."

"I doubt that very much."

They were alone inside the squalid hut that served as Stacy's prison cell. The other three young women had been sent outside when he arrived demanding privacy. At first Stacy feared she was about to be assaulted, but the truth was even more bizarre, more frightening.

The pirate captain was proposing marriage.

No, that wasn't right. He wasn't asking her to marry him. Rather, he was informing her of his decision, standing back and smiling at her with his yellow teeth, as if she ought to be delighted by the news. He plainly viewed the prospect of their marriage as an honor that should be apparent to the most thick-headed woman on the planet.

"Married?" She repeated it as if the word were foreign to her, not a part of her vocabulary.

"That's the ticket," Kidd replied, still beaming at her with discolored teeth. "You're prob'ly wondering about the service."

"Well—"

"I grant you, we don't have a rightful preacher," he continued, "but we have our differences with Mother Church."

"I can imagine," Stacy said.

Kidd chuckled to himself, appreciating her wit, but it was artificial, like stage laughter, there and gone. He still had more to say, and while he hadn't exactly rehearsed the speech, he still seemed bent on making certain points.

"The good news," Kidd continued, "is that I'm the captain of this scurvy lot, and maritime law gives me the authority to pronounce nuptials."

"So, you can marry yourself?"

Kidd blinked at that idea, as if confused, then frowned slightly. "Perform the rights, you mean? Of course. I grant you, it may not be strictly legal on the mainland, but I've long since given up on courting the opinion of landlubbers."

"This is so sudden," Stacy said. It was the ultimate cliché, but she could think of nothing else to say. Her mind was racing, jumbled thoughts colliding, jostling one another, but she had a feeling that it would be foolish—maybe even fatal—to show weakness in the presence of this man.

"You'll get used to the notion," Kidd replied,

"once we've been rightly hitched. You'll be my queen."

The final comment was so serious that Stacy almost laughed out loud. She bit her tongue instead and stood with eyes downcast, considering the best response.

"What sort of an engagement period were you considering?" she asked at last.

"Engagement?" Once again Kidd seemed confused. "To hell with that nonsense! Tonight's the night, my love. Your Chinky friend's already working on the menu."

"He's Korean," Stacy said, stalling for time.

"It's all the same," Kidd said. "You rest now. Get yourself shipshape for the big event."

"I don't have anything to wear!" she blurted out, the sheer absurdity of it all twitching the corners of her mouth into a near-hysterical smile that could just as easily have been a rictus of pain.

"No matter," Kidd replied. "We'll fix you up with something for the ceremony. Later on, of course, you won't need anything to wear."

He left her with a wink and leer in parting. Stacy stared after him until she was alone and fairly certain he wouldn't duck back to add some new announcement. She stiffened at the sound of shuffling footsteps, but it was her fellow captives returning. Megan came forward, while Robin and Felicia hung back, near the curtained entrance to the hut.

"I hear we're going to be bridesmaids," Megan said.

At that, a dam burst inside Stacy, and she stepped into the younger woman's arms, dissolving into tears.

CHIUN WAS WORKING ON A culinary masterpiece. It was to be a wedding feast, as he had been informed, and the ridiculous young men who thought he was their prisoner demanded "something special for the bride and groom."

Chiun intended to oblige.

The one-eyed cretin charged with guarding Chiun lurched to his feet as the Master Emeritus of Sinanju approached. "Need sumpthin', Chinaman?"

Chiun considered pulling off the pirate's arm and using it to rearrange his grubby features. It would be so easy. Once that simple chore was done, he could proceed to take the others as they came, one at a time, or in whatever combinations they preferred. There were no more than sixty-five or seventy in all. It would be child's play. If not for the prisoners. Surely the rabble would resort to using hostages once it became apparent that they were being picked off by an invisible killer.

How important, he wondered for the tenth time, were the prisoners, really?

Important enough to Emperor Smith, Chiun decided. He would be upset. As would Remo—and the bigmouthed boy would never let the subject rest. He would go on and on for weeks. Chiun would be in misery. He sighed mentally. He would have to wait.

But the waiting wouldn't be wasted time.

"Your captain wants a special feast," Chiun said, making his voice higher and slightly squeaky.

"Our cap'n?" parroted the goon behind the crusty eye patch.

"As I said." Chiun could be obsequious when circumstances called for it, though it would never cease to gall him. "I require some spices."

"We got salt," said the pirate, swinging at the single wooden shelf in the cooking sty. "And we got pepper."

"Not enough," Chiun replied, gesturing toward the forest that surrounded the encampment. "I must go and look for other things."

"Like hell," the pirate snarled. "Nobody tole me nothin' 'bout you leavin' camp. Forget about it, Slant-eyes."

This time, Chiun imagined reaching deep inside the pirate's chest and ripping out the withered lump of gristle that sufficed him for a heart. Perhaps, on second thought, it would be more instructive to crack open his skull and examine the tiny husk of his brain.

Both prospects made Chiun smile, an uncharacteristic expression on his ancient face, but the pirate didn't know him well enough to realize that death was near.

"I cannot argue with such evident intelligence,"

he said. "No doubt, you will explain to Captain Kidd why his instructions for the wedding feast have been ignored. He will, of course, be sympathetic to your reasoning."

"You tellin' me the cap'n ordered this?"

"His excellency's order is for me to fix the ultimate gourmet repast. I have little to work with. Producing a special feast from this miserable larder will demand, at the very least, some distinctive seasonings."

The pirate tried to wrap his mind around Chiun's statement, which had an awful lot of long words in it, then snorted. "Where in hell you think you're livin', Chinaman? These ain't the goddamn spice islands, for Neptune's sake!"

"I have some knowledge of these things," Chiun replied. "There is no doubt the jungle, there, will yield surprises for the palate."

Chiun's watchdog glared at the forest with his one eye, finally turning back to face the Master Emeritus of Sinanju. "I don't like the jungle," he declared.

"By all means, then, stay here," Chiun offered. "After all, how can I run away?"

"You'd like that, wouldn't you?" The pirate sneered. "Get me in trouble with the cap'n, jus' so you can go off playin' in the woods. No way you're gettin' off that easy, Slant-eyes."

"I will be most happy for your company," Chiun suggested, smiling pleasantly.

The gruff guard actually found himself amused by the tiny Chink codger, who had to be off his rocker. The old fart'd been prisoner here just a day and here he was happy as a clam.

The pirate might have thought differently if he saw the picture in Chiun's head—a vision of the pirate with his head cranked backward on his shoulders.

"How long's this supposed to take?"

"Not long," Chiun replied. "The sooner I can find what I am looking for, the sooner we come back."

"I dunno how you think you're gonna find a god-damn thing out there," the pirate groused.

"Jungles are much the same," Chiun informed his captor. "I have every confidence."

"Le's get a friggin' move on, then!" the one-eyed pirate growled. "I wanna get back here and stick to business."

"As you say," Chiun replied. "Your wish is my command."

CARLOS RAMIREZ WAS A CITY boy at heart, though he had spent his first half-dozen years in the Colombian back country, where he observed the coca trade firsthand. He felt at home with solid ground beneath his feet, and while he owned two yachts himself, employing them for floating orgies on occasion, he was never perfectly at ease once they left the dock behind.

Ramirez didn't get seasick, exactly, but he always

felt as if the deep water beneath his keel was in control, somehow, and he despised the feeling, as he hated anything that made him feel inadequate.

That afternoon, Ramirez had two boats to think about. He was aboard the *Macarena,* a sixty-foot luxury craft he had legally purchased in Miami two years earlier, allowing his then-mistress to name it. Iliana said it was "my favorite song from when I was a kid!" This from a girl still three months shy of being able to vote legally in her native Florida. But she was certainly grown-up enough to perform her duties as Ramirez's concubine.

A role without much job security, as Iliana learned about by the time she celebrated her eighteenth and final birthday. While Iliana was no more, the *Macarena* served Ramirez well enough. This day he shared the craft with Fabian Guzman, three crewmen and four soldiers. The second vessel was the *Scorpion,* a forty-foot speed launch with another two dozen shooters aboard.

"Carlos?"

Ramirez turned away from the port rail and found Guzman beside him, full lips curved into a frown.

"Still worrying?" Ramirez asked.

Guzman rolled his massive shoulders in a lazy shrug. "This business with the pirates," he replied. "I keep thinking you would be safer back at home."

"But for how long?" Ramirez asked. "If there was any doubt in Medellín or Cartagena that I had the capability to deal with locos such as these, how long before I find my enemies attacking me on every side?''

"If you fear treachery, Carlos—''

Ramirez leaned in close to Guzman, with their noses almost touching. "I fear nothing, Fabian! Repeat it!''

"You fear nothing. *Sí*, I understand, Carlos. Forgive me.''

"There is nothing to forgive, my friend. A mere slip of the tongue.''

"As for these soldiers, though…''

"I want them in reserve, as I've explained,'' Ramirez said. "There is no reason to believe that Kidd is planning to betray us. Should he entertain such suicidal notions, though, we will have force enough on hand to deal with him.''

"Three dozen guns, Carlos, if you include the two of us.''

"Are you not still a soldier, Fabian?'' Ramirez enjoyed the darkening of Guzman's countenance, the way his spine stiffened at the thinly veiled insult.

"You know I am,'' his second in command replied, "but they outnumber us two to one, at least.''

"They are as children,'' said Ramirez. "They are locos, Fabian. You said as much yourself.''

"Locos who aren't afraid to kill,'' Guzman replied. "They've proved that much. I simply do not trust them, Carlos.''

"A wise decision," said Ramirez. "Trust is difficult to earn among the best of friends. The best of families have traitors in their ranks, as you know well. Strangers like these..."

He made a vague, dismissive gesture with one hand and turned back toward the rail. The deck shifted beneath his feet, Ramirez stretching out one hand to grip the rail and keep himself from wobbling where he stood. Behind him, Guzman stood with his feet well apart, arms crossed over his chest.

A backward glance showed him the *Scorpion* a hundred yards or so behind the *Macarena,* keeping pace. Most of the gunners were belowdecks, as he had commanded. The *Scorpion* wouldn't be putting into harbor when they reached the pirate stronghold—not unless and until Ramirez felt he needed reinforcements on the scene. If Kidd or one of his subordinates had any questions about the second vessel, Carlos meant to answer that he needed crewmen for the new boat he was buying from the pirates. It was all they had to know, unless Ramirez had some reason to believe that there was treachery afoot. In which case...

Carlos wished that he could have his soldiers check their guns again, but logic told him that wouldn't be necessary. They were all professionals and would have seen to their equipment well before they went aboard the yacht. If there was one thing that his soldiers knew about, it was preparing for a fight.

Ramirez craved a glass of rum, but knew that it wouldn't be wise for him to begin drinking now, with less than two hours to go before he met Kidd and the other buccaneers. There would be liquor flowing at the camp, he knew, and it was critical that Carlos keep his wits about him every moment that he spent in the presence of those locos.

Rum could wait. There was no time, at the moment, to mix business with pleasure.

At the very least, he had another stolen boat to purchase from the buccaneers, blood money changing hands. If there was treachery afoot, as Fabian suspected, then Ramirez would be forced to deal with that, as well. A little killing might even help settle his stomach, after spending so much time at sea.

The thought made Carlos smile again, with feeling this time.

Perhaps, after all, it would be an enjoyable day.

"YOU HAVE TO UNDERSTAND," said Ethan Humphrey, "what it's like to have a dream come true, when you've been hoping for it—waiting for it—all your life."

"Some dream," Remo said. He was standing off to one side of the ex-professor, in the cockpit of the *Mulligan Stew*.

"It must seem absurd to you, I realize," the old man said.

"Absurd doesn't quite say it," Remo said. "Try demented."

"My academic life—my whole life, dammit—has been dedicated to a study of the buccaneers who plied these waters in the seventeenth and eighteenth centuries. From childhood onward, they provided me with hours of escapist reading, academic study—in short, pure enjoyment. A reason for living, as it were."

"All fine and dandy until you start living it out, Professor," Remo said.

"These men are purists, don't you see that?" Humphrey frowned and shook his head, red faced in a way that had nothing to do with the afternoon heat. His topic clearly moved him in the same way that politics or religion moved other men, to the point of fanaticism and beyond.

"Pure killers, would that be?" asked Remo. "Pure hijackers? Or maybe it's pure rapists that you had in mind?"

"Their ethics represent another time, another era," Ethan Humphrey said, apparently unfazed by Remo's comment. "It's unfair to judge them by the standards of the modern era."

"You've discussed this with their victims, I suppose?"

A frown creased Humphrey's face. "You see me

as a man devoid of sympathy,'' he said. ''No doubt, you find me heartless. But consider this, my friend—the world today is overcrowded. Men lead lives of quiet desperation, in the words of Henry David Thoreau. Are you aware how many innocents are murdered every day in New York, in Chicago, in Los Angeles?''

''I'd look it up,'' said Remo, ''if I figured it was relevant.''

''But everything is relevant,'' said Humphrey. ''Don't you see? So many sacrificed for nothing, while a handful put their puerile, wasted lives to better use.''

''As fish food?'' Remo asked.

''Sarcasm.'' Humphrey nodded like a wise man who expected no better from his intellectual inferiors. ''I understand that you have difficulty grasping what's at stake here.''

''Lives and property, you mean?'' asked Remo. ''It's a stretch, all right, but I can just about catch hold of it.''

''I'm speaking of a race, a culture,'' Humphrey said. ''What are a few lives in the balance, when it means the preservation of a cultural tradition?''

''Maybe you should ask the victims that,'' said Remo.

''Victims!'' Humphrey spit out the word with a genuine expression of contempt. ''Throughout recorded history, the sea wolves had been scrupulous in preying on the wealthy parasites who fatten on the lifeblood of society like ticks or leeches. Who else owns the yachts and other pleasure craft worth stealing? Who else can afford the ransom for a high-priced hostage?''

''So, if they're rich, you figure they're unfit to live. Is that about the size of it?'' asked Remo.

''The wealthy breed like roaches,'' Humphrey said. ''Look at the Kennedys, for God's sake. You can't swing a dead cat from Hyannis to Miami Beach without hitting some millionaire third-cousin of JFK's grandson. What on Earth do they contribute to society, beyond the weekly crop of tabloid headlines?''

''So, your pirates are a bunch of Marxist revolutionaries,'' Remo said. ''The Pirate Liberation Army. It's a quirky twist, Professor, but I've got a problem with it.''

''You miss the point. I merely meant to say—''

''They're killing people for the hell of it,'' said Remo, interrupting him. ''Sometimes they let the women live, I understand, but those who do regret it, when they get to know your noble savages. We also have good reason to believe they're selling boats they steal to narcotraffickers from South America, to help the cocaine trade along. Of course, in your view, I suppose that's just another way of keeping up tradition.''

Humphrey recognized that there would be no winning Remo over to his cause. His jaw was set now, lips compressed into a narrow slit below his nose, eyes fixed on the horizon.

"They'll be waiting for us," the professor said. "You know that."

"I'm counting on it."

"What does that mean?"

"Never mind," he said. "Just make damn sure that you don't lose your way. I understand the sharks are hungry hereabouts."

CHIUN SPENT FIVE MINUTES searching for the herbs he wanted. He found them, yanked the tuber out of the ground and into his kimono sleeve while his rather stupid guard was looking bored at a tree, then continued to search.

"Hey, slow down, would you?" the guard demanded.

"Do not tell me you cannot keep up with a bent old man such as myself," Chiun chided the guard.

The guard huffed along behind him.

There was indeed a small outcropping jutting from the jungle. It was of a black rock that contained many gaping spherical shelves.

Chiun scanned the rock, looking for bone fragments and found none. But that meant nothing. If this was *the* rock described in the Sinanju scrolls, then its shelves would once have contained the skulls of pirate victims. But that was three hundred years ago, and it was unlikely that they would still be here, where the exposure to the elements would have eaten them away long ago.

"I thought you was looking for spices. This is a rock."

"You are a very smart man," Chiun remarked. "But what I look for is a kind of flavorful spoor found in certain lichens. I see none here—are there any more such escarpments?"

"Any more what?"

Chiun smiled at the guard benignly. "Big rocks."

"Oh. No. Just this one. Everything else is all sand."

"I see," Chiun said with disappointment, but inside he was frolicking with delight. Only one such formation on the island and the description matched that in the histories.

This was the first marker.

He circled to the north side of the rock formation and found, as promised, a small vertical ridge in the rock, at the bottom of which was a small natural rock shelf on which a man could stand, a few inches off the ground. He stepped up onto it, peering at the rock. His guard watched him for a moment, then got bored and looked elsewhere.

Chiun immediately turned and faced out, north, and looked for the Two-Headed Tree.

It was gone. Of course it was gone. There had been

only the smallest chance that a tree in these climes would still exist after all this time.

With no two-headed tree, Chiun didn't know in which direction to walk. His treasure hunt was over almost before it had begun.

But not for long. This was just a start, really. There would be other ways, perhaps, of continuing the hunt.

He stepped up to within spitting distance of the daydreaming guard.

"Finished!" he clamored. The pirate jumped off the ground.

"Jee-zus, old man, you trying to get yourself killed!"

"I try to make feast for captain. He be velly angry you not get me back to camp fast." Chiun thought he did a pretty fair imitation of what an American would think an ignorant Chinese would sound like.

"All right, just don't go yelling at me like that anymore, will ya?"

"Velly solly!" Chiun screeched, louder than before.

16

"What is it?" Fabian Guzman asked the lookout, eyes narrowed to dark slits as he stared across the sun-dappled water.

"A boat, *jefe.*"

"I can see that, idiot! Give me the glasses!"

He snatched the binoculars and raised them to his eyes, adjusting the focus once he had the boat framed in his viewing field. It was approaching from the west, and while no name was painted on the bow, one glimpse told Guzman that the boat was not official. It wasn't Coast Guard or DEA, not Haitian or Jamaican or Dominican. An older boat, privately owned. Logic dictated that its presence, here and now, had to be coincidence.

And yet...

Suppose that he was wrong—then what? Guzman had been the strong right arm of his amigo, Carlos, for more years than he cared to think about, since they had risen from the mean streets of the barrio in Cartagena to command an empire stretching from Colombia to the United States and Western Europe.

The two of them hadn't survived this long by taking chances, banking on coincidence.

"Shall I fetch Carlos?" the lookout asked, nodding back in the direction of the cabin as he spoke.

"You mean Señor Ramirez, eh?"

"*Sí, jefe.*" The contrition in the lookout's voice seemed genuine enough. It should have been, considering the penalty that insubordination carried in the family Ramirez and Guzman had built up for themselves.

"Stay here," he told the lookout. "If that vessel should change course or try to overtake us, let me know immediately. Is that understood?"

"*Sí, jefe!*"

Guzman left him standing at the rail and moved back toward the flying bridge with long, determined strides. He climbed the ladder swiftly, ignoring the helmsman as he reached out for the radio, adjusted the frequency and hailed the *Scorpion.* Another moment, and recognized the voice of the *Scorpion*'s first mate, a stone-cold killer named Armand Sifuentes.

"We have company," Guzman announced without preamble.

"I see them," said Armand. "What should we do?"

"Take three men in the motor launch," Guzman replied. "Be careful. Use whatever means you must to get aboard."

"And then?" Sifuentes almost chuckled as he

asked the question. There could be no doubt about what Guzman had in mind for those aboard the aging cabin cruiser.

"Do what must be done," Guzman replied. "No witnesses."

"My pleasure," said Armand Sifuentes, sounding very much as if he meant exactly that.

Time crept along at a snail's pace while Guzman waited on the *Macarena*'s flying bridge for the *Scorpion*'s motor launch to appear with its cargo of gunmen. After a moment, Guzman realized that he was holding his breath, and he released it with a whistling sigh between clenched teeth.

Should he have checked with Carlos first, before he sent the gunmen off to deal with the intruders? Possibly, but he had judged that there was no time to be wasted in the present situation. Anyone aboard the weather-beaten cabin cruiser could identify the *Macarena* and the *Scorpion* from legends painted on their transoms. Granted, they were still miles from their destination, but Guzman had trained himself to think ahead, anticipate such problems and eliminate them in the embryonic stage.

Carlos would almost certainly agree with him, but Guzman would have wasted precious time by then. And if Carlos did not agree...what then?

Then Carlos would be wrong.

It startled Guzman, thinking in such terms, but he didn't regard it as betrayal of his lifelong friend. The best and wisest men still made mistakes from time to time; it simply proved that they were human, after all. A friend stood ready to prevent such lapses of humanity from turning into fatal errors.

There! The motor launch was setting off from the *Scorpion*'s port side, three gunmen leaning forward on the thwarts, while a fourth manned the outboard engine's throttle. Their weapons were nowhere in sight, but Guzman knew they would be close at hand, ready to open fire at the first indication of a threat from the old cabin cruiser.

In moments, they would draw abreast of the intruder. Moments more, and they would be aboard. A brief delay, while Sifuentes tried to determine if the new arrivals on the scene posed any threat to Ramirez and company, but it would make no difference in the end. Once they had stormed the cabin cruiser, everyone aboard would have to die. They were potential witnesses, and while the boat wasn't worth stealing, in and of itself, it could be scuttled, lost at sea.

Another mystery of the Caribbean, perhaps unsolved forever.

And if Carlos was displeased with the result, well, Guzman knew that he could reason with his old friend, given time. Their business with the loco pirates took priority, and nothing else could be allowed to slow them down.

He leaned against the rail and lit a cigarette, watching.

Waiting for the distant sound of guns.

"STAY COOL," REMO ADVISED the ex-professor.

"I don't recognize these men," said Humphrey, squinting in the late-afternoon sunshine as he watched the power launch approaching.

"Just remember," he warned Humphrey, "when the guns go off, you're standing in the middle."

"I don't recognize these men," the former academic said again. "Who are they?"

"Let's just wait and see."

Remo slid down the ladder and found a hiding place from which he could observe and overhear the new arrivals as they came aboard. The moments ticked away, Humphrey hauling back on the throttle as the strange craft approached. A voice hailed Humphrey from the launch, and Remo frowned. Their spotter didn't seem to recognize the old man, and he had what sounded like a South American accent. That wouldn't rule out a pirate, in itself, and yet...

There was a soft thump as the launch kissed hulls with the *Mulligan Stew,* and then boarders were scrambling over the rail, boot heels clomping on deck. Humphrey was agitated, calling down to them from his place on the flying bridge.

"What's the meaning of this?" he demanded. "What are you doing with those guns? This is—"

A stutter of automatic gunfire rattled overhead. Remo waited, half expecting a squall of pain, perhaps the sound of Humphrey's body sprawling on the deck above him, but instead he heard a scramble of feet as the professor ducked out of sight.

"Stand up, *pendejo*," one of the boarding party demanded. "There are questions joo must answer."

"This is a flagrant violation of—"

Another burst of gunfire silenced Humphrey, bullets smacking into bulkhead, one round glancing off the tarnished brass rail with a high-pitched whine.

"All right!" the old man shouted. "Please, stop shooting! Tell me what you want!"

"We gonna search joo boat," one of the shooters said. "Joo gonna tell us why joo're here."

"Look anywhere you want," the old man answered, groveling on the deck. "I have nothing to hide."

Remo heard footsteps on the deck, approaching his hideout. This was a nice spot, he decided. Out of sight of any binocular trained on the *Mulligan Stew* from the boat these losers came from.

He concentrated on the footsteps of the gunman who was closing on him, marking others as they moved off toward the bow.

The man who came around the corner was a twenty-something Latin, carrying an Uzi submachine gun in both hands, across his chest. Dark eyes went wide at the sight of Remo, but he had no chance to use his gun or shout a warning to the others in the split second of life remaining to him.

Remo grabbed the Uzi, grabbed its owner and inserted the former into the latter. The Uzi went pretty far down the gunman's throat, and with a little pushing and twisting it went in a lot farther.

Remo hoisted the gunner's deadweight and sat him in a bench seat in the cabin cruiser's galley.

Above him, on the deck, more footsteps. Remo could hear someone shouting at Humphrey, the sound of an open hand striking flesh, a cry of pain and outrage from the ex-professor. Whatever kind of search was under way, it seemed haphazard and disorganized.

Remo emerged from the companionway into sunlight. Most of the noise was coming from his left, the starboard side, so Remo moved to port. He knew there was a gunman above him, grilling Humphrey, and another somewhere to starboard. That left the one making footsteps in Remo's direction.

"Uh—" the gunner said.

"Bye," Remo said, rapping his knuckles on the gunner's rib cage. The gunner's eyes went wild as his heart rhythm revved out of control. Remo held the guy's mouth closed with one hand to keep the screams from escaping, stepped on both the man's feet with his own and pulled the spasming body taut to keep him from making any loud noises. A few seconds later the gunner had stopped making noises forever, and Remo dropped him.

Remo went looking for gunner number three. The *Mulligan Stew* was a sort of floating sounding board, and Remo could easily track everyone on board by the sound and vibration of their footsteps. That meant the hunt for gunner number three wasn't even a challenge. He just walked up behind the man. The gunner turned to face Remo—his head, that was in Remo's hands, turned to face Remo. His body stayed facing front. The gunner was dead before he had time to figure out why the world had suddenly started turning in circles.

That left the man up top guarding Humphrey.

''Wha' joo doin?'' the apparent leader of the boarding party called down to his team of thugs, not knowing the gun squad was, each in his own unique manner, very dead. Remo saw a bulky shadow moving toward the port rail of the flying bridge as he came up on it.

The commander of the boarding party was a stocky man, solid muscle underneath a layer of camouflaging fat. He had some kind of submachine gun and he brought it into play when Remo rushed him and struck at his gun arm.

The stocky man was confused as to why his gun was silent. Then he heard an abrupt splash off the side of the boat. He looked over just in time to see his submachine sinking in the turquoise Caribbean water, dragging his arm down with it.

But that couldn't be right because the man who had attacked him didn't have a knife. How could he have cut off a whole arm?

The commander of the gunners decided the question was too difficult and he wilted where he stood as the blood pumped out by the pint.

Remo gave him a side kick that launched the gunner in a long arc and ended with another, bigger splash.

"Are you all right?" Remo asked Ethan Humphrey. The old man was sitting, his hands supporting his upper body as if he was about to collapse.

"All right?" The ex-professor looked confused, as if he didn't understand the language Remo spoke.

Remo bent and gripped one of the old man's earlobes, pinching lightly, bringing Humphrey to his feet.

"Were those your friendly pirates?" he demanded.

"Pirates? Ow!" The old man struggled in his grip but could not break away. "Of course not! Those were total strangers. Kidd's men wouldn't try to kill me!"

"Then we'd better get a move on," Remo said. "Find out what kind of speed this tub can handle."

"Speed?"

"Unless you want to see how many other guns these guys are packing."

"Oh, I see. Yes, quite."

The old man turned and grabbed the throttle, pouring on the power.

"YOU'RE GOING THROUGH with it?" Felicia asked.

"Don't be an idiot," snapped Megan. "What choice does she have?"

Stacy had asked herself that very question, time and time again, and still no ready answer came to mind. Of course, she could reject Kidd's offer, but would that accomplish anything? If she refused to play along with the pathetic marriage ceremony, would it stop the pirate chief from claiming her, forcing himself upon her?

No.

The grim truth was that Stacy had no viable alternatives. Escape or suicide would place her beyond Kidd's reach, and at the moment, the two words appeared to be interchangeable. And whatever her plight, the second hard truth was that Stacy Armitage wasn't prepared to die. Not yet.

Not while her brother's death was unavenged.

"Are you okay?" Felicia asked.

"Christ, that's a stupid question!" Megan snapped. "She's got a shotgun wedding to a psycho killer coming up in—what, about two hours—and you ask if she's okay? Did someone drop you on your head when you were little?''

''Just get off my case, all right?'' Felicia's eyes were flashing, angry tears about to spill across her cheeks.

Stacy Armitage almost didn't hear them. She had spied one bright spot in the otherwise unrelieved darkness of her waking nightmare. If she was ''married'' to Kidd, labeled his private stock, it meant two things. First, the other pirates would be kept away from her, her suffering and degradation minimized. And, more importantly, it meant there would be times when she was left alone with Kidd, no bodyguards or chaperones. And sometime, sooner or later, the pirate would let down his guard.

And when that happened, it would be her time to strike. She would require a weapon, then, but there was time to pick one out. She might not find an opportunity the first week—or the first month, for that matter—but her time would come. One chance was all she needed, and it didn't matter if the effort cost her her life, as long as she could take Kidd with her.

As for Chiun, she didn't know what the Korean had in mind, but it was growing more apparent by the moment that she couldn't count on him to help her.

''Penny for your thoughts,'' Megan said, frowning.

Stacy's voice was grim as she replied, ''It's nothing, really. I'm just looking forward to my honeymoon.''

"YOU THINK THEY WERE Kidd's men?'' Carlos Ramirez asked.

"Who else?'' Guzman replied.

Ramirez scowled across the *Macarena*'s railing, standing with his fists clenched at his sides. The battered old cabin cruiser, *Mulligan Stew* her name was, had managed to outrun his newer boats despite their crews' best efforts. It was obvious someone had been tending to the old tub's engine—one more indication, if Ramirez needed any, that an ambush had been planned.

By whom? he asked himself. Who else but Captain Kidd and company knew that Ramirez would be visiting the pirate stronghold, sailing through these waters at this particular time? Who else could have prepared the ambush that had claimed four lives?

Ramirez had found one of his men floating dead in the water, minus an arm, when the *Macarena* started to pursue the enemy. The others had been jettisoned during pursuit, one already savaged by barracuda before they reached his body. There was no point hauling them aboard—more awkward questions if he should encounter a patrol boat on the prowl—but even when he let them go, urging his pilot to the utmost speed, the *Mulligan Stew* still pulled away from the pursuit craft, ultimately vanishing among the islands of a nameless archipelago.

"What shall we do?" asked Guzman.

"What do you imagine, Fabian?"

Ramirez didn't know why Kidd would turn on him, betray him after they had worked together for so long. It hardly mattered now. Ramirez had a list of enemies that ran from spring to Christmas, taking special care with his security, but none of those he watched his back for on dry land had known where he was bound this afternoon.

It had to be Kidd, unless...

Ramirez had considered simple chance, and just as quickly ruled it out. The four men on his boarding party had been armed professionals, adept at killing for a fee. Armand Sifuentes had been something of a one-man army in himself, with better than two dozen murders to his credit. It defied all logic to assume that simple fishermen or tourists could have dealt with men like that and managed to escape unharmed.

There hadn't even been gunshots. They would have heard them. These men could never, ever have been brought down that quickly unless the ambush had been well planned and flawlessly executed.

That kind of work required stone killers. Thomas Kidd and his community of pirates might be loco, but they also knew their business, and killing at sea was their specialty. Who else made a more likely suspect, in the circumstances?

"Bring us back on course for Île de Mort," Ramirez ordered.

"We're still going, Carlos?" Guzman sounded dubious.

"Indeed we are, amigo. If I'm right, the captain won't expect us now."

"We take him by surprise," said Guzman, smiling now.

"We take him by surprise," Ramirez echoed. "Now, full speed ahead!"

17

The root Chiun had discovered on his quick tour of the jungle wasn't precisely what he sought, but it would do. He had sliced it and diced it—with a knife, since using his fingernails might have been considered unusual—and sprinkled it into the simmering pot.

Pirates were drifting in from their appointed duties, some of them already having changed from their grubby clothing into more colorful garb. Chiun had yet to see one of them bathe, nor was he looking forward to the sorry spectacle. In fact, from the effluvium that wafted off their unwashed bodies, Chiun didn't imagine that he would be dwelling on the island long enough to glimpse such a unique event.

Nor, he surmised, would anybody else.

His stew was almost ready, its aroma spreading through the camp. From the reaction of prospective diners, several of them passing by and peering down into the pot, he knew that it would do the trick. There might not be enough to go around, but even if he only reached two-thirds of his opponents, it would be sufficient.

The potion was indeed mere window dressing for his master plan. Chiun had no fear of his "captors," needed no tricks to defeat them singly or en masse, but it amused him to distract them from the woman while he made his move. The root he had selected was fast-acting, and should bring results within fifteen or twenty minutes after it had been consumed. The camp would be a great deal more malodorous once his surprise kicked in, but Chiun reckoned there would be little time to savor the result—or suffer through it, as the case might be—before he had to make his move.

It had been ordered that the feasting should precede the wedding ceremony. That was fine with Chiun; in fact, it suited him no end. He knew the hasty ritual would have no standing anywhere beyond the pirate stronghold, but it pleased him to consider frustrating the would-be king's design.

There had been no time for him to discuss his plan with Stacy Armitage, but that didn't concern Chiun. White women had a way of letting their emotions run away with them in crisis situations, and he understood that redheads were the worst of all in that regard. Brunettes were more sedate, if only by a matter of degree, while blondes were often too disorganized and witless to perceive real danger.

Chiun had learned that much from television,

studying his favorite soap operas, where men and women acted in accordance with their roles in white society.

He wouldn't wait on Stacy, then, or trust her with the details of his plan. If she was not in a position to assist him, neither would she be a stumbling block when he began to smite their enemies.

In general, the Master Emeritus of Sinanju favored subtle killing, the ideal assassination having been defined as one in which no third party suspected assassination, but he also recognized that there were times when subtlety fell short of the desired result.

Times such as this.

Chiun watched the pirates lining up with plates and bowls in hand. The first man in the line was one of those who had repeatedly described him as Chinese. Chiun smiled and ladled out a double portion of his special gumbo to the unwashed buccaneer.

"Smell's durn good, Chinaman," the buccaneer said.

"You will velly tasty, you bet," Chiun answered. In his head he added, You be velly dead velly soon, ignorant white man.

And he meant it.

"WE'RE ALMOST THERE," said Ethan Humphrey, pointing with a hand that trembled now, despite his effort to control himself.

The island loomed in front of them, two smaller

lumps of jungle-shrouded rock flanking it on either side. The center of attention, christened Île de Mort, according to his skipper, was a mile long, give or take, with rugged peaks along its spine. Only the crags were naked stone; the rest was clotted jungle growth from mountain slopes down to a reeking mangrove swamp at water's edge.

"The anchorage is on the northern side," Humphrey explained. "We'll need another half hour to get there."

"I see an inlet there." Remo pointed toward the mouth of what appeared to be a brackish stream, amid the looming mangroves. It was wide enough for Humphrey's boat to pass. The water course might narrow inland, but he didn't care, as long as they could pull the cabin cruiser out of sight from any stray patrol boats that might happen by.

"You can't be serious," the ex-professor said.

"Not up to it?" He cracked a mirthless smile. "No sweat, Professor. I'll just take her in myself."

"You will not, sir!" His voice was stern, but Humphrey clearly realized that he could not stop Remo from seizing control of the boat if he was so inclined.

"Do they post lookouts?" Remo asked, as Humphrey nosed the boat toward shore.

"It's possible," said Humphrey, "though I've never asked. Myself, I think they trust in isolation here."

Humphrey drew back on the throttle as they neared the inlet. Remo's nostrils flared at the smell of rotting vegetation from the swamp, a stench primeval from the dawn of time.

The mangroves closed around them, branches drooping low, scraping the canopy above the flying bridge. Daylight was fading fast, but it was even darker in among the trees, a sudden twilight.

They had already moved some fifty yards inland when the cabin cruiser's hull struck something with a scrape and a shudder, groaning underfoot. Humphrey immediately throttled down and let the engine idle, turning to Remo with a worried frown.

"We can't go any farther," he insisted. "This is madness."

"Listen, Professor, you've got a bunch of friends who say 'yar' and wear puffy shirts. Nothing I do can ever be considered 'madness' by comparison. We'll take the skiff."

"If it's all the same to you," Humphrey replied, "I'll just wait here."

"It's not the same to me," said Remo. "I still need a guide. You're it. Let's go."

"I've never come this way," the old man said. "We may get lost."

"Then we'll get lost together," Remo told him.

"But—"

"Let's put it this way. I don't mind leaving you

behind. Look how many other guys I left behind on this little three-hour tour.''

Now Humphrey got the point and grimaced, starting down the ladder from the flying bridge. The skiff was stowed astern, a smallish aluminum rowboat with paddles for two. Remo untied it, dropped it overboard and hopped down from the transom, holding it steady while Humphrey came aboard.

In front of them, some twenty yards ahead, the stream forked at a clump of cypress, smaller brackish channels splitting off in a rough Y shape. For all Remo knew, they might join up again beyond the wall of trees, but he wasn't prepared to risk it.

''So, which way?'' he asked of his reluctant guide.

''From where we are, it should be westward.''

To the right, then, if the old man wasn't lying to him, stalling in an effort to protect his friends.

''Be sure,'' said Remo.

''As I said, I've never tried to reach the camp from this direction. There's a possibility—''

''Be sure,'' Remo repeated. ''I don't have the time or patience for mistakes. You're still expendable.''

The old man thought about it for another moment, biting on his lower lip, then nodded. ''Westward,'' he said again.

THE DRESS THAT STACY WORE wasn't a bad fit, pinned beneath the arms to take it in, floor-length blue satin, just a trifle loose around the hips. She thought about the woman who had worn it first, wondered what had become of her and how Kidd's pirates had obtained the formal gown. On second thought, she didn't want to know.

"You look really nice," Felicia said.

"Felicia, Jesus!" Megan scowled and shook her head.

"Hey, I was only saying—"

"Never mind, for Christ's sake!" Megan turned to Stacy once again, the frown still on her face. "You do look nice, though. I mean, for the circumstances."

"Thank you."

There was no mirror in the hut that served as their prison cell. Indeed, she would have been surprised if there was one in camp. Some of the pirates combed their hair, after a fashion, and most of them shaved— at least irregularly—but it was apparent from their general appearance and their hygiene that none of them spent much time before a looking glass.

"I like the flowers," said Felicia. Then, as Megan turned to glare at her again, she stuck her tongue out. "Well, I do, so there."

"I like the flowers, too," Megan admitted grudgingly. "God, this is so damn weird!"

The flowers were an added touch. Meg and Felicia had retrieved them from the forest near the camp, while Robin stayed with Stacy in the hut. She wasn't company, in any recognized sense of the word, but Stacy could talk freely to her, venting her fear and

anger in full confidence that Robin would not inter-
rupt her. Indeed, there was nothing to suggest the girl
had understood a single word.

Megan had plucked the flowers carefully, long
stems intact, and then had woven them into a kind
of wreath that nestled in her hair. Stacy had no idea
where Megan found the bobby pins, but she had
come up with a pair of them to fix the wreath in
place. Stacy imagined how she had to have looked—
some kind of hippie princess, dressed up for a love-
in—and her stomach churned.

The blushing bride, she thought, and felt like
throwing up.

"What's going on out there?" she asked of no one
in particular.

Felicia peered through a hole in the curtain that
served as their door, shifting positions several times
as she tried to get a full view of the compound.

"Eating," she replied at last. "The goons are lined
up for some kind of stew. They've got your friend
dishing it out."

So much for Chiun taking out the pirates on his
own, Stacy thought. But what had she expected, really? He was one old man against a veritable army.
Even if he used to know some kung fu moves, he
was still outnumbered sixty-five or seventy to one,
by younger men with guns and knives.

"Is this the shits, or what?" Felicia asked.
"They're having the reception first, and they don't

even feed the bride? What kind of weird, ass-backward deal is this?''

"You're sweating etiquette?'' The tone of Megan's voice conveyed a mixture of dismay and gallows humor. "Jesus, Fe, you didn't pay that analyst of yours enough.''

"That's cold,'' Felicia said, eyes smoldering as she returned Meg's glare.

Megan ignored her and addressed herself to Stacy. "So, have you decided what to do?''

"Looks like I'm getting married,'' Stacy said.

"I mean, after,'' said Megan. "When you...you know...?''

Stacy wondered how much she could tell the younger woman without further jeopardizing herself. It took all of a second and a half to decide that her troubles could get no worse, barring an immediate sentence of death. Megan was still Kidd's prisoner, his enemy. If she betrayed Stacy, it might get her killed, but death was coming either way. It was only a matter of time.

"I'm going to kill him,'' Stacy said.

"Kill who?'' Megan's voice dropped to a whisper as she spoke, and she glanced nervously over her shoulder, first toward Felicia, then toward the vegetative Robin.

"Kidd,'' Stacy replied. "Who else?''

"But...I mean, shit!'' Megan was at a loss for words. "You'll never get away with it, you know?''

"I'll never get away, period," Stacy replied. "We're prisoners, in case you hadn't noticed. We're not going anywhere. They'll never let us go. Is any of this getting through?"

Anger flashed in Meg's eyes as she replied, "I hear you, dammit! And I've been here longer, in case you've forgotten. Anything that's waiting for you has already happened to me, to us."

"I'm sorry, Meg. I didn't mean—"

"How would you do it?" Megan interrupted her. "Kill him, I mean?"

"I'll have to wait and see," Stacy replied. "Of course, I'll need some kind of weapon. That could take a while, but I'll find something. All the guns and knives around this place, he'll have to let his guard down sooner or later."

It hardly qualified as a plan, but it was the best Stacy had been able to come up with, in the circumstances. One opportunity was all that she would need. No matter how long she was forced to wait, she meant to grab that chance and make it count.

"Are they still eating, Fe?"

Felicia peered outside again before she answered. "Yeah, still chowing down. The line out there, I'd say another twenty minutes, anyway, before they all get served. Then, figure some of them want seconds, and—"

"Enough, already!" Megan chided. "Next thing,

you'll be telling us what kind of silverware they're using.''

''Some of them are using fingers,'' Felicia said, ''if you really want to know.''

''We don't,'' Megan assured her. Turning back to Stacy, she went on, ''I wish to hell there was some way we could get out of here.''

But there was no point wishing. Just now, Stacy required all of her wits and nerve to face the grisly prospect of her wedding night.

Meanwhile, she hoped the feast would last for hours, and that the liquor would flow like water. It was one time when a stinking-drunk bridegroom was preferable to a sober one.

With any luck at all, Kidd might drink so much that he passed right out the moment they had gone to bed. If not...

Her stomach churned again, and Megan seemed to pick up on it from Stacy's expression.

''What?'' she asked.

Stacy managed a smile as she replied, ''Oh, nothing. I'm just hoping that they let me cut the cake.''

CARLOS RAMIREZ COCKED his semiautomatic pistol, thumbed on the safety and slipped the weapon back into the shoulder holster worn beneath his stylish jacket. It was hot, despite the hour, and although Ramirez had already sweated through his shirt, he balked at taking off the jacket. He had a certain image to protect, and killing off his enemies was only part of it.

Whenever possible, he also had to be the best-dressed killer on the block.

Ramirez knew the way to Kidd's encampment, how to find it from the sea, but he wasn't prepared to land directly in his enemy's front yard. He still had no idea why Kidd would turn against him, but there was no arguing with facts. Four of his best men were dead, and Carlos knew of no one else in the vicinity who could have pulled it off without sustaining losses in the process. Even for a group of wily pirates, it would be a challenge, but the ease with which the killers had escaped him told Ramirez that they knew the local waters well indeed.

Ramirez and his men had been outnumbered when they sailed from Cartagena, and the odds weren't improved by losing four good men. Ramirez still had faith that he could win the day, but he was counting on surprise to make it possible.

They landed near the west end of the island, roughly half a mile from Kidd's compound. No lookouts were in evidence, but Carlos took no chances, posting sentries of his own while he addressed the others.

He had formed a simple plan after the ambush out at sea. His men would land well back from the encampment and march overland to take the pirates by surprise. There would be no need for discussion, nothing in the nature of a warning to the men he meant to kill.

Carlos Ramirez was no woodsman, but he reckoned he could hike for half a mile through even the most savage jungle, with the ocean on his left to help him find his way. It would take more time in the dark, of course, and night was falling fast. A handful of his soldiers carried flashlights, but they had been ordered to refrain from using them except in the most dire emergency, since strange lights in the forest would betray them to their enemies. They could afford to take their time, spend half the night walking if necessary. In truth, Ramirez thought it would be better if he found his enemies asleep, but he didn't intend to waste the whole night waiting unless it was absolutely necessary. Better to surprise the pirates at a meal, for instance, while his men were reasonably fresh, than to risk them getting jumpy, trigger-happy, maybe even dozing at their posts.

Ramirez gave no thought to snakes or other perils of the forest. He was wholly focused on revenge, the mental image of his lifeless enemies eclipsing any thought that might have made him hesitate. He stumbled over roots and vines, scuffing his handmade alligator shoes, snagging his tailored slacks, but they meant nothing. When they reached their destination, Carlos would have more use for the Uzi submachine gun slung across his shoulder than he would for slick designer clothes. If anything, Ramirez wished that he had brought a Kevlar vest along, but there were none among the *Macarena*'s stores.

It didn't matter.

When the shooting started, Carlos hoped to see his enemies cut down like grass before a scythe. There would be—should be—nothing they could do to help themselves. If all went well, they would—

Ramirez heard the sounds of revelry before he saw the torchlight flickering among the trees, still well ahead. He raised a hand and hissed an order to the nearest of his soldiers, waiting for those close at hand to pass it on.

Some kind of gala party was in progress…or, he thought, perhaps the pirates celebrated this way every night. Their lifestyle was admittedly bizarre, more outlandish than his own, although Ramirez knew the buccaneers had no wealth to compare with his. They wouldn't sleep in filthy hovels, living hand-to-mouth and wearing rags if they had cash to spare. As for the money looted from their victims, or the sums Ramirez paid them for the boats they stole, he didn't know or care what happened to it. This wasn't a raid for revenue.

"Take special care," he warned his men when they were grouped around him like a soccer team, awaiting their instructions for another play. "Ramon and Lucio, you both have silencers, so you will lead the way and deal with any guards we meet."

The soldiers didn't argue. They were paid to follow orders, kill upon command, and they had always known there would be risks involved. On sunbaked city streets or in the steaming jungle, they were still professionals, and they would do as they were told.

"The rest of you, be ready for my signal, but control yourselves. In no case must you fire, unless I give the word or we are fired upon. You understand?"

He scanned their faces, watched them nodding acquiescence. No one spoke; no answer was required. Each of them knew Ramirez, knew exactly what would happen to the man who disobeyed.

When he was satisfied, Ramirez sent his scouts ahead and followed several yards behind them, with the others trailing after.

18

The stew kicked in as Stacy was preparing for her long walk down the aisle. Of course, there was no aisle per se, since there was no church in the pirate camp—no chairs, in fact, since those in camp seemed to prefer sitting on the ground, or on rough stumps where trees had been cut down to clear the compound. If anything, her march to the altar would be more like running a gauntlet, with pirates lined up in two ranks, waiting for the bride to pass.

They weren't looking at her, though—a fact that struck the redhead as peculiar. She had grown used to the eyes that followed her each time she left the hut that was her prison cell, lewd comments muttered as she passed, but now the pirates had apparently experienced a change of heart en masse.

Could it be Kidd's influence? Stacy knew that he had killed one of the pirates for objecting to his wedding plan, but this felt different somehow. Several of the grubby men were actually making faces at her, grimacing, rolling their eyes, baring discolored teeth. One clutched his stomach, fingers digging in like claws. As Stacy neared him, he hunched forward, closed his eyes and spewed a stream of vomit in her path.

Stacy recoiled, disgusted, but the spectacle was only getting started. As the bearded pirate retched again, one of the men beside him doubled over, grabbing at his midsection, and followed his example, splattering his own feet with the remnants of his latest meal.

In no time flat, a wave of gastric panic swept the audience. Some of the pirates were vomiting, while others clutched themselves and took off hobbling toward the tree line, cursing as they soiled themselves. Stacy stood rooted to the spot and watched them scatter, her nose wrinkling in disgust at the sights and smell surrounding her. Her own stomach was rolling, but she hadn't eaten when the others had—nothing, in fact, except some rice at breakfast.

Some fifty feet away, Kidd stood beside a bonfire that had been constructed to provide the central lighting for the wedding ceremony. He wasn't looking at Stacy now, however, but rather was sweeping the camp with fierce eyes, watching his men as they seemed to go mad. She watched a hand slip underneath the too small velvet jacket he had donned for the occasion, probably in search of hardware, but this was no attack that he could meet with force of arms.

In truth, he seemed to have no more idea of what was going on than Stacy did. Whatever plagued his men, it seemed to have no hold upon the captain. Kidd stood firm and straight, watching all but a handful of the others as they fell apart.

She glanced at Chiun, still in position near the cooking pot, as if at work on something for dessert, and an idea began to form in Stacy's mind. Chiun caught her watching him, flashed her the bare suggestion of a smile and cocked his head in the direction of the forest.

What? She almost mouthed the word, but caught herself, afraid that Kidd would see her and react with paranoid aggression. In the circumstances, he might open fire on Chiun, and then what would the old man do?

The gunfire shocked her. It wasn't Kidd who started firing, though—nor, Stacy saw, had any of the pirates opened fire. As Stacy turned in the direction of the noise, crouching instinctively, she spotted muzzle-flashes in among the trees. One of the stumbling pirates took a hit and went down, wailing. Almost instantly, she saw another fall, and yet another.

Chiun was instantly forgotten in the chaos that erupted, and she gave no further thought to breaking for the trees. The prison hut would be her only sanctuary now, and Stacy bolted for it, heard the long gown rip along the seams with her first stride.

Behind her, screams and gunfire made the night a living hell.

THE TWO-MAN SKIFF HAD seen them through the mangrove swamp, hungry mosquitoes trailing them along the half-mile course, but they were forced to ditch it when the stagnant water changed to spongy earth and forest. Humphrey's enthusiasm for the journey had been slight enough to start with, but he balked now at the thought of trekking through the jungle after nightfall.

"We'll get lost," he said. "I can't—"

"So stay," Remo replied.

"Very well," Humphrey said reluctantly. "This way."

Humphrey might be a sailor, but his woodcraft left a great deal to be desired. He lurched and staggered every third or fourth step, reached out to brace himself against the nearest tree and muttered nonstop oaths that would have startled his old colleagues at the university.

As night descended on the forest, it began to come alive. Insects picked up their trilling songs, competing shrilly from the undergrowth, while night birds shrieked their raucous mating calls.

Ethan Humphrey stumbled yet again. He didn't catch himself this time and went down on his face, grunting in shock and anger as the breath was driven from his lungs.

At that moment Remo heard a whisper of sound far ahead and got a fix on its source. Shouting. Cheering. It sounded like some kind of wild-ass party going on, and Remo guessed that he had found the pirate hangout he was looking for.

He only hoped that he wasn't too late to join the fun.

"I'm going on. You want to take a hike, feel free," he told his guide.

"Where should I go?" asked Humphrey, sounding timid now.

"Your call," he said. "Just stay the hell out of my way."

Remo left the old man standing in the darkness and moved through the night swiftly, his ears and instincts leading him. He made less sound in passing than a night breeze whispering among the trees. No man would hear him coming.

The sounds ahead of him began to change, grew even more bizarre. Instead of cheering, shouts and laughter now, it sounded more like gagging, interspersed with coughs and garbled curses.

Remo was picking up his pace when yet another sound erupted in the night. Staccato, sharp, like heavy-metal thunder. Gunfire.

What kind of party did these wack-job pirates throw, anyway?

CHIUN WAS IRRITATED. He had hoped his special stew would buy himself more time for the treasure hunt while Remo dawdled, but the arrival of gun-toting South Americans spoiled his plans.

Now he would have to find and protect Stacy Armitage. He couldn't let her be shot. He would never hear the end of it.

He moved through the camp, a shadow flitting amid the chaos.

A pirate lurched into his path. This one hadn't been wounded yet, but suffered only from the effects of Chiun's culinary masterpiece. He had already emptied out his stomach, judging from the dark stains on his chin and faded denim shirt, but that didn't prevent his doubling over, retching with the dry heaves.

Chiun was merciful. He sent the buccaneer to his reward with a stroke that was barely more than a caress. At that, it was enough to whip the pirate's head around and snap his neck as if he were a chicken. When he landed in the grass he was already dead, the cramping in his stomach mercifully forgotten.

Chiun pressed on, here dodging bullets from the forest, there dispatching pirates as he met them, with a touch, a jab, a kick. He left a trail of broken mannequins behind him, lying twisted where they fell.

When he had almost reached the prison hut, a burst of automatic rifle fire streaked through the air above his head and stitched its way across the hut's thatched roof. Inside, a woman screamed—not Stacy Armitage; Chiun would have recognized her voice. As he gained the doorstep of the hut, one of the three young hostages who had been here before him rushed outside.

Chiun didn't know her name, but he recognized her as the one who had withdrawn into herself, as if from shock. Whatever else she had become, the woman hadn't lost her voice entirely, nor had she forgotten how to run. In fact, if Chiun hadn't been there to stop her, she would certainly have run into the middle of the firefight, to her almost certain death.

The girl was several inches taller than Chiun, and she outweighed him by as much as thirty pounds, but she seemed weightless as he looped an arm around her waist and whisked her back inside. The other three, including Stacy Armitage, stood gaping at him in surprise.

"Robin!" the blonde spit out. "What's wrong with you?"

"Chiun, can we get out of here?" The question came from Stacy. She stood watching him, arms crossed, hands clasping her elbows as if to stop herself from trembling. "Well, can we?"

It didn't sit well with Chiun to leave before the job was finished, but it sounded very much as if the buccaneers were being massacred without his help.

"This way," he said, and moved directly to the side of the hut that was farthest from the door, farthest from the gunfire rattling outside.

Its roof aside, the hut was built of scrap lumber.

The wall he chose was plywood, and it shivered at his touch. He took a step back from the wall, examined it and lashed out with one hand. The steel-strong blades of his fingernails slashed through the plywood once, twice. A freshly made archway was left as the wood pieces fell to the earth.

Chiun turned to face the four women, his face impassive.

"Now we go," he said.

KIDD TRACKED ONE OF THE raiders with his revolver, framed the runner in his sights and squeezed off two quick shots. Though he had never seen the man before, it pleased him greatly when his bullets struck and spun him in his tracks, dumping him facedown into the dust.

Some of his men were starting to recover, fighting back in something that recalled their old, familiar style. The sickness that had gripped so many of them earlier still sapped their energy and made their movements awkward, but they clearly recognized the danger that confronted them, and those still fit to use a gun or blade would not go down without a fight.

The first outbreak of gunfire had come close to paralyzing Thomas Kidd. It stunned him to imagine anyone had found his secret compound, much less that the unknown enemies could mount a raid and take him by surprise. The shock had lasted but a heartbeat, though, before Kidd told himself the law had found them somehow. But no sooner had the notion taken shape than he rejected it. Lawful authorities, he knew from prior experience, came bearing papers from the courts, announcing their arrival with all manner of lights and sirens, demanding surrender before they opened fire.

Which told him that the men around his camp were outlaws, like himself. How had they come to be here at the very moment of his wedding? And why had they attacked like this, without apparent motive?

There was no time, in the heat of battle, to answer such questions, and Kidd had barely drawn his revolver when the answer came to him, as plain as day. Along the west side of the compound, several raiders were already breaking from the trees. One of the faces shown to him by firelight was familiar, after all.

Carlos Ramirez!

Kidd had known the cocaine lord was coming for another boat. The bargain they had struck was lucrative for all concerned. He had expected the Colombians to show up sometime following his wedding ceremony, while the celebration was in progress, to join in the festivities. Now, instead, here they were with guns blazing, and led by Ramirez himself!

Logic meant nothing in a fight for life. It didn't matter why Ramirez and his men had gone back on the bargain, shifting from allies to mortal enemies.

All that mattered now was stopping them—and that meant stopping them forever, dead in their tracks.

His first shot had been aimed at Carlos, but Kidd rushed it, jerked the trigger instead of squeezing it, the way he had been taught, and the bullet had missed by inches. Ramirez had gone to ground, beyond the firelight, and then everyone had been firing at once. Billy Teach had found his M-60 machine gun, staggering to battle with it tucked beneath one arm, his shirt and denim pants still reeking with the remnants of his recent meal.

The Chinaman would pay for that, whatever he had done, but that wasn't Kidd's first priority. Old men could wait their turn to die, when there were younger men with guns around, demanding his attention at the moment.

One of those, in fact, was charging Kidd's position, firing from the hip with some kind of stubby automatic weapon. Kidd swiveled to face him, raising his revolver in a firm two-handed grip, sighting on the shooter's chest before he squeezed off two quick rounds.

The young Colombian was staggered, lurching sideways, firing even as he fell. The bullets raised a storm of dust between himself and Kidd, but none came close enough to cause the pirate chieftain any harm. Instead, he watched his dying enemy collapse, twitch once and then go slack in death.

Around him, as he scanned the compound, Kidd

saw numbers of his own men sprawled among the slain. He gave up counting at a dozen, knowing that there had to be more, but he believed their enemies were still outnumbered. If his men stood fast, despite the sudden illness that had weakened them before the sneak attack, they had a chance.

And if they won the fight, what then?

That problem had to wait until another time. He saw Ramirez now, just rising from behind the cook fire in his fancy clothes, the jacket spoiled by soot or gun smoke, Kidd couldn't say which. Nor did it matter, as the pirate leader rushed his business partner turned would-be assassin, closing the gap between them with long, loping strides.

Ramirez saw him coming, but it was too late. The drug lord swung his weapon to the left, in Kidd's direction, finger clenching on the trigger, but he had already spent the magazine and was rewarded with only a sharp metallic clicking as the hammer fell upon an empty chamber.

Kidd wasn't about to waste his golden opportunity. The revolver thrust in front of him, he squeezed off three rounds and watched the bullets strike his target, the once-stylish jacket rippling with the impact of his lethal rounds. Ramirez staggered, dropped to one knee, staring back at Kidd before he toppled slowly onto his back.

One down, Kidd thought, but taking Carlos down wasn't the same thing as a victory. Kidd's crew and his community wouldn't be safe as long as one of the attackers lived.

"Come on, you scurvy swabs!" he shouted to his men who were still alive and fit to fight. "Have at 'em, lads, and get it done! It's time to be true pirates again!"

REMO MET CHIUN EMERGING from the shattered back wall of a thatch-roofed hut. The Master Emeritus of Sinanju had four women with him, one of whom was Stacy Armitage. She wore some kind of formal gown that had been pinned beneath her arms and ripped along the seams, revealing shapely legs. A handmade diadem of flowers sat atop her head, askew and dangling from one side, although she didn't seem to notice it. She recognized him in the darkness, and her mouth fell open like the jaw hinge had suddenly broken. She made noises as if she were trying to speak but couldn't.

"Looks like I missed the party," Remo said.

"You are certainly tardy," Chiun squeaked in irritation.

"I had to catch a ride from where you dropped me off," Remo explained. "I would have walked, but you know how it is."

"Excuses," Chiun snapped. "Now clean up this mess while I convey these young women to a safer place."

Remo knew better than to argue, even with the

sound of automatic weapons hammering his eardrums from the far side of the hut. Chiun was moving toward the tree line with the women, even as
Remo prepared to join the shindig in the pirate compound. Stacy seemed as if she had something to say,
but simply squeezed his hand before she followed
Chiun into the night.

He went in through the open back wall of the hut.
A bullet slapped into the wall as Remo neared the
entrance, but he paid it no attention. Peering out into
the camp, he glimpsed a strange, surrealistic battlefield, where pirates brandished swords along with
modern firearms, squaring off against opponents
dressed in flashy suits and pointy shoes.

The strangest, and least pleasant, aspect of the battle was the smell.

Remo could only guess who the invaders were, but
it was no concern of his. They weren't police—that
much was obvious—and he wouldn't allow them to
impede his mission. Now that he had found the pirate
stronghold, and Stacy was out of the way with Chiun,
he knew exactly what he had to do.

He slipped outside, keeping to the shadows,
watching the gunners he could see. A ragged-looking
pirate came at Remo, slashing at him with a cutlass
in his left hand and a metal hook that had replaced
his right. Remo ducked the blade, grabbed the hook
and maneuvered it. The pirate saw what was coming
even if he didn't understand how it was happening.

"Yo-ho-ho," Remo said, then with a lightning stroke forced the pirate to rip his own throat open.

A spray of bullets rippled past him, and he sidestepped them instinctively. Remo sought the shooter and found one of the raiders scowling at him, grappling with a compact weapon that was either jammed or empty. Remo closed the gap between them in a flash, moved around the SMG his adversary swung as if it were a club and struck back with an open hand. The shooter's head snapped backward, eyes already glazing, as the front of his skull shattered and sent shrapnel ripping through his brain.

Remo moved through the grappling, cursing combatants like a shadow of death. He was everywhere at once, lashing out, thrusting, jabbing with stiffened fingers like daggers. Wherever he paused for a heartbeat, another man died on one side or the other, pirate or invader. At the same time they were so engrossed in their loud, confused melee they never even suspected he was there as they continued killing one another without letup, guns rattling, blades flashing, doing Remo's work for him.

It struck him that the pirates seemed to be at a disadvantage, even with their greater numbers on the battlefield. Most of them had a sickly look about them, as if the attack had caught them in the middle of a grievous hangover or bout of ptomaine poisoning. It had something to do with the ungodly stench

about the place. He didn't stop to consider it now—
he was on a roll and headed for the finish line.

He came up on the blind side of a pirate with wild
red hair, who was strafing the camp with a modified
M-60 machine gun, three of the stylish invaders jittering before him as the bullets tore into their bodies.
Remo let him finish it before he slipped an arm
around the gunner's neck and twisted sharply, hearing the snap-crackle-pop of vertebrae as they separated, shearing through the spinal cord and cutting
off all signals to the angry brain.

The killing ground fell silent, but one figure still
remained upright. Remo had never seen the man before, but from his garb, he guessed that this was a
ranking officer—if not the leader—of the pirate crew.
He held a shiny automatic revolver in one hand and
raised it.

The pirate discharged the weapon.

Remo approached him, walking.

The gun fired again. And again. The final three
shots were fired from just a few steps away, and confusion etched itself in the features of the pirate as his
target refused to drop. When the pistol's hammer
clicked down on an empty chamber, the pirate flung
it aside with a sound of disgust and drew the sword
that weighted down the left side of his belt. The
blade was long and highly polished, glinting in the
firelight.

"You don't have the same look as these other scurvy bastards," the pirate said.

"I'm alone," Remo replied.

The pirate glanced around, saw bodies scattered everywhere and said, "It would appear that I am, too."

"It's over," Remo said, advancing slowly toward the sole survivor of the pirate crew.

"Is it?" He wore a crooked smile. "I started on this island alone and look what I built. I'll do it again."

"Yeah, but why?" Remo asked. "I mean, what's with all this Captain Hook stuff?"

Still smiling, Kidd lunged forward with the sword, but Remo dodged easily. The pirate tried a backhand slash that would have left him headless if it had connected, but the blade sliced empty air instead.

"You're quick, my friend," the pirate said.

"That's only half of it."

"Indeed?"

"I'm not your friend," said Remo.

"I suppose I'll have to kill you, then."

So saying, his assailant charged, sword flashing overhead and down toward Remo's face. It would have split his skull down to the shoulders if he had been willing to stand still and wait for it, but Remo was in motion even as the strike began. He removed the sword from the pirate's hand. It was strong, old steel but it snapped easily enough at the hilt.

"God! Oh no!" Kidd exclaimed.

"What?" Remo asked, snapping the blade again and again until it was nothing more than a handful of inch-wide scraps that tumbled into the dirt. The hilt fell there, too.

"That was the sword of my grandfathers!" the pirate said.

"I don't think they need it anymore."

"That sword shed blood around the world," he moaned. "The Kidd family terrorized the oceans for generations."

"So you're just following in your father's footsteps? That's why?" Remo asked.

Captain Kidd spit angrily. "That on my father. He was a pathetic loser, no better than his father. I was the first real man in the Kidd family in generations—the first Kidd in a century to devote himself to the calling that is our heritage."

Remo guffawed. "Kidd? As in Captain Kidd? Come on!"

"Don't laugh at my family name, swine!"

"Oh, sorry, I'll try to show a little respect for the human slime that drips from your family tree. I got news for you, Cap'n—rapists and murderers are nothing but scumbags, even if they did wear white puffy shirts."

Kidd made a guttural noise of fury and charged Remo with bare fists.

At that moment the killing ground was shattered

by a piercing sound like a doggie squeeze-toy played through the amplifiers at a rock concert. "Hold!"

Remo knew better than to disobey a thunder-squeak like that. He put out one hand and gripped Captain Kidd by the scalp. Kidd flailed at Remo's face, then his arms. Remo lifted him high enough off the ground that further struggles caused excruciating scalp pain.

"Do not dare to kill that man, Remo Williams!"

"I'm not, see!" Remo shot back. "But why, I wanna know?"

"He must be questioned," Chiun, Master Emeritus of Sinanju, declared solemnly.

Huh, thought Remo. He could feel it coming. Finally. "This guy's got nothing to tell us. And Smitty wants him dead."

"You do not know this," Chiun retorted.

"Have you see my official job description? It's just two words—'Kill people.' If Smitty sends me after somebody, I'm supposed to assassinate 'em and that's that."

Chiun stood before him. "And you'll get the chance, but first we talk."

"I will tell you nothing, cook!" Kidd said through gritted teeth as he struggled in Remo's grip.

"This is the Island of Many Skulls," Chiun said matter-of-factly.

Captain Kidd stopped struggling. He hung there, almost on his tiptoes with his face and neck stretched out absurdly by the hold Remo had on the top of his head. All that was ignored now as he gazed wide-eyed at Chiun.

After a moment, Kidd said one word in a near whisper. "Sinanju!"

Chiun's head moved in the briefest of nods.

"You are the Master?"

Chiun nodded again.

"Hey, I am, too," Remo spoke up.

"Actually, he is simply the Reigning Master," Chiun explained. "I am the Master *Emeritus*."

"Oh, brother." Remo rolled his eyes.

Kidd looked from Chiun to Remo and back again. "You killed my great-great-great-grandfather!"

"Not me personally," Chiun said, frowning with his forehead. "But one of my own forebears rid this part of the world of the man who settled this island once, centuries ago."

"You stole the family fortune!" Kidd shouted.

"You stole it first," Chiun retorted. "How many human beings died because the Kidd pirates lusted for trinkets and females?"

"We lived by a code of honor and discipline!"

"So does the Mafia and they're slime, too," Remo said. "I knew you had some secret going on, Chiun. Are you telling me one of the Masters was on this island fighting pirates?"

"Yes. Once. There is something you should know," Chiun added with quiet amusement. "The gold that belonged to the Kidd pirates never left the island.''

Kidd looked as if he had just been slapped. "Liar!" he retorted hotly.

"A Master of Sinanju never lies," Chiun responded.

Remo snorted. Chiun gave him a glare and continued.

"My ancestor found where the chests were dug up," Kidd rattled off. "They searched everywhere. There was no trace of any other digging. They knew the island, every square inch of it. If the gold was here they would have found it.''

"But the Master was still here," Chiun said. "And when he was bored with their games he wiped them out. Would he leave with the gold and come back again?''

"Yes! He must have!" Kidd replied fiercely.

"No."

"We know he left without the gold after murdering my ancestors—that is how the family history tells it! He did not have the gold then!''

"Correct," Chiun said.

"So it must have been removed prior to that!''

"Incorrect."

"No, no, we would have found it. They searched. They came back and searched again. Even though we stopped pirating, my family came here for three generations, always searching for the treasure. If it was here, it would have been found!''

Kidd was emphatic. To believe that the treasure had always been right under his nose for all these years was simply too bitter a pill.

Hands in his kimono sleeves, a slight smile touching his mouth, the tiny, ancient Korean man said, ''It is here.''

''Where, then? Prove it!''

The smile became slightly more amused. ''It was never removed from where your ancestor buried it. My ancestor simply dug deeper into the hole that the old Kidd made for it.''

''No. My ancestors thought of that. There's the water table. If you try to go deeper, the water just makes the hole keep filling itself in again with sand. It's impossible to penetrate any deeper.''

''Impossible for you. Impossible for your flea-bitten ancestors. No problem for a Master of Sinanju.''

Kidd sneered. ''You lie.''

''No.''

''Prove it.''

Chiun sighed. ''If I must.''

''What? Huh? Why can't we just kill him now?'' Remo demanded, his patience running thin.

Chiun shot him a baleful look, but his voice was almost buttery. ''This man deserves to know his heritage before he is removed from this world. We'll allow him to see the gold of his ancestors before he goes. Remo, take him.''

"Why don't you take him?"

Chiun wrinkled his nose. "I think not. He has soiled himself.''

Indeed, although Kidd himself had hardly noticed it, the stew had finally caught up with him, and his baggy-legged trousers were sloshy and stinky.

"You're the one all fired up about getting more gold," Remo complained. "Like Sinanju even needs more gold.''

Chiun's face reddened in the firelight. "Sinanju always needs more gold! Have I taught you nothing, imbecile?''

"All right, don't have a sea cow. Come on, Cap'n. Could you at least see to the prisoners, Little Father?''

"Of course," Chiun said magnanimously.

"HE'S LYING, you know," Kidd said.

"Been known to happen," Remo conceded.

"He said the Masters of Sinanju never lie!''

"That was an untruth. How far is this place?''

"Just up ahead," Kidd said. "We'll see what you dig up. I know the treasure is not there. I know it.''

"Okay. Fine.''

"I know it. I mean it.''

"Okay, okay, you know it! Is this the place?''

They were in a clearing in the trees no more than

eight feet in diameter. The soil was sandy. "It's one of the lowest points on the island," Kidd said. "The chests were eight feet down, about. It's been dug up over and over in the last three hundred years. At twelve feet you hit water in the sand. You can't get through it. It's been tried a dozen times. You just can't."

"Fine," Remo said.

"The treasure is not—"

Remo paralyzed the malodorous pirate with a pinch and propped him up against a tree. Then he started digging with his hands.

The sand flew out of the ground as if some high-tech piece of machinery were pile-driving into it. Captain Kidd, mute, paralyzed and stinky, watched the hole appear as if by magic, frowning deeper by the second.

Then he noticed where the sand was going—flying into the air and sprinkling down on his head and shoulders, and piling up around his legs. His feet were already covered—he could see his shins disappearing if he really strained his eyeballs.

Soon he felt the cool pressure of the sand reach his crotch. By the time he was chest deep in the sandpile, Remo was out of sight, so deep was he in the hole he had created.

But it had only been maybe fifteen minutes—this was impossible! Kidd tried to tell himself this was all a bad dream.

Kidd was now buried to his chin.

The sand coming out of the ground was now soggy, and it landed on his head in globules. Seawater trickled down his face.

The ancient Korean appeared in the moonlight and bent to peer into the hole. "Are you not finished yet?"

"Hey, I don't see you in here shoveling dirt!" Remo cried from the hole.

"Nor shall you," Chiun answered.

"Are the prisoners all right?"

"Yes, yes, the healthy ones are succoring the unhealthy ones. They found a stable in the rear where the used-up prisoners were housed in filth until they finally died—some forty of them. The loudmouthed daughter of the senator is supervising the rescue. She has already called for medical assistance on one of the boat radios."

Kidd's mind was sidetracked violently. Senator's daughter? Who?

"So what was she doing playing dress-up, anyway?" said the voice from the hole.

"Getting married," Chiun said impatiently. "We do not have all night, lazy boy! Keep digging!"

Kidd's vision was swimming. *Stacy* was the senator's daughter?

"Okay, I'm at the water level. Now what?" Remo called.

"Now go in and get the treasure! Before the authorities arrive would be ideal!"

"It's muck!"

"It's sandy water. It is not a challenge to a skillful master. I'll come and get you if you don't surface."

"Fine! Whatever!"

Kidd heard some sloshing, then nothing.

Had the white man really slithered into the wet sand of the water table? If so, he would never, ever pull free! But the little Korean didn't look worried.

Ten minutes passed. Kidd knew the white man had to be dead, but something told him he was wrong. The old Korean stood watching the hole calmly.

Then came more sloshing.

"Next time you want me to go swimming in mud," said Remo from the hole, "I ain't gonna!"

"Give those to me," the Korean demanded. He pulled one heavy chest, then another, out of the hole. They were corroded chests, but they clearly hadn't been constructed of wood. They looked intact.

The Korean was dancing. It was almost a jig. Kidd looked on in horror. All this time it had been there. For all these years he had been this close to unfathomable wealth.

"Hey, Chiun," Remo said, brushing at the damp sand that was caking his body, "was it Shang-Tu?"

Chiun became still and looked at Remo in surprise. Kidd rolled his eyes at Remo, too, clearly recognizing the name.

"I do not recall ever telling you of this episode in Shang-Tu's life," Chiun said.

"No, but he's the loser who let the king of Siam rip him off, right?" Remo said, proud of his deductive historical insight. "Right time frame, and he seemed like the kind of knucklehead who would get his hands on a pirate treasure and then lose it again."

"Shang-Tu did not lose the treasure. He simply could not bring it with him when he left the island and planned always to return for it. He never had the chance, and the instruction he left for finding it proved to be inadequate," Chiun explained.

Then the old Korean turned on Captain Kidd. "One thing more you should know, pirate. I looked for the burying place this afternoon. I could not find it. I must thank you for leading my son to the spot."

The bitterness became a bonfire in the body of Thomas Kidd.

"Remo!" Chiun called. "More sand!"

"Sure thing."

The wet soggy sand reached Kidd's mouth, his nose and finally his blazing eyes.

Kidd was thankful for it.

Death, now, was a mercy.

19

Remo placed the call to Folcroft Sanitarium from the *Melody* when they were just an hour out of Nassau. They had found the boat floating at anchor at the pirate's dock and made their getaway before the first rescue craft could get to the scene.

"You made the evening news on CNN," Smith said. "You were successful, I assume."

"It went all right," Remo allowed. He had not watched the news and did not plan to, but his curiosity was piqued. "Who's cleaning up?"

"Authorities from Martinique have claimed the jurisdiction," Dr. Smith replied, "although their provenance is far from certain. As it happens, they're cooperating with our friends from DEA."

"Your friends," Remo corrected him.

"Carlos Ramirez and his bevy of Colombians were quite a bonus, Remo."

"Should I recognize the name?"

"He's low profile—or, he was—but I'm informed that he ranked third among the DEA's 'most wanted' fugitives from Columbia."

"Do I get a bonus?"

Smith cleared his throat. "In any case, aside from shutting down the pirates, you apparently took out the leadership and first-string soldiers of a leading cocaine ring in Cartagena."

"Well, I had some help," Remo reminded him.

"Of course, and that's another bonus. To the media, it looks like Kidd and this Ramirez person had some kind of private feud in progress, and they wiped each other out."

"That's pretty close to the truth."

"It's convenient." Dr. Smith was on the verge of sounding happy.

"Don't get all exuberant on me, Smitty. I don't know if I can take it. Did they find Ethan Humphrey?"

"Yes, the professor was found in the forest, buried up to his neck in the sand," said Dr. Smith.

"Wonder how that happened."

"The ants got at him and he nearly died—"

"Aw."

"But they choppered him to the mainland, and he was treated in time. They think he'll pull through."

"Aw."

"The man is an accessory to murder, hijacking, assorted other felonies. Police in the Dominican Republic want to have a talk with him and see if he can finger any more associates in Puerta Plata," Smith explained.

"Well, I wish them luck."

"There's still the matter of Stacy Armitage," said Dr. Smith. "Her father is concerned, as you may well imagine."

"Right. It's getting closer to election time."

"Remo—"

"She's fine. I'll have her on a plane this afternoon."

"Fine."

The connection was severed.

"Thanks. You take care, too. Bye-bye now," Remo said sarcastically and pressed some buttons. The display on the phone was supposed to go dark. Instead it said, "Menu Options: 1) Program Caller ID. 2) Program Quick-Dial Numbers. 3) Activate GPS."

Remo pressed more buttons. The little green display wouldn't turn off. In fact, it was still glowing green when the phone sank beneath the waves a hundred yards off the port bow.

Stacy, on the beach chair, lifted her sunglasses to watch it disappear, then haughtily allowed them to drop back in place.

"I hate phones," Remo explained.

"You hate a lot of things," she observed without rancor.

"I do like your bikini top."

"I'm not wearing the top." She grinned.

"You saucy wench, that's what I like about it."

"Eeee!" The wail came from the bridge of the *Melody,* where, above them, Chiun was busily inventorying his long-lost treasure chests and, when he had time, keeping the craft on course to Nassau.

"What's the matter with the old fart?" Stacy asked.

Remo smiled. He really liked it when Stacy called Chiun "the old fart."

"Tell the young harlot this!" Chiun cried out, and the rest of his instructions were too softly spoken for Stacy to hear.

"Well, what did he say?"

Remo grimaced. "It's not very nice."

"So clean it up enough that my delicate sensibilities will not be offended."

"Uh," Remo said. "Well, in a nutshell, he said if he has to listen to any more of our, uh, sexually charged banter that he'll be forced to kill us both or himself."

"I see," Stacy said, expression unchanged behind her sunglasses.

"And could we please just go belowdecks and commence quote rutting unquote so that he is not forced to endure any more of said sexually charged banter."

"I see." She sipped her bottle of water and stood, and a second later she was doing the same thing with the bikini bottom as she was with the top—not wearing it.

"He's not going to spy on us, is he?" she asked.

"Naw," answered Remo. "The old fart won't leave his gold."

"For your insolence, I am not giving you a share!" Chiun squeaked from the bridge.

"Big surprise," Remo said. He took the hand of the beautiful, naked senator's daughter and led her inside the *Melody*.